W9-ANF-125

MELODY AND CORDOBA

MELODY AND CORDOBA

A WESTERN TRIO

MAX BRAND®

FIVE STAR

An imprint of Thomson Gale, a part of The Thomson Corporation

THOMSON
™
GALE

Detroit • New York • San Francisco • New Haven, Conn. • Waterville

LIBRARY OF CONGRESS CATALOGING-IN-PUBLICATION DATA

Brand, Max, 1892-1944.
    Melody and Cordoba : a western trio / by Max Brand.—1st ed.
        p. cm.
    ISBN-13: 978-1-59414-561-2 (alk. paper)
    ISBN-10: 1-59414-561-X (alk. paper)
    I. Title.
PS3511.A87M39 2007
813'.52—dc22
                                                                    2007017542

First Edition. First Printing: October 2007.

Published in 2007 in conjunction with Golden West Literary Agency.

Printed in the United States of America on permanent paper
10 9 8 7 6 5 4 3 2 1

CONTENTS

THE BLACK SIGNAL 9

LEW AND SLIM 97

IN THE RIVER BOTTOM'S GRIP 185

EDITOR'S NOTE

Frederick Faust's first Western story in Street & Smith's *Western Story Magazine* appeared in 1920. The popular pulp would remain an important market for him, almost an exclusive one throughout the 'Twenties, through 1933. Except for one serial and one short novel, all of Faust's output in 1925 was published in *Western Story Magazine*—six serials and seventeen short novels. Three of these short novels dealt with the adventures of Lew Melody. The first to appear was "The Black Signal" in the issue dated March 21st, followed by "Lew and Slim" on April 4th and "In the River Bottom's Grip" on April 11th. As many of Faust's young protagonists, trouble is Melody's natural element, and except for Tom Travis, a minister and the narrator of the story, and Cordoba, the money-lender, Melody has few true friends. Things only get worse for him when he falls in love with Sandy Furnival and makes a promise to her.

★ ★ ★ ★ ★

THE BLACK SIGNAL

★ ★ ★ ★ ★

I

I never thought that Lew Melody was to blame, but the society into which he was born was at fault. This conclusion I arrived at before the real trouble ever began, and I know that I was not alone in that feeling. Others had the same thought, although they could not express it so clearly, and, when the true explosion came, to which all the rest had been minor preparations, not a voice was lifted in behalf of Lew Melody except my own— and in such matters the minister's voice is never much heeded.

No minister, in fact, is supposed to be at home in dealing with a narrative of such odd, ridiculous, and terrible events as the history of Lew Melody, but, nevertheless, I think no one is better acquainted with the facts than I. At this statement Sheriff Joe Crockett would smile, I know, but to many of the details I was an eyewitness, and to all I have the testimony of fairly honest men. Some of it is my own imagining, I admit, but I have an idea that my own imaginings are perhaps truer than the facts. All our words and all our actions are only partial expressions of the thing that is in us. However, I must not forget that this is not a sermon.

But to go back to my first statement—if Lew Melody had been brought to his early manhood somewhere in the jungles of India or the wild heart of Africa or if he had had tigers and lions and leopards to contend with, he would have been a mighty hunter and a valuable member of society.

But the wilds of the West could offer to young Melody only a

11

few grizzlies of a race that had been gun shy for half a hundred years and a scattering of pumas that were cowards by nature and by education. So Melody, with his soul of fire, turned otherwhere. He hunted among men.

But at first he was discreet. I challenge Sheriff Joe Crockett to deny that he once vowed to me that nine-tenths of his hardest work was performed by the hand of young Melody. For Barneytown lay in a snug valley that pointed south toward Mexico and the Mexican trail. In the older centuries, along this trail the Comanches swept south, crossed the Río Grande, burned, murdered, robbed, and then rode back, driving their captured herds of cattle. Along this trail, also, Mexican punitive expeditions worked north and struck with desperation, but usually in vain, at the elusive redskins. What farmer in the valley has not turned up ancient bones of cattle—and of men? And in the brown summer the old trail is marked with a dotted line of chalk—the skeletons that wolves and buzzards picked clean in the long ago.

If the railroads have turned the main channels of travel in other directions, still the old warpath of the Comanches served purposes of its own, for down it rode in continual train fugitives from American justice, and up it wandered Mexicans who had escaped across the Río Grande. They pooled in Barneytown.

I do not mean to say that our little town was the constant resort of malefactors or that they forced us to breathe an atmosphere of crime. No, much as I differ with Sheriff Joe Crockett in many of his opinions, let me pay high tribute to him now. If he could find crime, he never lacked the courage or the strength to crush it. It was an underground river, if I may call it that, composed of a north and a south current, each of which bobbed above the surface at Barneytown for a quiet hour or two to get provisions, rest, and perhaps buy ammunition, before it slid away once more on the long trail. And it was among these that Lew Melody hunted; it was from them that he received his training.

He was a scant fourteen when the first crash came. Up to that time he had been busy in minor affairs, such as thrashing with his fists every boy in town during the winter school months when he was not at work on his uncle's ranch. But at fourteen he felt himself enough of a man to hunt for greater trouble. He went to find it in the tramp jungle just north of Barneytown, and he did not have to wait long for what he wanted.

Afterward, he managed to drag himself back from the hollow and onto the high road. Don Carter passed in his buckboard and brought the boy back to the town, a well-soaked mass of still running blood from knife wounds that had searched for his vitals and missed them by a miracle. I think he was two months in bed after this adventure, but when he was questioned, he refused to explain. Only when the sheriff went to him, he said through his teeth: "There was two of 'em." But who the two were he would not say.

The reason was that he promised himself to take an ample vengeance later on. For the remainder of that year he became the most industrious, soberly quiet boy in the whole valley. Some people hoped that the lesson had not been too dearly paid for, and that Lew would be a grave man the rest of his life and one who respected the prowess as well as the rights of others. But others observed that he worked nearly all the time with knife and gun, studying ways and means of offense and defense. The very next winter he began to show the effects of these ardent studies.

Once again he repaired to the jungle, and the next day some odd stains were discovered on the clothes of young Lew Melody, while, in the jungle, there lay the body of a tall Mexican with a knife thrust in the hollow of his throat. The sheriff went straight to Lew, of course, and accused him.

"I dunno what you mean," Lew said with a gracious smile. "After my lesson last year, I guess I wouldn't hunt for no trouble of that kind again. Not by a long shot."

"Look here, Lew," said Crockett, "this might have been a serious thing, I admit, if it were another man. But I have a description of this fellow from old Mexico. He was a murdering skunk down there, and they wanted him pretty bad."

"Is that so?" said Lew.

"So talk up, son," said Crockett. "There's a reward, in fact. I don't know how much."

"I dunno what you're talking about," said Lew Melody.

And that was his attitude always. He made a point of never claiming the victories in any of these secret battles of his.

I must pause here to say that my good wife has just leaned over my shoulder to see what I am writing in the way of a sermon; it is a habit with my dear Lydia. Even what my poor pen has to say possesses a peculiar interest for her.

"Tom, Tom!" she cried. "Are you going to write a sermon about that terrible Melody boy?"

"Perhaps," I said, "it will be a sermon, after all."

"Ah!" she cried in revolt. "Nothing but murder . . . murder . . . murder!"

I cast about in my mind for an answer—usually some pat trifle is enough to stop her.

"To the pure all things are pure," I said gravely.

"Heavens, Tom," she said. "What nonsense are you talking?"

I must admit that the quotation is a little wide of the point. I explained: "Perhaps his very violences may in the end show a way to a greater and a better. . . ."

"*Tush,*" said my dear Lydia. "Don't sermonize me."

"I doubt that word as a verb," I said.

"What do I care about verbs?" said Lydia. "I'm interested in sense."

"An ungrammatical mother makes ungrammatical children," I said.

"Ungrammatical fish!" Mrs. Travis exclaimed.

"I am very busy, my dear," I said coldly.

"I think it is a disgrace for a man of your position, Tom Travis, to justify such frightful crimes that. . . ."

I reached for my pipe and began to fill it. Presently I wafted a large cloud in the general direction of my wife.

"*Phaugh!*" cried Lydia. "Will you put out that nasty thing and tell me why that young demon ever enlisted your sympathies?"

"My dear," I answered her, "you must permit me to have my one poor dissipation."

She flung something sharp over her shoulder as she went out of the room. So I have written this down, not that I wish to discredit my Lydia, who is an excellent housekeeper and a very good mother, but because I wish to let you know how opinion about Lew Melody was divided even in my own house.

How the details of Melody's crimes—if you wish to call them that—will affect you, I cannot guess. I put them down in the true spirit of the historian, although Lydia accuses me of loving his crimes for their own sake. That, of course, is ridiculous!

I begin again by repeating that, when he was fifteen, his first man fell at the hands of Lew Melody, while the scars of his terrible battle of the year before were still red on his body. But having the taste for blood—I am sorry to use such a strong expression—he went down into the same jungles for the third time, and within a week from his first killing there was a second, and this time of an American. But he proved to be a vicious scoundrel who had journeyed all the way from Montana, leaving a dead man behind him. Once more Lew refused to claim the credit—or accept the blame, if you wish to look at it from that viewpoint—but by this time young Melody was beginning to be a known man. And I think it was not more than a week after the second killing that a stranger rode into Barneytown and shot Lew down in the streets, and fired twice into the senseless body as it lay there.

He was not killed. It was the brother of Lew's second victim who had done the shooting, and Lew declared that he would have to live in order to get back at the man. The very next year he had his chance, and he used it.

You will think that this is to be a bald chronicle of slaughters, which I do not intend it to be, but I wish to give you an understanding of how Lew fell into ways of violence with some irresistible instinct leading him. From the time he was fourteen to the time he was eighteen, he was continually in hot water. How many battles, deadly and otherwise, he entered upon I shall not say. I have the list of them beside me, but such figures are too grossly suggestive; I shall quote nothing more from them. Until his eighteenth year, however, I think he suffered almost as much as he inflicted. Everything happened to him short of death, and, although he recovered, he was a mass of scars. I have seen his body when he was in swimming at the pool, and it was literally checkered and criss-crossed with wounds. Only his face was clean of any hurt, except for a single knife scar in the center of his forehead that gave him the appearance of a slight frown even when he was smiling, and made his eyes grave even when his lips were laughing.

However, after his eighteenth year, all calamity turned its back upon Melody and shrank away from him. It was in his eighteenth year that his uncle disowned him because of his stormy life. Some people said that since Lew was thrown entirely upon his own resources, he could not afford to be laid up with wounds of any kind.

His habits remained as they had always been. He had to work for a living, now, of course. But in the intervals he rode to Barneytown and dipped into the river of evil that flowed up and down the valley. His exploits, at length, grew so numerous that the very river itself shrank away to nothing. That flow of criminals turned aside and sought routes more difficult for horse or foot travel, but safe from the terrible hands of this lover of battle.

So he went on to his twenty-second year, when the fatal disaster came. I must admit that Sheriff Joe Crockett had foreseen the evil day before it arrived.

"This kid needs work for his hands," said the sheriff to me one Sunday when he had remained after church to argue with me some point in my sermon. "He's turned the crooks away. He's made this valley a real bad lands for 'em. And now what'll he do?"

"He'll settle down and be a sober man," I said, because I confess that I had always loved the dauntless face of that boy.

"The devil he will!" said the sheriff. "Trouble is his natural element. He's got to have it. Can a fish breathe when it's out of water?"

II

All the prejudices of Barneytown against Melody were not entirely groundless. Perhaps you will think that, because he rid the place of the gunfighters and the Mexican knife experts, he had good grounds to expect popularity. And, as a matter of fact, he was popular with many, because I presume that Barneytown was as rough and as filled with hardy men as any place in the mountain desert, so that there were plenty of people—chiefly the young men—who looked upon Melody as a sort of Achilles, fated to a short but a glorious life. But there was something a little unnatural in the daring of Melody. There was something frightful in that hunger for danger that led him into perils that thrilled the blood of other men in the mere telling. How many blood feuds were started by his terrible right hand in action I cannot so much as guess, but I remember a time when Barney-town grew solemn because three Mexicans, ugly-looking specimens, entered the village, declaring that they had come for the scalp of this man destroyer, this fiery Lew Melody.

I presume that a round dozen friends of that youth hunted for him to warn him of his danger, but when they found him, he filled them with wonder and horror by deliberately riding out on the trail of the three—and into the night. The details of that night were never known, because Lew Melody never talked of his doings, but the three Mexicans were never seen again, and Lew came back the next morning. It was generally believed that he wounded one or more of them in the very beginning of the battle, and that after that they trusted to the fleet heels of their horses rather than to their own courage and skill. At any rate, this affair made such an immense impression upon the Mexicans—for the three were all known men—that, I think, no man south of the Río Grande would have considered facing Melody from that moment forth. They looked upon it as suicide.

At the same time, I think the affair ended the period during which Lew was looked upon as a young hero; from that time forth he was considered a sort of mysterious devil of a man. I remember that Hank Loomis, the old frontiersman, asked Sheriff Joe Crockett if he would attempt to arrest Melody single-handedly.

"Do I look like a fool?" Crockett was not ashamed to say.

Other men felt the same way about it. Even the bravest of them would not have crossed Melody, any more than they would have bared their heads and matched their agility against the flash of a thunderbolt. Because Lew was so very young, so hand-some, so smiling, I think that the horror people felt for him was increased more and more. In another century he certainly would have been accused of witchcraft, and the very incident of the three Mexicans would have been enough to send him to the stake.

In the meantime, danger gathered about the head of Melody, but in a new form. I have said that he made no trouble in wrong directions. Whatever were the exploits of Lew, they were performed at the expense of scoundrels who were better off the earth than on it; I have quoted already the opinion of the sheriff, and this opinion, I am convinced, was not exaggerated. But the tragedy began, as you will half suspect, with the face of a pretty girl.

Lew had his hands so full of work on whatever ranch employed him, or in making his pleasure excursions past the danger line of Barneytown—that is to say, the old, tumbled-down district beyond the bridge, where the rascals found refuge when they arrived—that he had never turned his hand to social accomplishments. He never felt the need of them until he decided to drop in at a dance in the schoolhouse one night. He had come in to watch many a dance before that, of course, but this dance was made different by the presence of Sandy Furnival.

Mr. Furnival had bought the Fitzpatrick place on the western hills that rolled up from Barney Valley. We were glad to have such a man in the community. He was not rich, but he had plenty of means. He bred good horses and was willing to buy more at a good price; he was willing to put money back into his cattle herd to improve the grade of the cows; he looked like a solid addition to the valley. He rode in to hear a sermon of mine the first Sunday after he arrived, and he remained to talk with me about it as the others were leaving the building. He was a very blunt, downright man who walked with a limp, due to a fall from his horse. He had a heavy, husky voice and a very terse habit of speech.

He told me briefly his name and where he lived; he told me

that he was not particularly interested in churches for himself or for any other man, but he thought that they were good for women, and that he had a girl who he would make a regular member.

"She's got a voice that you can use in your singing," said Mr. Furnival in his practical way, "and I'll be as much interested in your church as though I hankered after your sermons . . . which I don't. By the way, that hoss shed out yonder is sort of falling down. Do you know it?"

I admitted that it was, and he told me that he would begin by putting the place in repair. And he lived up to his word. In short, he was a hard-working man who was willing to pay for what he got, and a little bit more for the sake of making friends. He did not drive hard bargains, and he did not expect to have people split pennies with him. On the other hand, he was as blunt as an English squire—than which there is nothing more heavy-handed. I remember calling his attention to our new altar, which was the pride of every member of the congregation.

"If that was a cow or a hoss," said Mr. Furnival, "I might be able to say something worthwhile your hearing, but I ain't up on fancy stuff. I'll say that it's got a sort of a fussed-up look to me."

After such an introduction to Mr. Furnival I cannot say that I looked forward to having his daughter in our choir, because I was afraid that her voice might spoil the very pleasant effect of our singing in the church. But I might have known that Furnival would not offer us a useless gift. When Mrs. Cheswick, who handled the choir for me, reported on Mary Furnival, she was in a trance of delight.

"Well?" I said.

"In the first place," said Mrs. Cheswick, "she is a dear."

"I'm so glad, Missus Cheswick," I said. "And her voice?"

"She has the finest, dearest pair of eyes I've ever seen," said

Mrs. Cheswick, "barring those of my poor dead Theodora."

"But her voice, Missus Cheswick?" I said.

"And the loveliest pale-gold hair . . . how ridiculous that people should call her Sandy!"

I was in despair. "The voice . . . the voice!" I cried, feeling that it was probably a frightful squawk.

"Oh, she sings like a bird. A real soprano . . . a solo voice . . . a perfect jewel. It will make all the rest of us seem as dark as croaking crows when you hear her open her throat."

Which was exactly what it did. She had an untrained voice that was not overly powerful, but so perfectly true, pure, and rounded, that her lightest notes cut through the rest of the music of the choir like the flash of a diamond half buried among bits of colored glass. Her voice was not all of Mary Furnival, however. I suppose that I am the only man in the valley who will still maintain that she was not classically and perfectly lovely. As a matter of fact, she was not. There was not enough regularity in her features for perfection or anything near it, but beauty is like spring water—continually welling up from within. It is a matter of spirit rather than flesh, I have always felt, and I have never seen a statuesque beauty who was really a charmer of men or of women. The bright eyes, the smile, the voice, the ways of Mary Furnival were the type of beauty. She was so thoroughly feminine that she took hold upon my middle-aged heart in five seconds, and, when I sat down to dinner opposite my poor Lydia an hour or so later, it seemed to me that my wife had aged by ten years. If she did that to me, you will imagine what she did to the other men of the town. There was no sleep for the youths of twenty to thirty. They spent all their money on fine clothes and rode like madmen up and down the road from the town to the Furnival Ranch.

For a fortnight they broke their hearts about her, proposed to her by the dozen—and, when they had been refused, they wakened to the fact that Mary was probably for none of them, and that in the meantime they had better enjoy her as freely as they could before someone came out of the distant regions of culture and wealth and carried her away as his wife.

The instant they adopted this attitude, all was happiness and the hearts no longer broke. She distributed her favors with perfect equality; she seemed to like all men and every man; she seemed to be just as happy to talk to women, old or young, as she was to talk to adoring males. And the result was that we had our wives and our daughters as deeply in love with Sandy as the men.

Yes, that was the crowning touch, and it will help to make you understand what she was. With all her charm, and with all her beauty, and with all her wealth of grace, she was as simple as a ruled line. She could laugh at a man's joke and smile at a woman's gossip. She could stand up and sing at anyone's request, and she could do a foolish Irish jig, with a great many whirls and shouts and stampings, until it convulsed a whole circle and warmed every heart to watch her. In seven days, she had ceased being called Miss Furnival; she was never Mary, but in a trice to the whole valley she was Sandy. Even her last name was lost. That was her charm.

Ah, well, I have looked over what I have written now about her, and I see that I have done a wretched job of it. I begin to wish that I had written more poems and fewer sermons; I have listed in my mind a thousand facts about her—but nothing will do. I am going to trust to your imaginations to help me and to assure you that no matter what picture of a girl fits most exactly into your heart, our Sandy would have fitted just as well.

I take you back from this digression to the moment when Lew Melody sauntered into the schoolroom, with men giving place to him right and left, and his gray eyes went straight across the floor to the farther corner, where Sandy sat, surrounded by her usual court, laughing and chatting and loving every moment of her life. I say that Lew Melody saw this and turned on his heel and left the schoolhouse and mounted his horse. It was the beginning of the end.

III

Not knowing Melody as our valley knew him, you will be surprised when you hear what he did. Any other man, having lost his heart at a single glance, could not have kept from going straight to the lady and asking her for the first vacant dance on her program, but Melody was not like others. I dare say that there was little that was boyish and simple about him except his handsome young face and his smile. What he did was to spur his horse through Barneytown and straight across the rickety old bridge over the danger line into the Mexican section.

In the old days—which had their glory, too—Barneytown had begun as a mining town. There had been the usual rush. A hundred times as many men had come to the placer deposits as could possibly make money out of them, and the town, growing like an ugly weed, spilled across the river and down the hollow and up the hill beyond. Afterward, when men learned that there was more gold to be found in the rich black loam by plows than by picks and shovels, the population dwindled suddenly—the western quarter across the river was deserted, and the eastern half grew into a solid, prosperous little community of farmers and cattlemen from the ranches on the hills. After a time Mexican laborers began to seep up through the valley to work the farms and ride herd on the ranches, and they took up the half-wrecked shanties beyond the bridge. They repaired them enough to make them habitable; when some of them tumbled down, adobe, squat-shouldered buildings took their places, and so the Mexican quarter came to have an ugly, interesting, jumbled face of its own. When I speak of the bridge and the river as a danger line, I do not wish you to understand that the entire population consisted of villains. I am not, in the first place, one of those who feel that because the people from below the Río Grande have different ways and darker skins they are necessarily a whit beneath us in the eyes of God or man, and the vast majority of the people beyond the river were honest, humble, simple, hard-working people with merry hearts that loved festivals.

The priest who tended their little church was as good a man and as near a saint as it has been my fortune to meet, and on the whole the land beyond the river was perhaps ten times more interesting than the dull, solid cattle village to the east. But still it was in this quarter that the fugitives from justice, whether Mexican or American, habitually took refuge, and there were sure to be some skulkers there, even after the fame of Lew Melody had been noised abroad as a warning to them. Therefore, Barney River was truly a danger line, and above all to Lew Melody, whose exploits in that part of the village were enough to make every man look upon him as an uncaged tiger. Yet he loved the place—not only because he was familiar with the people in it, and their ways, but also because beyond the danger line was his country of adventure, as well as the tramp jungle down the river. To this place of peril it was that Melody rode on this night.

I wish that I could take you with him—or that you could come with me now to the window of my room and look down to the staggering old wooden bridge with a froth of water around each pier, or beyond that to the confused Mexican village, tumbled on the hillside without plan or reason. The moon is broad and high on this night; it was broad and high on the night when Lew Melody crossed the river, and every feature of the valley lay before him as though under the sun, except that the moon gives with its light a beauty as of another world. And when young Melody looked beyond the town to the sheer face of the range beyond, and three noble mountains, grand and calm and headed with white, be sure that his heart must have leaped.

Perhaps he paused, when he crossed the bridge, and looked up and down the shining river. Perhaps he listened there, also, to the delicate sounds of music that a bright moon was sure to call out from the guitars and the mandolins and the sweet voices of the Mexicans. Yes, at this very moment a dainty harmony floats to me through my open window.

Ah, what sadness and what happiness there is in my heart as I listen.

Then from that bridge, spurring his horse until the crazy old structure rocked beneath its hoofs, Melody swept up the street until he reached a house that had been built around and out of an old miner's shack, retaining the characteristics of a shack through all its growth. It was the house of the rich man of the quarter.

How far his brown hands reached up and down the valley, with a loan here and a loan there, no one has ever known, but he was rich, even from an American viewpoint. However, these quarters were good enough for him, and in these quarters he did his business—sometimes loaning a few dollars to a laborer, sometimes loaning a few thousands to an American rancher, but I think that his lights were, after all, more Christian than those of any *gringo* bank that I have ever known.

Under the balcony, which extended above the street, Melody stopped his horse, and, with the butt of his revolver, he banged against it, and presently the door from the balcony to the second story of the house opened.

"Who is there?" said the voice of *Señora* Cordoba.

Now, although Melody spoke very blunt English, as a rule, and although his Spanish was far from the purest, but mixed oddly of unbookish Mexican slang and ungrammatical sentences, yet when he spoke Spanish, he scattered flowers—but always with a grin that was salt with the sweets.

"Is it you, light of my life?" said Melody to this fat *señora*. "Is it you, my rose, my jewel?"

"Ah, scoundrel!" said the *señora*, chuckling. "Ah, *Señor* Melody . . . whose throat have you cut tonight?" She came to the edge of the balcony and looked over the railing down to him.

"*Don* Luis," she said, with a shudder in her voice, "why do you come here at night? Look! There are a thousand shadows, and in the heart of every one of them there may be a knife ready for you. Come quickly into the house . . . come into the light."

"My dear mother," said '*Don* Luis', "only to see you is to be happy . . . only to see you is to be safe. But tell me if Juanita is with you tonight?"

"I know," said the wife of Cordoba. "Oh, cunning young liar, *Don* Luis. You do not come to see a fat old woman . . . but only because of my girl."

"It is false," Melody said. "It is only because she is your daughter that she is worthy of a glance. But is she in the house?"

"If a man has a diamond," said *Señora* Cordoba, "does he toss it out in the street, or does he keep it in a strongbox?"

"I shall be with you instantly," said Melody. He threw the reins of his horse, jumped up in the saddle, and, while the mustang flirted its heels in the air, he leaped upon the balcony and stood beside her. She looked on him half in terror and half in affection. I could never learn from Lew Melody himself what service he had rendered to the money-lender, but I half suspect that on some dark night he kept the purse, and perhaps the throat, of Cordoba from the knife of some thief. At any rate, he was free of that house, as you have seen. And he walked in with the *señora* like a son of the family.

It was very comfortable, inside, but quite simple—an odd mixture of Mexican-shepherd simplicity and American modernity. There were sheepskins here and there on the floor, and it was said that Cordoba himself preferred to squat on them rather than sit in a chair. There were sheepskins, too, to cover the stools and chairs with which the room was furnished, and yet, oddly out of keeping with these things, was a fine American piano in a corner of the room.

Cordoba was stretched on a couch, napping, with his hands folded on top of his fat stomach, but he wakened now and looked sleepily toward Melody, who was looking at him.

Lew Melody bowed to him. "*Señor* Wisdom, *Señor* Tranquility," said Lew Melody, "I have come to tell you that I shall give the *padre* the price of a Mass to be said for the welfare of your soul tomorrow."

The money-lender grinned at him and pushed himself into a sitting posture.

"Welcome, *Don* Luis," he said. "But am I about to die?"

"I have only come for your daughter," said Melody.

"Shall I call her then?" said *Señora* Cordoba. "No, she has heard you. She would hear your voice through the walls of a mountain, *Don* Luis. And here she is coming."

She came in at that instant, with her dark eyes shining, I have no doubt, and her dark hair combed back to show the smooth height of her forehead. Lew Melody went to her and kissed her hand.

"Silly boy!" Juanita exclaimed, delighted. Juanita was just seventeen, and she looked askance at her mother, to see if she disapproved. But *Don* Luis could do nothing wrong within the walls of that house.

"Look," Cordoba cried, "he is acting like a prince out of a fairy story!"

"I am the witch, then," said the *señora*.

"You are the fairy godmother," said Melody. "Will you let Juanita dance for me?"

"Dance? Dance?" Cordoba chuckled. "That is good! I shall see Juanita dance, also."

"I shall not," said Juanita, seeing that she was sure to be overruled. "I am not in the mood."

"Here," said Melody, "is a flower that has magic in it. It will make you, Juanita." With this he broke off a rose, a full-bloomed rose, musty red, and kissed it first and then slipped it into the hair of the girl, calling to the *señora:* "Now, my dear *señora*, music, if you please! The finest music, which will run down into the slender ankles of Juanita and give them wings."

"See of what he speaks," said Cordoba, shaking his fat sides with laughter. "There is no modesty in this young devil."

IV

But here the music began. Cordoba had married above his caste a girl of many graces and some accomplishments, and among the rest she could play the piano very well. Some said that all the life of Cordoba had been spent in the making of money, not for the love of gold, but to repay his wife. But he could give her very little. She, wise woman, knowing that she had married a peasant, would not make him ridiculous by trying to lead him into the life of a gentleman. That was the reason that they had not moved to the eastern side of the river. That was the reason that they did not live in a great house at the top of the eastern hill. That was the reason that they did not have many servants—only one old woman to help with the housework. Many people attributed the poverty in which they lived to the niggardly instincts of a money-lender. But I had occasion to learn that this was not true. The life of Cordoba was for his wife, and hers was for him, and there was no home in the valley into which so much content was poured and kept as in that odd old shack across the river. And it was the great wisdom of the *señora* that kept it there.

In the meantime, the *señora* was playing, sweeping grandly and strongly into a dance theme and looking over her shoulder to watch Juanita begin, which she did a little stiffly, a little self-consciously, laughing at herself and at the gray, watchful eyes of *Don* Luis. But presently the rhythm reached her blood and ran through her supple young body, and tingled in her hands and in her feet until she was swaying and tossing around the big room like a leaf in a pool of wind. There was not enough for her hands to do. She snatched from the little table its chief ornament, which was a long yellow scarf with deep orange fringes, and with this she danced, making it swerve into wild, swift, graceful lines, like her own body, or letting it flutter straight behind her, as though a gale bore it up.

Melody, leaning against the wall with one arm tucked behind his head, waved a hand with half-closed eyes to keep the time with her. She ended suddenly with a stamp and an upward fling of her arms. Then she flung herself down by her father and laughed at his enthusiasm with sparkling eyes, for he was swaying back and forth, chuckling and clapping his fat hands together.

"Are you pleased, *señor?*" he said with mock humility.

Lew Melody answered curtly, leaving Spanish for his own tongue: "This is only a beginning. We must have more, after this. Next, you must dance with me, Juanita."

How she clapped her hands and cried out, I can imagine. She was not old enough to be afraid of this ominous youth, and to her he was still no more than a hero and no less.

Then he added: "Can you teach me to dance as they do in a waltz and a two-step?"

The money-lender and his wife broke into loud laughter.

"There is the answer to the riddle for you," *Señora* Cordoba said. "I knew that we should find it very soon. He will learn to dance. It has found him at last! In another month or two we shall go to his wedding. Will you invite us, *Don* Luis?"

He tilted back his head a little after a way that he had and looked at her with his smiling lips and his grave eyes. "I shall do in all things as you direct me, *señora* . . . and you, *señor.*"

"You see," said the *señora*, "that even the devil loves music. Who will you marry, *Don* Luis?"

"A girl like Juanita," he said, staring at her shamelessly.

Ah, how she blushed, and then bit her lip; and blushed all the harder because she was ashamed of it.

"See!" cried her mother and father, and they began pointing at her and laughing like two children.

"But will you marry me, Juanita?" said Lew Melody.

"Never!" she cried.

"Someday when I am as rich as your father?"

"When you are as good as he . . . then, perhaps," Juanita said, and threw her arms around the fat man, because she felt a need of hiding her face.

"You are so bad, *Don* Luis," said the money-lender, "that even I seem a better man. And yet I am old. And am I not wicked?"

"He is full of evil," chuckled his wife. "Stand up, Juanita, and teach *Don* Luis the steps."

"Never," Juanita insisted into the shoulder of her father.

"You must do something with her," said the *señora*. "She is too stubborn for me."

Lew Melody went and leaned over her. "Sweetheart," he said with his wicked grin, "do you not love me?"

"No!" said Juanita.

"But only a little?"

"Not this much!" she said, and whirled around on him with a

snap of her fingers.

Poor Juanita. Could she have known then what the guitars and the wind-hidden voices are singing over the river at this moment, and how the sweet, small sound comes to me, drowned with moonlight—but I must go slowly with this history.

"However," said Lew Melody, "if I were to give you the pinto mare that you said you liked. . . ."

"Ah, Luis! Do you mean that?"

"She is a beggar!" cried her father, delighted nevertheless. "She is a hard trader! Oh, she is my true daughter, is she not?"

In a trice Juanita was where she wished to be—with the hands of Luis in her hands and his eyes fixed upon her dainty feet.

"Now when you hear the beat . . . do you see? . . . ta, ta, ta! That is it. Then one step to the left, and bring up your other foot, and then again with the first foot . . . not too quickly. And turning . . . so!"

They moved slowly around the room. "I am like a hobbled horse," Lew Melody said.

"You are not!" she cried in enthusiasm. "You are doing it wonderfully well! Is he not, Father? Is he not, Mother dear . . . for one who has never danced before? Who could guess it? Oh, it is very well, Luis. This, then . . . quicker, quicker . . . with the beat always in your mind . . . see, when my finger presses on your hand . . . that is the beat. Look, Mother, he has it already. It is wonderful. *Don* Luis . . . now your arm around me, and with your left hand take my hand. What is the matter, Luis?"

"Is it modest?" Melody asked, grinning at the *señora*.

"Modest?" she cried. "Oh, *Don* Luis, there is no modesty in these bad days. There is no modesty left, at all. Do not think of modesty, or people will call you a fool."

"Ah, well, then," Melody sighed, and put his arm around the girl.

"You are a silly child," she said. "Now the music, Mother . . . but very slowly. No, no, Luis! Watch! When I press your hand . . . that is the beat . . . do you see? And step as the music steps . . . it is all the music . . . it is not us. We go with it, like a bit of wood on a river . . . so, so! That is better."

The money-lender went beside the piano.

"Are they not a pair?" he murmured, beneath the sound of the music.

"They are like two beautiful pictures."

"And I have a thought," Cordoba said. "I did not know before tonight that Juanita was so nearly a woman."

"You are a great, stupid creature, then. I was your wife at her age."

"Ah, my dear." He patted her shoulder, then: "But listen to them talk. Where is there such another wild man as this Luis of ours?"

For Lew Melody was saying: "How shall I talk to you, Juanita?"

"You are not to talk. I shall do all the talking, *Don* Luis."

"I cannot stand so close to you without talking, Juanita. I cannot!"

"Hush. You are stumbling, great, awkward thing. You are treading my feet to rags."

"What is the fragrance in your hair, my dear?"

"Oh, there is no fragrance . . . and mind the time. Here at the corner, turn so. You hold me too tight. Luis!"

"I cannot help it," said *Don* Luis, grinning in his strange way over her shining head at the money-lender, who grinned in return.

"You must help it."

"You are so pretty, Juanita, that my heart is beginning to hurry like a drum."

"Wicked Luis. Are you making love to me?"

"Is it love? I cannot tell."

"Shall I believe that?"

"Truly. I know nothing of such things. But I know that your eyes are lovely things."

"Luis!"

"Is it wrong to tell you the truth?"

"I shall not dance with you."

"Are you angry?"

"Ah, very!"

"But you are smiling, sweetheart."

She flung away from him and broke into laughter. "Father, he is a terrible man . . . he is making love to me without shame!"

"Ah, villain!" the money-lender cried, roaring with mirth. "I shall cut his throat!"

"One more, Juanita. This time I shall not speak a word. But you are cruel to me."

"Not another step!"

"You break my heart . . . besides, the pinto mare. . . ."

"Well, I shall give you this one time to try to be good."

"If I do not talk, I shall do some terrible thing, Juanita."

"Now what do you mean?"

"I shall be in danger of kissing you, I am afraid."

"No! Even you would not dare. Now the music, Mother . . . the beat, Luis . . . the beat."

V

This was not an unusual evening, from that time forth. Every night Lew Melody was at the house of the money-lender. He had quit his job on the ranch; he was making far more money playing poker, at which he was altogether too clever, and he was spending part of that money in buying clothes much more elegant than any he had ever worn before. He was so changed, and so extravagantly elegant, that if it had been any person other than he, he would have been smiled at.

In the meantime, rumor was busy—for where could rumor have found a more attractive subject than this handsome, reckless, fire-eating boy, who was now said to be paying his court to the daughter of a Mexican money-lender? And, of course, every whisper of the news came to me. Truly it is wasted time for a minister to read the newspaper unless he has a foolish devotion to accuracy. It is so much more pleasant to let the parishioners detail the gossip and the great event. The good ladies of my parish can turn a tale of a broken leg into a narrative as thrilling as a pitched battle between two great armies, and the narrative of how the grocer tried to raise the price and was foiled is more stirring than a famous debate between two orators.

In this manner I received the story of the addresses that Lew Melody was paying to the little Mexican girl, and, when I heard the tales, I did not pause to enjoy them as I should. Some of them were delightful pieces of fiction. Instead, I began to sift those rumors for what small gold of truth I could find in the sand and the broken rock of invention. I found enough to worry me, and on an evil day I decided that I must take my young hero to the side and talk with him soberly.

All elderly men have the feeling that with their wisdom they can unlock all the mysteries of the future for the benefit of the foolish young, just as middle-aged women feel that they can smooth the paths of their daughters and leave nothing to chance in the selection of a proper husband. However that may be, I could not rest until I had met with the man-slayer on the street.

When he saw me, he tipped his hat to me, and, when I began to speak, he remained with his hat in his hand. Why he should have taken up this custom, I cannot tell, but it was always his habit. Not that the rascal was greatly interested in my work, for he had never been inside the doors of my church—at least, not when a sermon was in progress; however, I must put it down as one of his queer ways. A very attractive way, I confess I thought it, and, if I am a little more honest, I presume I must admit that this little trick, more than any other thing, won me over to him and kept me true to him when every voice was the voice of his enemy. Perhaps I may explain this novel way of his by saying at once that it was not because he had a peculiar respect for me, but I believe that he felt there was something in my office that was worthy of a little reverence.

"I have been eager to see you for a good many days," I said.

"You should have sent for me, sir," said Lew Melody.

"I did not know that you would come, in the first place."

"I'm sorry you doubted that."

"You are an odd chap," I said with too much frankness. "But tell me why it is and how it is that you find such good grammar when you talk with me."

He looked at me with those steady gray eyes, and that sudden smile that was almost boyish, but not quite.

"On Sundays, sir," he said, "I always put on my best clothes."

"And so . . . well, that is very good, Lew Melody." I could not help laughing, although I did not wish to begin that interview in a spirit of levity. There was very little mirth in my heart. "And yet, you rascal," I said, "you never come to hear me preach."

His answers were as ready as the tongue of a woman. He looked at me with his guileless eyes and said: "You have never said that I might come, sir."

"The devil," I said. I do not swear. I cannot swear, of course, with a regard to what I am supposed to be, but the naïve impertinence—no, the subtle gravity—of this remark made the oath pop out of its own accord. "Oh, Lew," I said, when I saw that he maintained his perfect gravity in spite of my last word,

"I'm afraid that there is too much wisdom in your young head."

He said as simply as a child: "I am sorry if you are angry, sir."

I melted like a silly grandmother. *"Tush,"* I said. "I am not angry. But put on your hat before you have sunstroke."

"Thank you," said this odd boy, and obeyed me at once.

"You will believe that I am one who wishes you well?" I said, making a rather clumsy opening.

"I do hope it," he said.

"Well, Lew, will you tell me, in the first place, why you are spending so much money on clothes?"

He hesitated a bit. "Why," he said, "if you think I have been cheated . . . I'll go back and talk to the storekeeper."

He spoke very quietly, but a chill was thrust through me by his words. In that instant, I promise you, that I saw the bald head of the poor merchant fallen on the floor of his shop, and blood pooled about his body—and this through my agency.

"No, no, no!" I exclaimed to him. "However, I only wonder at you, Lewis, because you have always been so moderate in your clothes."

"I have always dressed like a beggar," he said studiously, looking down at himself. "But if these are too much. . . ."

"I'll leave the matter of the clothes. I suppose there is no hidden reason why you want gayer things lately?"

He flashed at me a glance from his gray eyes so coldly penetrating that I remembered—well, at that moment I remembered how this mild, gentle-voiced youth had ridden alone on the trail of three desperadoes who were pledged to take his life. It quite scattered my wits. "I think there is no hidden reason," said Melody.

"Very well, Lew . . . very well," I muttered. "I do not want to lecture you today. But may I speak freely?"

"I hope that you will, sir."

We had turned in at my gate.

"I have been filled with alarm," I said, "by following the stories that I have heard about you, and that every one else has heard . . . of fights with guns and knives . . . of dead men, my dear boy."

He nodded. "It is a bad thing in me," he admitted.

"And what I want 'specially to point out is that sooner or later your gun may hang in the holster and drag at the instant of the draw."

"I keep the sight filed off," said this innocent man-slayer.

"Very well," I hastened on. "Or, on the other hand, you must remember that somewhere in the world there are men capable of meeting you on equal terms . . . though you have met none as yet. I think of my own ancestors who first came to this village. Ah, Lew Melody, I am a withered little man. I have no strength. But they were giants, and they were terrible warriors with weapons of all kinds. Those men would have given you trouble, Lew."

"I have no doubt, sir."

"And there are other men in the world like them. Though there are few who could do what my granduncle did . . . for he lifted that great rock that you see by the steps, and he put it there . . . though the foolish fellow strained his back so that he was never the same man afterward. But I dare say that there are hardly two men in the mountains who could budge that stone now . . . let alone lift it."

"It is very large," said the youngster, and straightway I saw a glitter in his eyes, and he laid his hands upon it.

I could not help smiling, for no matter how dreadful a fighter he might be, I saw that he was not very large—surely not a whit above six feet, and built roundly, but not in massive fashion. I was to witness that strength in man is like beauty in woman—a thing of the spirit rather than of the flesh alone. For I saw the heels of Lew Melody's boots driven deeper and deeper into the soft garden sod as he increased the pressure of his hands. Then, with a slight sway, the huge stone came up from the ground, making a little sucking sound against the air. Melody turned with that monstrous burden; he stepped with it; he set it down on the path.

When he turned to me, his face was redder with shame than with his exertion. "I hope that you don't think I have been showing off," he said.

"No, no," I muttered, seeing one of my dearest family legends torn to insignificant shreds and feeling my own small stature and importance diminished accordingly.

"Besides," said the gentle voice of Melody, "you know that bits of the rock may very well have chipped away in the winters. . . ."

"That is very true. That is very true," I said. But it was only a small mercy, considering the weight of the blow that had just fallen upon me.

"Come in, Lew," I said, "and we'll have a cup of tea . . . or coffee, if you wish it."

He went in with me and sat down while I found my wife and told her what we wanted. She started at his name and grew a little pale.

"Heavens, Tom," she said. "In our own house?"

"Is he a leper, woman?" I said, very much moved, and drawing myself up to my full height.

"Isn't he something a lot worse?" Lydia asked, drawing herself up, also.

Alas, she topped me by a full inch, and her puffed hair made her advantage seem even greater; I could only slink back to the library where Lew Melody waited. But I had been through so much that I was blunter than I should have been in what followed. I shall never forgive myself for it.

VI

You will consider in justice to me that I did not at this time have the slightest knowledge of what was in the mind of poor young Melody concerning Sandy Furnival. All his hopes and his aspirations that turned around that girl were a blank to me, and, so far as I could tell, there was no woman in his mind except the pretty Mexican girl who lived beyond the danger line.

I said to him: "If I talk too frankly, you will stop me, Lew?"

"You cannot talk too frankly, sir," said Lew Melody.

"I begin with gossip that has been going around the town," I said, "concerning you and little Juanita Cordoba. . . ."

I thought it was a beginning, but I found that it was an ending, rather. My guest leaned forward in his chair with a look, as the old poets would have said, as grim as any lion.

"There has been gossip about that?" he said.

"People will talk about anything," I replied.

He answered me carefully: "You mean that two or three have been talking about this?"

"It is over the entire town," I said.

A frightful blunder, if I had known about Melody and Sandy—but how could I know? I saw, however, that I had moved Lew Melody more than I could have guessed. He merely sat back quietly in his chair, but there was enough in his face to tell me that I had cut deep.

"What does the town say?" he asked.

"That you intend to marry the Cordoba money," I told him, blunter than ever.

"Do you think so?"

"I think that you go over the bridge for adventure, Lew," I said. "I don't think that you would go there to get a wife, although Juanita is a pretty girl," I added with some diplomacy.

"She is," said Melody.

"If this had happened a year or two ago," I said, "no one would have whispered about it, but in the meantime you have been growing into manhood, and growing so fast that I wonder if you yourself are aware that you are no longer a boy?"

"Perhaps I haven't thought of it," he said.

"But that is the fact," I said. "Now, my son, when we grow into manhood, the attitude of the world toward each one of us changes. We may play for a certain length of time . . . we may amuse ourselves very much as we please so long as we are children, but as we come into manhood, society begins to make demands upon us. You will be surprised if I say that people have a right to talk about you and your conduct from this time forth?"

"A right?" Lew Melody echoed with a sharp emphasis. "What do I owe to anyone?"

"A great many things," I said. "You owe your existence, for one thing."

"To my dead mother and my dead father," said Melody.

"No," I said, "they were only the representatives of society. Your debt is not to them but to your village, your state, your nation. You are a member of society, and you exist for society just as much as society exists for you."

I grow not a little ashamed when I see how I was spreading my elbows at the board and rolling the taste of my wisdom over my tongue, but I put down exactly what was said. It is not for me to cover my folly.

"How does society exist for me?" asked Melody with a frown. "What has it done for me?"

"It adopted you when you were a helpless little orphan," I informed. "That was the beginning."

"My uncle did that," he said.

"Your uncle merely acted for society. If he had not taken you in, someone in the town would have done it . . . and, if that had failed, the state would have put out its hand and gathered you into an institution where you would have been well fed, clothed, educated, and equipped to become a useful member of the community."

"I am glad that the state did not have to treat me like a beggar," Lew Melody said coldly.

"The state would have been glad to do it," I said, "for it knows that every uneducated pauper is a drain on it, a possible thief and wrongdoer, a menace to the peaceful. It knows that every workingman is an addition to its strength, a taxpayer, a good, strong muscle in its body. Do you follow me?"

"I think that I do," he said, sitting stiffly in his chair. "But if I don't choose to be dependent on the state then . . . ?"

I broke in: "You can't help it. You need our help as much as we need yours. While you live a single life, you will not feel it so keenly, but someday you will marry and settle down to make a home and to raise a family. It will be then, Lew, that you will understand how the law . . . which is the voice of the state . . . stretches an arm around you, keeps you from the depredations of criminals, guards your house, your wife, and your children while you are away at work, furnishes you with roads on which you can haul your crops, gives you big, fair markets to sell your goods, lends you money through its banks when you are hard up, builds schools, and employs schoolteachers so that your children may be educated. In a word, Lewis, you will see, if you look at the matter with a little care, that you and the banker, and the schoolteacher and the farmer, and the lawyer and the humble minister, are all cogs in a great machine, one cog fitting against another, and the whole turning out life. We cannot exist without one another. A great general needs us humble people in his ranks as privates and corporals and sergeants and lieutenants . . . a great artist needs us as an audience to praise him . . . and to pay him. None of us lives for himself alone."

He went straight to the point of all my talk, before I had

finished thrilling over my own eloquence: "By all of this you mean that I have been leading a selfish life, Mister Travis?"

"My dear boy, my dear Lew," I said with emotion, "you have been doing what all boys do . . . you have been playing. But now you begin to be a man . . . and what is right for a boy is not right for a man. You have gone across the bridge and the danger line to play with pretty little Juanita . . . very innocently, I have no doubt . . . but I know, Lew, that you do not intend to marry her."

He started violently at this. "What makes you say that?" he asked.

"Am I right?"

"You are right," he admitted. For the first time I had really impressed him. For the first time he began to listen with more than a polite attention. I hastened to strike heavier blows.

"Here is the time when we expect you to settle down as an earnest, hard-working citizen. We expect you to find a girl, sooner or later, to your liking. We expect you, finally, to marry her and become a steady member of the community. And what a power you could be, Lew! Think what it means to he considered the bravest and the strongest man in the whole valley . . . in the whole stretch of the mountains, perhaps."

"You are very kind," Lew Melody said gloomily.

"But instead of doing these things," I said more harshly than before, "you are no longer working, but you are taking honest money of other men by your skill at cards, and, while you live on that, you spend your evenings in the house of a Mexican money-lender, courting his pretty daughter, who may be the sweetest girl in the world . . . but, nevertheless, she is not your kind. That is why people talk about you, and that is why they have a right to talk. Let me go still further. This gossip is only the warning thunder. It means that society is becoming suspicious of you. It means that the law is getting ready its great steel hand. And if you wander on in this careless, pleasure-loving, idle path, and if you come to a crime . . . then the law will stretch out its hand toward you and crush you, Lew . . . crush even you, in spite of your strength. Because the power of a hundred million men and women and children is in that hand!"

When I ended on such an ominous note, I was watching his face with the greatest care, because I was very curious to know if he would be sullen, resentful, rebellious, or simply impressed by some truth in what I had to say. I was a happy man to see that his eye remained clear. And he said to me at once:

"I suppose this is in the nature of a last warning?"

"By all means, consider it such."

He astonished me by answering: "I'm going to get work on a ranch this same day . . . I'm going to give up cards . . . and Juanita . . . and I'm going to start hunting for an American girl to become my wife."

"My dear Lew," I said. "I do not mean to say that all of these things should be done at once. For marriage, after all, you're rather young. I only meant this . . . that you ought to point in certain directions."

"And why not get there as fast as I can?" he asked. He began to grow heated with excitement. "Oh," he said, "you must not think that I have been closing my eyes to what people think of me. They call me a snake . . . they hate me, and they're afraid of me, but I want to show you and all of them that I can keep inside the law as well as the best of them. I want to show every one that I can be as straight as the best of them. Do you believe that I can do it?"

I answered him in an ill hour: "I do not. Not so long as you carry a knife or a gun on your person. Temptation will be too strong for you."

His answer was as quick as the sound of an echo: "Then I'll never wear either a knife or a gun again."

"Can you keep such good resolutions, Lew?" I asked, bewildered by so much fire from him, and in such a right direction.

"You will have a chance to see," he said. "Today I intend to find a job, and tonight I'm going to the dance at the schoolhouse . . . without a gun."

I felt—I can hardly say how—but very like a man who scrapes a villain and finds a saint. But, of course, if I had known what Sandy meant to Lew Melody, I should have considered him a little less saintly and a good deal more human.

However, I was very soon to find out. But now Mrs. Travis came in with a tray of tea, only to find that our guest had rushed away.

"Of all things!" she said.

"Yes," I said, "you have just witnessed the end of the best day's work of my entire life."

I write this foolish speech frankly; you will see the true results of my talk with Lew Melody soon enough.

VII

Of course there had been only one reason—or one controlling reason—for those steady visits of Lew Melody to the home of Cordoba. With his characteristic thoroughness, having decided that he must not meet Sandy until he had added some social accomplishment to his list, he had spent that month arduously pursuing the study of dancing, with amazing results. Most youngsters learn to dance by stumbling about a floor a few times with some good-natured girl, and then they dance at random, now and again, and confirm their faults. Lew Melody made a profound business of it for an entire month, and on the day he left me, so filled with his new good resolutions, he was proficient, to state it mildly.

Since I knew that Lew was to be there, it was not hard for

me to let Mrs. Travis persuade me to attend that dance, and accordingly we went to the schoolhouse in the middle of the evening. I did not intend to stay long because, much as I wanted to see Lew's debut into society, I never felt at ease in such gatherings. Partly because the size of my dear Lydia is never more apparent than when we are dancing together, and partly because I know that a minister's presence is always a damper on parties of young people. I do not know why it is that a minister of the gospel is supposed to possess all the disagreeable qualities of a saint and none of the good ones.

However, when we arrived at the dance, Lew Melody was not there, and I had the privilege of seeing him enter at the very moment that I was taking Mrs. Cheswick to her seat after a dance. She did not sit down, however, but stabbed a forefinger at my ribs and whispered: "Look. If that isn't the terrible Melody boy. Has he brought his Mexican girl with him?"

Which proves how very far gossip had gone in that matter, for Mrs. Cheswick was not a malicious woman. Lew Melody advanced a little from the door and stood at his ease, looking over the crowd. There was not a great deal of talking at that moment; the laughter ended as abruptly as though someone had raised a hand to hush the room. I presume that every young fellow in the schoolhouse wondered if he had offended Melody, and if that famous warrior had come for him, and every sentimental girl wondered if her beau were about to be challenged by this destroyer. Even the perspiring violinist on the musician's platform—which was where the teacher's desk ordinarily stood—stopped mopping his face and neck, to watch what Lew Melody might do next. All other eyes were upon him. He was as cool under the pressure of those eyes as though he were the only man in the room, and all of the rest were the merest cattle. Then he saw me and came straight toward me.

When it was seen that I was his goal, it was as though a signal had been given that all was to be peace and goodwill, even with the terrible Lew Melody in the room; the talk and the laughter commenced again, and so there was enough noise about us for Melody to be able to speak to me without danger of being heard by others.

It was a beautiful specimen of his directness. He merely said: "I am not wearing a gun or a knife, sir. I have found a job. I have given up gambling, and now I have come to find a girl to marry me."

He smiled as he said it, but there was enough seriousness in his manner to make me stare at him.

"Have you picked out the girl you will take, Lewis?" I asked.

"I have picked out the girl I intend to marry," he said very gravely. "She is sitting in that corner . . . the one with the men all around her."

"Good heavens, Lew!" I exclaimed. "You don't mean Sandy Furnival?"

"Is that her name?"

"It is!"

"What's wrong with her? Is she married already?"

I could only gape on him, for it was evident that he was perfectly serious, and at that moment I saw the tragedy spread out before my prophetic eye, dimly, but a prospect filled with shadowy dangers.

So I laid a hand on the arm of Lew Melody; the stringy muscles were working a little under the tips of my fingers, and by that token I could read the excitement that he kept out of his face.

"Lewis," I said, "every young man in the valley has proposed to that girl during the past six weeks. Are you going to follow where the rest of them have made the way?"

"Is she like that?" he asked. "Is she a flirt? Well, that makes no difference."

"I don't mean that. Only consider, Lewis, that. . . ."

I could not find the fit words to continue. After all, how could I say to him: "There is the prize of the mountains, whose sweetness and whose gentleness have won all hearts. And here are you, famous for your fighting only, suspected by everyone of being capable of the most frightful crimes, without a penny in the world, with a future ahead of you as dark as your past, and every prospect of leaving the woman you marry a widow in a few months . . . unless you change all your ways suddenly and unless the grace of the Lord wipes all thoughts of vengeance out of the minds of your thousand enemies."

I could not tell him this. I could not tell him that everyone would be pleased and amused if he chose to fall in love with any other girl, but that all people would be shocked if he aspired to this charming Sandy. My own blood was a bit chilled by the prospect. And if she refused him—what then? What would his violent nature suggest to him if he fell violently in love with her and if she held him off? All of these things were swirling through my mind.

"Be wise, Lew," I said, "and choose again."

He only said: "I want you to introduce me."

There was nothing for me to do but to lead him toward that corner group from which half the noise of laughter went musically out across the dancing floor. When I approached, or rather when Lew Melody was seen coming close, the wall of men in front of the girl parted and fell back. And in the faces of those youngsters—brave fellows every one, I have no doubt—there came such a shadow as though this were a tiger that I led beside me. Little Sandy Furnival stood up to shake hands with me, and so I introduced Lew Melody to her.

After that, I retired to Mrs. Cheswick and found her in a state of consternation.

"Why did you do that?" she asked me.

47

I said with some irritation: "Is the boy a monster? Is he a demon?"

"He is," she said with much assurance. "And you know it as well as I do, Tom Travis."

There is nothing so annoying as to have one's mind read by a woman; I felt that it would be easy to hate Mrs. Cheswick on that night. Besides, it was only a partial truth. For there were other qualities in young Melody besides his powers of destruction.

"Look," whispered Mrs. Cheswick. "He's making a dead set at her . . . and . . . merciful heavens! She likes it!"

She was not the only one that was whispering. A murmur passed ominously around the entire dance floor, and I, turning with a lump of dread in my throat, saw that she had not exaggerated. The lithe and graceful form of Melody stood over the girl like a tiger over a lamb, and the rest of her admirers had found other business that took them elsewhere. But it was not Melody who interested us most then. We could take it for granted that he would be entranced by our delightful Sandy just as every other man in the valley had worshiped her in turn. It was not that which we scanned so eagerly, but the face of Sandy herself, and there we saw what promised a sad story in the making.

We were well enough accustomed to her smiles and her pretty ways with her eyes and her blushes and her laughter, but, upon my soul, it was not hard to see a change in her the moment she heard the voice and saw the face of Lew Melody with the smile that he wore and the grave eyes above it. She sat quite stiff and straight in her chair, with her hands locked together in her lap and her head tilted back a little as she looked up to him. She looked like a little pupil hearing a lecture from a teacher; she looked like an enraptured child staring at a lighted Christmas tree. There was so much mingled wistfulness and pleasure in her eyes—she had grown suddenly so timid, whereas she was usually so easy and so gay, that it was not difficult for everyone in that hall to see what was happening.

I told myself that it could not be true—that the girl had too much sense and had seen too many young men before Lew ever came near her—but when the music began and they stood up to dance, I knew that the worst was upon us. They glided together around that floor like creatures that the music was not only leading, but had made, also. And every moment we could see a new chapter of the story that was being written—first the flushed, happy face of Sandy, and then the gray eyes of Lew Melody, filled with fire.

Mrs. Cheswick, at my side, uttered my own thoughts, and the thoughts of everyone in the room, I have no doubt, when she said to me in a moaning voice: "What is to be done about it? Tom Travis, what is to be done about it?"

"I don't know," I said miserably. "Who could have guessed that they would both break into a flame at the same instant? It's fate, Missus Cheswick . . . it looks very much like fate."

"Like witchcraft!" she cried, full of energy. "And if there are six real men in this valley, they'll see that Melody boy hung up by the neck on the tallest tree by Barney River before they'll allow him to carry off our poor, sweet Sandy!"

So it was Mrs. Cheswick who struck the second ominous note, and she was a prophet, also.

The dance ended, but it was not the end of Sandy and Lew Melody. They sat down together and talked and laughed in one another's eyes, and saw not another soul in the rest of the room. The group of admirers did not gather again; not a youngster came near her, for they saw the handwriting on the wall, and, when the music for the next dance began, Sandy, the just and the wise and the fair, never partial in the distribution of her favors, stepped out on the floor with Melody again. By that I saw that the seal was put upon the mischief. I could not stay to watch it progress further, but I took Mrs. Travis and we started home.

VIII

Nothing else was talked of in the village, as a matter of course. Barneytown was not big enough to contain the news, but the last person who I expected would come to bear me tidings of any affair between a pretty girl and a valley boy was Sheriff Joe Crockett. Yet I could not help thinking the better of him for it. He came in to me while I sat in my office, jabbing my pen at a piece of paper and pretending that I was making a sermon. He even forgot to take off his hat and sat down with it pushed to the back of his head, which angered me a good deal. When a man is small, as I am, there is a vast deal in the proper way of an approach. And particularly from a large fellow like Joe Crockett I like a certain measure of respect. If that wildfire, Lew Melody, would stand in the street with his hat in his hand when I addressed him, why should not the sheriff at least take off his hat when he entered my house?

Ah, well, I shall not dwell on these little things, except that the sheriff's large and lounging ways made me a bit sharp with him on that morning.

He began by saying that the devil was loose, and I cannot tell what other vague and gloomy things, until I snapped out and asked him what he was talking about. At this, he considered me with a heavy frown for a time.

"You know a good deal better than I do, Tom Travis," he said. "You know what I mean."

"I am too busy to waste my time guessing at trifles," I said, more pettish than ever.

"Is murder a trifle?" asked the sheriff.

"Has it come to that?" I shouted at him. "Has he gone that far already?"

The sheriff could not help smiling, when he saw that he had pried me out of my shell of discontent.

"It'll come to that before long," he said. "The trouble is gathering thicker and thicker."

I could not keep in my impatience any longer. I admitted that I had left the dance before the second dance between the pair had ended, and I begged him to tell me whatever he knew. The sheriff was a reasonable man, and he went into all necessary details. He had received the news that Lew Melody was at the schoolhouse, monopolizing Sandy Furnival, and he had gone straight to the point of danger. He needed only one glance at them to see what was the matter, although he admitted that his eye was not sharp for such business as that. However, when he reached the dance floor, Sandy and Lew Melody were so full of one another that the rest of the world was quite shut away from their eyes. They could do nothing but sit and stare and stare at one another, or else they danced with the rapt look of sleepwalkers. Love was a disease that had stolen their brains. They left early, however, and Lew Melody had taken her to her home, driving the Furnival buggy, with his own horse walking behind.

"Walking?" I said weakly.

"Walking," said the gloomy sheriff. "They took their time. What we want you to do, Travis, is to go out and talk to that girl . . . and if you can't talk to her, bring Furnival to time."

It was an ugly task, but someone had to undertake it. So I saddled my old gray mare and thumped up the road over the hills to the Furnival house. There I found Sandy Furnival. She answered my rap at the door, coming with a trail of song behind her. She had her sleeves rolled up—I think she was washing windows, for there was a white rag in one hand. She wanted to know if I wished to see her father, but I told her that my business was first of all with her. So she led me into the parlor and raised the shades, and offered me the rocking chair with the leather pad on it. I told her that I preferred to stand. When I am taller than the other person, I always find it better to stand, and the reverse when I am out-topped, which is usually the case, alas.

I said to Sandy: "We are worried, my dear."

"Worried?" she said. "Who?"

"The whole valley, Sandy, about you and Lew Melody." It was half delightful and half sad to see her blush. "I suppose that you know what I mean," I said.

She was very calm and steady about it; she looked me well in the eye and told me she understood that she must have acted very foolishly the night before, and that a great many people must be talking about her now.

"Pitying you, Sandy . . . but I'm glad to know that you feel it was foolishness. I suppose one touch of daylight brought you to your senses, Sandy."

Who could have thought that there was so much blood in the girl? She grew angry at once, and asked me if I meant that as a detraction from Lew Melody. But this was too important a point for me to slide over.

I said: "Sandy, when we love you so dearly, can we be happy to see you step into such a marriage, which is bound to end in sadness?"

She did not see why it would end in sadness, and she told me so.

"If people wonder at me because I love Lew Melody," she said, "I don't care. And if they think I'm flighty for knowing in the first instant that I wanted to marry him . . . that makes no difference, either. Only tell me why our marriage must end in sorrow."

"Because sooner or later Lew will be a fugitive from justice."

"He is going to settle down," said our Sandy. "We've talked over everything. Do you think that Lew is a sneak or a coward? No . . . he told me his whole story . . . all that I wanted to hear, at least."

She shivered a little, and I wondered how many steps Melody had described of his career in violence before she stopped him.

She said: "People all stand by expecting him to do something wrong. Is that fair? All except you, dear Mister Travis. And he spoke with a very warm heart about you and your kindness and your good advice."

It brought a foolish tingle of tears to my eyes to think that he should have been praising me when I was preparing to strike at his happiness.

"Let Lew marry where he will," I said, "and I wish him the best of good fortune . . . but I don't want any experiments made with the heart and the soul of our Sandy."

"Ah," she said, "it is all settled. He will not even wear a weapon. He is working now, hard and steadily."

A dark spirit of prophecy swept over me, and I cried to Sandy: "If you'll not marry in four weeks, before that time ends I'll swear that Lew Melody will have killed another man."

"Mister Travis, you speak as if you hated poor Lew."

"I speak because I love you, my dear child. And so do we all. But will you promise me that?"

"Of course I'll promise it," she said. "It will be too easy. Oh, I'm as sure as can be about it."

"But if he should not keep his promise . . . ?"

She looked at me in a very puzzled way. "But he has given me his word, you know," said Sandy. "And he couldn't break that. Oh, no, there's no danger at all of that."

"In spite of having given you his word . . . what if within this month . . . ?"

"I should shut him out of my heart even if it killed me!"

cried Sandy Furnival. "I should never want to see him again. I should hate him and I should scorn him!"

"Do not be too savage, Sandy," I said, "but just give me your hand on that."

She did it, with a grip that put the strength of my own fingers to shame, and then I went out to see Mr. Furnival. I found him superintending some changes that he was making to enlarge his barn. He sat on the ridge of a low shed, with a hammer in his hand, while I stood below and told him what I had done and asked his approval.

He merely shrugged his shoulders. "Whatever Sandy does is good enough for me," he said.

"Very well . . . but if Lew Melody breaks his word to her and does fight within the month, you'll help her to keep her promise to me?"

"If a double-barreled shotgun, loaded with slugs, can keep him away from her after that, I'll promise you to keep him away," promised Mr. Furnival without heat.

When I went back to get onto my horse, Sandy came running out to me and stopped me.

"Dear Mister Travis," she said, "you're not like all the rest . . . you don't hate poor Lew?"

"No, no, no," I said. "I want nothing more than happiness for both of you. And very few really hate him . . . but everyone is afraid . . . mortally afraid of what he's apt to do. The world is like tinder, my dear, and your Lew Melody is a burning match. Do you see?"

I went back to Barneytown feeling that I had done an excellent day's work; I was so proud of myself that I spent some time finding the sheriff, and there I told him of what I had accomplished. He listened with a very apparent pleasure, and he agreed with me that everything was well. With the sheriff's approval behind me, it was only natural to go home and confide my success to Mrs. Travis. My dear Lydia is not one who readily agrees with her husband, but on this occasion she was even enthusiastic. Of course, after I had told her, I knew that the tale would be over the town in no time, and I was right.

I received as many congratulations as though I had been made a bishop.

"But," I said, "suppose that he manages to last out the whole month."

Everyone smiled at the idea and pointed out that young Melody had gone almost half a year, now, without getting into serious trouble. In short, the idea was discussed back and forth from every angle, and it was generally agreed that my plan was a masterpiece—if only the girl would stick to her word if Lew fell from grace. We had considered every possibility except one, I say, and that was the chance that some scoundrel might manufacture trouble for Lew, no matter how hard the poor boy tried to keep out of it.

And that was exactly what happened. All that my fine plan in the end accomplished was the setting of a deadly trap for young Melody.

IX

Bert Harrison, as we know well enough now, was the villain. But at that time there was not the slightest suspicion turned upon him. I must begin by saying that Bert, in the first place, was a most respected member of the community because he was what is called a self-made man. Any youngster who at the age of seventeen or eighteen starts out on his own resources and struggles to make a living, who discards from his soul every thought except that of money, and who plugs away at it until he has coin in the bank, a house on the hill, and a servant to open his door, is considered a leading citizen and is pointed out with pride when, as a matter of fact, he has simply coined his heart into dollars and has left everything else behind him.

Bert Harrison was this type of self-made man. He had been a simple young cowpuncher, no more virtuous than any other when he was eighteen, but at that age he had sat in, it was said, at a poker game where luck flowed his way. Some people declared that it was a little more than luck, but of this there is no proof. At any rate, he sat down poor and rose up with $4,500 in his pockets. The possession of that large sum changed the life of Bert Harrison. His joy became not the mere hoarding of this money, but the addition to it of fresh stores.

He put that money in the bank and went on plugging away at his ranch work, but on the first of each month, instead of blowing in his wages on a spree, he added them to the bank account. In a few months he found an opportunity to buy a mortgage and take over a small ranch. It was partly cattle land and partly good river bottom, but it was not big, and it was not improved—everything about it was tumbling down. Bert Harrison threw himself into the upbuilding of that little estate with a furious energy. First of all, he cut down the old apple orchard, of which every tree was cursed with a blight, and he put in the planting of a new orchard, five times as large. He started at the basement, and from foundation to the roof he propped and strengthened and rebuilt the place. He put in new plumbing while he was arranging the rest of the repairs, and arranged a large bathroom, among the rest of his improvements. Then, one spring, he grew more ambitious and put up an entire fresh wing to the old ranch house. He worked at the sheds and the barns and the fences in the same way.

Not that the regular ranch work was neglected. No, for Bert Harrison worked according to an unusual scheme. He put in a straight ten-hour day on the usual affairs of the ranch, the planting, cultivating, sowing, mowing, and all the rest, plus the labor on the cattle. And he worked so fast in those ten hours that it was admitted that he was better than two hired laborers. But ten hours was not enough for Bert. He was one of those people who are sometimes called lucky because they can get on with only five hours of sleep a night—although I have never seen one who did not break down in one way or another before he reached old age. At any rate, Bert Harrison worked ten hours and slept only five, which left him nine whole hours to put on other affairs. As for cooking and such matters, Bert wasted no time on them.

"How do the Chinese live and keep fat?" said Bert. "On rice!"

And like a Chinaman Bert lived. I don't believe that he spent $5 a month for food. And that was almost his only expense. He did all the work on that little place with his own hands, except at harvest time. And those extra eight or nine hours of each day he put in at his fence building and carpentry and plumbing. He did not know a monkey wrench from a hacksaw when he began, but he taught himself as he went along, and mastered each problem as it came up. For instance, under the broken roofs of the sheds there was a quantity of junk—broken-down wagons and plows and harrows and seed sowers, and there was more of the same stuff left to rust in the open. Bert went after that rubbish, furbished up the working parts, replaced rotten wood with new, and rusted iron with forge work of his own rough doing, and presently he had an actual surplus of tools and comforts of all sorts.

In five years, people pulled up their horses to look at the handsome white house behind the screen of the orchard's greenery, and they went away talking and wondering. That same year the little farm took the eye of an Easterner, who gave Bert $20,000 in cash above the value of the mortgages. And two months later he had bought in another place for the amount of the second mortgage and a little extra cash. This time it was a big, sweeping affair on the crest of the eastern hills, and Bert began the same sort of work over again. I think it was four years before he made a new move. When he moved, he had more than $100,000 in cash. He looked about him, and bought again in the same way; it was a cattle ranch again, and every year he turned the cows into greater floods of gold. No matter what he did, it turned out well. His prices were always the best, partly because he improved the strains of cattle on that ranch and partly because he knew when to sell and when to hold on. He also knew how to farm the best land on his ranch and pasture the rest. At the time when he enters my narrative Bert was thirty-two or three years old, worth a quarter of $1,000,000, and fairly certain to get the other three quarters before he was fifty. There was nothing he wanted that he could not have, with one exception, and that was Sandy Furnival.

Which ties him up with the main narrative at once. Ordinarily one would never have taken Bert for the sort of man who would lose his head over a woman, no matter how charming. But the great and the small went down before Sandy. Twice a week, on Sunday afternoons and Wednesday evenings, he rode to the Furnival house, a few miles away, to call on Sandy. If there were other callers, he contented himself with chatting with Mr. Furnival. If she were free, which sometimes happened, he would ask her to play for him, and, while she played and sang, Bert Harrison sat in a stiff chair and hungered after her with a wistful smile on his lean, grim face. I suppose that he had never said three moving words to her in all the time of this odd courtship; his system was that of the slowly dropping water that is supposed to wear away the stone.

So, when the rest of the valley heard of the promise that Sandy had made to me, while all the rest nodded and grinned and said that all would turn out well in the end, Bert was the only man who rose to act. He suddenly declared that he would take a few days for a vacation—the first in fourteen years. His vacation was a railroad trip into dusty Nevada. There he got off at a little station, bought a horse, rode fifty miles across the desert to a tiny crossroads town, and asked for Stan Geary. The following evening he was in Stan Geary's shack.

I suppose that he took the precaution of leaving his pocket-book behind him, for Stan Geary was famous as a man who would cut a throat for $5. He had spent fifteen of his forty years in the penitentiary, and on his last trip he would have gone to the death cell had he not turned state's evidence and supplied an astonished district attorney with data that landed half a dozen rogues behind bars.

Stan Geary's hired man—a weird little fifteen-year-old desert rat—wakened from his bed on a straw pallet in the attic and, through the trap door that communicated by a ladder with the room below, heard the following:

"My name is Bert Harrison. I come from Barney Valley."

"I was jailed there once," said Stan Geary. "What might bring you up here?"

"I've got a job for you," said Bert, "if you've got the nerve to tackle it."

"If I had as much money as I got nerve," said Geary, "I'd be sitting in a steam yacht lookin' at the pictures of my race hosses hangin' on the cabin wall. What kind of nerve do you mean?"

"Knife or gun," said Bert. "It don't make no difference which to me."

"Have a drink," said Geary. "The more you talk, the more sense I see that you got."

"I ain't a drinkin' man," Bert said honestly.

" 'Scuse me, then. *Ahem.* My throat gets more rawer every year, it seems to me. The time I've spent in jail sort of softens it up, I guess. Or maybe it's this alkali dust."

"Maybe," Bert agreed.

"All right, old son. This is the size of it . . . you ain't a fighting man, and you need a job done."

"In the first place, can anyone hear us talk?"

"There ain't nobody in earshot, except a kid that does the chores for me, and he'd sleep through the shootin' of cannon."

"Take a look at him now and see if he ain't got an ear cocked at that trap door."

The desert rat was far swifter than his employer, and after Geary had climbed up, he returned to report to his guest: "It's just the way that I said. He's snorin' his head off. I keep him busy enough to make him need no sleepin' powders at night. Take off the ropes and let 'er buck, old-timer."

"Have you heard of a young gent that goes by the name of Lew Melody?"

"That sounds like a stage name, and I ain't no theater-goer. What might be his act? Song and dance?"

"He makes the others sing and dance, too. But they do their dancin' on the flats of their backs. He's a fightin' man, and the most of a fightin' man that ever was in Barney Valley."

"The devil," Geary said. "That's a lie and a loud one, because I was in that valley once myself. But go on. What's this bird done?"

"Nothing but raise the devil for eight years."

"Only eight years? I ain't afraid of nobody that ain't had real experience. How old might he be?"

"Twenty-two," said Bert Harrison.

At this Geary tilted back in his chair and laughed heartily. "Twenty-two!" he exclaimed. "Well, son, I dunno that I'd take on a little odd job like that. But what might there be in it?"

"Have you a price?"

"I ain't a union man." The brutal Geary chuckled. "I've worked cheap and I've worked high. Just now I feel sort of high. I dunno . . . lemme see . . . say four or five days to get down there, and about the same to come back . . . and a week to look things over and do the job. That's the best part of three weeks, ain't it?"

"It is."

"And three weeks is the best part of a month, ain't it?"

"Naturally."

"Well, old son, for high-class work like this . . . this kid being a fightin' man, as you say . . . I suppose that I'd ought to be ashamed to ask less'n five hundred dollars . . . eh?"

"For a month's work?" said Bert Harrison.

"I'll make it four hundred," said Geary.

"Four hundred dollars, then. I agree on that. But it's the price of three good posses."

"I know it is," Geary said, "but these ain't the old days. Take Larry Mason . . . that gent would bump off a 'puncher for a ten-spot, and then spend the ten treatin' the gent that hired him. But them good old days ain't no more. Things has been runnin' downhill for a mighty long time, ain't they?"

"I guess they have."

"Four hundred dollars, and a hundred down."

"Come to town tomorrow and I'll give you that hundred."

"I'll do that. You ain't startin' back so soon?"

"I've got to start back, and start pronto."

"One drink before you go, old son."

"Nothing. I ain't used to it. So long."

"So long, then."

All that night the young desert rat lay awake, turning the great thought in his head, but finally he decided that where a man like Geary had already killed so many, one more would do no harm. Besides, this Melody was proclaimed as a fighting man, and it was fitting that one rattler should destroy another.

X

I myself saw the brute Geary not many hours after he arrived in Barneytown. He had signalized his arrival by attempting to prove that the head of the waiter in the hotel dining room was an eggshell and that his fist was intended by the Lord to crack it. A dozen men threw themselves on the monster, and it was almost impossible to drag him away from his victim. He was killing the poor creature with his great hands when a lariat noose was slipped over his neck and he was choked off as a dog would be dragged from a fight.

The sheriff opened the jail for Stan Geary and went to his cell for a little chat as soon as Geary had stopped raving and swearing that the world was a rotten banana and that he was going to smash it under his heel. The sheriff took me along.

"I want you to see the bottom of that pit you talk about now and then," he said. "I want you to see what they look like that live down there right along."

I followed Joe Crockett to the jail, and he brought me in front of an abysmal brute, truly. He was a great lump of a man, fat-bellied, fat-jowled, and yet suggesting both strength and activity in prodigious measures. His lump of a head was dropped fairly upon his shoulders, for the reason that no neck could have been devised to bear the weight of it, and his enormous arms were cast around his knees, as he sat on his cot and stared out at us without shame.

"This is our sky pilot, the Reverend Thomas Travis," said the sheriff, nodding to me, "and I thought you might want to talk to him."

Stan Geary rolled off the cot and swayed to his feet. The black monster came roaring with laughter to the bars. He laid hold on two of them and pressed his face against the strong steel while he stared at me with little, bestial pig eyes.

"That's good, Sheriff," said Geary. "That's pretty good, I say.

Me and a sky pilot. Say, Travis, would you get me into heaven?"

I was too disgusted by the face and the voice and the horrid body of the brute to speak in reply. At this, he thrust his bulky arm through the bars and extended his huge, dirty paw toward me. I could not help giving him my hand as he said: "No hard feelin's, Mister Travis."

But the instant he had my hand in his, he jerked me violently to the bars.

"You little rat!" he hissed, letting me see his yellow teeth as he snarled at me. "I ain't good enough for you to talk to, eh? Why, I hate you, and, if I had a chance, I'd tear you into pieces."

He released me, and I staggered away against the wall, thoroughly sickened and fairly cold with fear. I shall never forgive the sheriff for subjecting me to such treatment. No man with any dignity could.

"You let him go just in time, Stan," said Joe Crockett. "I was about to save the hangman a lot of trouble with you."

"I was watchin' you," returned the monster, grinning. "But I'll tell you what, there ain't no rope that'll ever break my neck."

"How come?" said Joe Crockett.

"Well, look at it. And then tell me if a rope could make it snap."

With this he passed his hand around his throat, and by a tension of the muscles made the great tendons distend and the muscles themselves swell until his head became merely the crest of a pyramid. It was such a frightful and inhuman sight that I had to look away from it. Joe Crockett, however, merely laughed.

"You got a good neck, Stan," he said, "but I got a lot of faith in a good old, stretched-out piece of hemp rope that ain't got no give to it, and a fourteen-foot drop, or more, with a weight on the bottom of your feet. I'd put my bet on the rope."

"I'll take you!" this evil beast said instantly. "I'll bet you fifty dollars to two hundred that they can't hang me."

"Who'll pay your bet to me if you lose?" asked the sheriff.

"Well," said the giant, still grinning, "I didn't think you'd see that point . . . but you got one of these here fast-thinkin' heads on you, ain't you?"

"Not so fast. But it gets along over the ground sometimes. Now tell me what was in you when you blew into town?"

"It was the rotten stuff that they call whiskey on the far side of the river," said the brute sadly. "Besides, I made another big mistake."

"What was that?"

"I tried to be a cyclone in a town where there was already a pretty high wind blowin' the opposite way."

"Meaning what?"

"Meaning just you."

The sheriff was foolishly pleased by this cunning tribute. He could not quite suppress the smile that came to his lips. But at least he was modest enough to change the subject.

"Well, Stan," he said, "if you keep on in other places the way you started in Barneytown, you will never get to the rope . . . and that's a fact. You'll have a knife slipped between your ribs. Or a bullet through your head."

"It'll be a bullet," the brute stated solemnly. He wrinkled his forehead in thought, and then he laid a finger between his eyes. "Right about here," he said. "That's about where it'll hit me. And that's why I ain't never been particular excited about being jailed, no matter what they jailed me for. I knew that I wasn't gonna be killed by no rope. Bullets is the things." This hideous remark he made without great emotion, as one who spoke of a most casual matter.

"That's your hunch?" asked the sheriff.

"That's my hunch."

"Now, Stan, tell me why you've busted loose so soon. Most usually you ain't on a rampage for a few months after you get out of the calaboose."

"I'll tell you how it was," said the huge criminal seriously. "I was aiming to drift down Mexico way. I ain't been across the river for a pile of years, and I hear that things has changed. I hear that they got more law and less fun down there than they used to have . . . which I don't believe in, and I'm gonna give it a look. Well, here I stop off at Barneytown, remembering the place by the time you pinched me. When was that?"

"About five years back."

"While I was waiting, I drifted into a Mexican dump and asks if they got any whiskey floating around loose. They said they had, and they brung me a glass of it. I swallered that glass, and then I started wallin' my tongue around my mouth, tryin' to get the taste of it.

" 'Is that whiskey?' says I to them.

" '*Sí, señor,*' says they.

" 'You lie,' says I. 'It's equal parts of mescal, varnish, and poison. But gimme another glass so's I can make sure.'

"Well, sir, about five minutes later I was beginnin' to roar and rampage, until finally I wind up in that there hotel and see a waiter with a head that looks like an egg to me. What was more nacheral, then, than for me to try to break it? Who could've resisted tryin' that?"

He said this to the sheriff with an ingratiating grin on his face. The sheriff, to my real horror, grinned back. There is really no understanding these men of action. Their ways are wonderful, passing the ways of women—even my dear Lydia's.

"Look here," said the monster to the sheriff, "you're a good guy, Crockett. The whole mountain desert knows that you ain't the kind to lay a little misplaced liquor ag'in' a gent. When you drink, d'you expect to be pourin' fire into your brain instead of fire into your stomach? No, you don't. Now, about that there gent that I mussed up in the hotel . . . suppose that I was to

65

give him fifty dollars . . . that's a month's salary. He'll get well before the month is up, and he'll get twice as many tips as usual because I colored up his face a little."

"You tore his coat all up," said Joe Crockett.

"All right. You throw the coat into the pot and I throw in ten dollars. Does that call you?"

"Nope . . . I raise you with a tooth that you knocked out of his face."

"I disremember any tooth," said Stan Geary. "But if they's a tooth in the pot along with the rest of the stake, I'll call you with fifteen more. Seventy-five bones for him, Sheriff. Is that a call?"

"That's a call," said the sheriff.

"You're a white man," said Geary. "When do I get out of this dump?"

"Are you in a hurry?"

"I never hurry a friend," said Geary. "And if you want to keep me here a while, it's for my own good."

"I can't turn you loose on the same day . . . but I'll let you go tomorrow evening . . . when the lights are low . . . and you can cut south or north, so long as you get well out of Barney-town and Barney Valley. You understand?"

"If it was wrote out in letters a foot high," said the wretch, "I couldn't understand you no better."

"So long, then, Stan."

"So long, Sheriff Crockett. You take that coin out of my wallet."

"I have already," said the sheriff, and he laughed in unison with the prisoner as he passed out through the hall from the nest of cells. I could hardly wait until we were by ourselves before I began to ask some extremely pointed questions, but the sheriff chose to look at me as though I were a child.

"Did you ever fight a boy or a man in your whole life?" he said to me.

"I am glad to say," I answered, "that I haven't descended to the level of a brute very frequently."

"That's your glad, then," said the sheriff. "Did you ever arrest a man?"

"Of course not. What are you talking about, Crockett?"

"Did you ever hang a man?"

"Certainly not!"

"Travis," said Crockett, "take my advice and don't meddle in these affairs. It's your business to save souls . . . it's my business to hang 'em up to dry and cure in the smoke. It's a shame to waste good hangin' material on a dinky little county jail and a dinky little three-month sentence, which is about the most that the judge could give him, even with his record behind him. Let him go loose, and pretty soon he'll come to what he wants and needs to get, a bullet or a rope or a knife."

I was too shocked even to attempt an answer. I began to mutter something, at last, about the frightful danger of turning loose such an atrocious creature to prey upon society, but the sheriff would not listen. I jammed my hat on my head and stamped through the door in a rage, but with a thrill of pleasure, also, for I began to feel the first sentences of a stirring sermon form in my throat, and my hands itched for a pen as violently as the fingers of any villain ever itched for the handle of a knife. The large hand of Crockett stopped me as I went through the door, however, and turned me back.

"Be a good fellow, Travis," he said, "and don't go away all choked up and full of words it'll take you a week of Sundays to get rid of. Besides, you got to remember that I'm doing more for that poor gent that Geary smashed up than the law would have done for him by sending Geary to jail for a few months."

Perhaps, in the long run, it might have been called wisdom;

there is no doubting the honest purpose of Joe Crockett. But, at the same time, the sequel was to show what the sheriff had loosed upon Barney Valley.

XI

On the evening of that day, just as I settled down behind a book and was thanking heaven for a brief respite during which no thoughts except the printed ones of another man must run through my mind—just as I was relaxing and shaking from the tired shoulders of my brain the load of the troubles of my parishioners that I had borne about all the day, there was a call to the front door, which Lydia sent me to answer because she was in the midst of the dishes. So I went, with a sigh. It might be almost anything—from a birth or a death to a sickness of body or soul—for to a humble shepherd like me the sheep blat out all their little troubles, as well as their great ones, and the doctor himself is not hurried away from his home more often than I. Also, may I be permitted to say without bitterness that he is paid for every call? Ah, well—it is not that I envy him, but on that night, as I rose from my book and put it on the table with a weary sigh, I could not help wishing that I might be rewarded with even a small fee for this effort. But when I opened the front door, I saw my reward as suddenly revealed to me. I saw the tonsure and the white face and the smile of *Padre* José.

I hurried him into my little library; I sat him down and offered him a glass of Lydia's homemade wine. He merely shook his head at me. I saw that he must be in the midst of one of his fasts—he was a little paler, a little more thin of lip and bright of eye than ever. And so, with awe and a sickness of the heart, I begged him to take a little food.

"I have just dined very comfortably," said this holy liar.

Ah, Father Joseph. If he had one regret in this world, it was that he could not multiply himself into a million bodies and torment them all, doing penance and more penance, and greater penance still to redeem the sins of this wretched world.

Now there are many in my own church who disbelieve in such things, and surely I disbelieve in them, also, and do not see how pain of heart and body can be pleasing to the Lord; nevertheless, whenever I was with *Padre* José, I was overwhelmed by a sense of my own smallness and by a sense of the great heart of this man. He was of pure Gothic blood, an old Castilian strain—his hair was blond, and his eyes were blue. Even now I cannot think of his goodness, his soft voice, his immense courage, without a sigh, which says to me: *Tom Travis, Tom Travis, what a petty little man you are. You could hardly have made a way in the world, except through the church, but the* Padre José *could have been an artist, a statesman, a warrior . . . but he chose to be a saint.*

In this manner I looked upon that blessed man, sorrowing over him and loving him, but with my heart full of awe. He had not reached his thirtieth year, but I could have dropped on my knees and let him teach me the will of the Lord like a child.

"I have come to speak to you about the daughter of the money-lender, Cordoba," he said, with his usual soft voice and his usual directness. "I have come to talk about her and about a young man who you know, if he is known at all . . . I mean him who is called *Don* Luis. The young man named Melody."

I was a little shocked by the subject that the *padre* suggested, but I could not say no to him. I told him to ask me what he pleased, and I admitted that we had heard a great deal of the attentions that Lew Melody had paid to Juanita.

"Every night for thirty nights," said the *padre*, "the young man was at the house of Cordoba, where he was already more than a son . . . and every night for thirty nights he told her with a smile that he loved her. Now, my brother, this girl is seventeen, but womanhood comes early to her race. Consider her as one of your own people who has passed the twenty-second year . . . her blooming has reached that point. But at seventeen a girl cannot jest too long concerning love . . . the very word has a power over her . . . it is an incantation. She taught him to dance, do you see?"

When he said that, I saw a great deal, for my eyes were suddenly opened to the craft of this strange young man who was able to plan so far ahead and work so patiently all the time. At the very moment when I had talked with him so seriously about the attentions that he was paying to the Mexican girl, the rascal had not the slightest seriousness of intention toward her. I could see that now, and I felt that I had played a good deal the fool in this matter. However, be that as it might, I had to confess the truth to *Padre* José.

I merely said: "Dear Father, I will confess to you that I love this young man in spite of his faults, which are very many. I think that he spent that entire month learning to dance so that he could appear in a more favorable light before another girl . . . one of his own people."

The face of the good *padre* withered with pain. He stood up at once, saying: "Ah, well, it is not the first time that I have had to carry sad tidings. God forgive him. Since you love him, I shall pray for him, but where is there such cruelty as that of man to woman, my brother? What my poor girl has heard of *Don* Luis and Miss Furnival is true?"

I could only nod, and the padre left me and walked out into the night. I could not help thinking then, with a little more humility than is generally granted to me, that if Lew Melody had had such a spiritual adviser as Father Joseph, his life might have been changed.

The next morning, black destiny took a hand in this history again. It happened that on this day the rancher for whom Lew Melody was working sent him to town with two empty wagons and eight mules on a jerkline to haul out several tons of baled hay; on that same morning the sheriff relented and, instead of setting Stan Geary free in the evening, he discharged him from the jail just in time to saunter down the street as Lew drove past, singing out to his mules, and checking them deftly down the street to avoid the chuckholes.

All that Geary knew of the appearance of Lew was a description that he had picked up the day before while be was in the town, but a child of three could have described Melody unmistakably, his eyes were so solemn and his smile so constant. So Geary knew him as well as if they had been old acquaintances.

I have often wondered why the butcher did not simply snatch out a revolver on the spot and send a bullet through the head of Lew; there could have been no resistance, for it was afterward known that Lew, according to his promise, did not carry a weapon. However, a man never seems so feeble as when he is poised on a high seat of a wagon with a bulky team stretched out by spans ahead and a pair of coupled trucks rolling behind. I suppose that Geary, staring up to the youngster as the seat rocked back and forth while the wagon rumbled over the rough street, told himself that he might as well do his work in a way that he always preferred—with his bare hands.

"How about a ride?" he sang out, and without waiting for an answer, since he had a monkey's agility in spite of his bulk, he swung himself up to the lofty seat and stowed himself at the side of Lew Melody.

No one knows exactly what passed between them; I can imagine the great beast leering at Melody with a swinish and terrible hunger in his bright little eyes. At any rate, before that wagon had rattled on for half a block the two had gripped one another. The little son of Mrs. Graham saw everything. He told afterward how Geary had grappled with Lew Melody, and how, after a few seconds of struggle, the one aim of Geary seemed to be to disentangle himself from this battle rather than continue with it. It was like trying to disengage himself from the claws of a panther, however, and in Geary's fury and astonishment and terror he flung himself blindly off the seat and carried Melody with him to the ground. That shock would have half killed normal men; it merely served to untangle this pair of warriors. The youngster saw them roll to their feet and watched Melody leap in at the big man through the cloud of dust that they had raised.

He declares that he saw the flash of steel in the hand of Geary, but whether it were knife or gun, it was not used, for as it appeared the driving fist of Lew Melody smashed home against the face of the monster. There was no resisting that blow. It struck the bridge of Geary's nose and flattened it against his brute face as though a swinging sledge-hammer had thudded home there. The weight of the stroke knocked Geary fairly from his feet and plunged him into a pool of liquid white dust.

The mules, in the meantime, had taken the first symbol of trouble as an excellent opportunity to rest. Melody now climbed back to his seat and drove on toward the warehouse, leaving Geary behind him. Only the Graham boy saw the giant lurch up out of the dirt, his nose closed and his breath drawn through his gaping mouth. He looked wildly around him for a moment, and then started rapidly back up the street.

No matter how stunned he was, I presume that he understood the town would not be safe for him if the sheriff heard of this last transgression. He took his horse and left at once for the road over the eastern hills of the valley—in other words, toward the Furnival Ranch, because he had heard by this time of the affair between Lew and Sandy.

As for Lew Melody, he came to find me as soon as his load was stowed on his wagons. He told me everything that had happened, and he swore to me that he had not provoked the attack.

"I thought that he was drunk," said Lew, "except that there was no whiskey on his breath. He went at me like a crazy man, and I had to fight back. Will this go against me, sir?"

But I, having seen so much of Geary, having followed the brute workings of his brain, felt that there was nothing wonderful in this affair except that a man so much smaller than the monster had tamed Geary with his bare hands. Then I remembered the lifting of the great stone that stood beside my porch, and the mystery was not so great. Of course, I assured Lew that he deserved nothing but praise, but again I begged him to be careful.

XII

It turns me sick even now when I conceive the intoxicating malice that must have been pouring through the soul of Stan Geary as he rode out of Barneytown on the eastern road. Two or three people saw him go in that direction, but they did not connect it, naturally, with the Furnival place. If the word had been carried to me, I think that I should have put two and two together and guessed that the direction in which Geary rode had something to do with an attack upon Lew Melody. However, no word was brought to me. For once my system of gossiped news failed to function.

The intention of Geary, beyond any doubt, was to secret himself near to the Furnival house and wait for the next chance visit that his quarry paid to the lady of his heart. Nothing could have been simpler, nothing could have been more delightful than this, from his viewpoint. Having experienced the deadly grip of Lew's hands in actual combat, having been crushed and subdued by one man for the first time in his life, there is no doubt that he would not risk a fair fight with guns thereafter. What he planned was murder as secretly and as safely as the exploit of any scalp-taking Indian.

At any rate, he lurked near the house the rest of the day. Perhaps he may have seen, in the distance, the winding dust cloud that the laboring wagons of Lew left in the air as the mules tugged up the long slope toward the ranch where he was working. But if he recognized the wagons, he was not tempted to make his attack on the open road again; perhaps the very sight of the wagons made him feel that they were bad luck for him. However that may be, he remained in covert until the falling of the dusk, when Sandy Furnival, bound home in haste, cantered her horse across the hills toward her father's house, singing as she came.

The men in the bunkhouse heard the sweet, sharp sound of her voice and hushed their own chatter to listen to it; they heard the voice stop abruptly, and, when they went to spy out the matter, they saw that she had stopped her horse and that she was conversing with a huge shadow of a man on a huge horse. By that dull light they could make out no more.

Presently Sandy broke away from the man and came hurrying toward the house, and past it to the bunkhouse. There was no song in her face as she stopped before the cowpunchers. She asked them if any of them had seen a giant with a smashed face, and who he was—and how he had dared to stop her.

She got no further than that. That anyone in the world should have dared to stop their darling Sandy was an incredible horror to those fiery cowhands. They shot into saddles in a trice and ripped through the dull light of the evening with curses spitting from their lips and guns ready in their hands. However, the beast was gone.

They came back reluctantly and vowed that they would make a more careful search for him when the daylight came again. What could have tempted Geary to ride out and expose himself to the eyes of the girl, thereby betraying his presence? I am not able to tell. The creature was so close to animal that it is impossible to analyze his emotions. For my part, I think that when he heard the clear voice of Sandy, and, when he saw the lithe outline of her body swaying over a hilltop, with the darkening colors of the west behind her, the very beauty of the girl raised up the devil in him. He started out into her path with who can tell what evil intent—or perhaps with merely a blind brute hatred of all that was beautiful and therefore belonged in a world different from his. Yet his senses came back to him when he confronted her and her own dauntless courage made his hand drop from her bridle rein.

He gave her enough of a shock, however, to make her break out with the whole story the moment that she saw Lew Melody, when he galloped over to see her that night. She did not quite finish, for, before the end, Melody had run to a gun rack in the corner of the hall and caught up a revolver and opened it to make sure that it was loaded. Then he started for the door.

She saw what she had done, then, of course. She threw herself in front of him and begged him to stop. He merely brushed her aside, but then she stopped him again with her mere voice and made Lew Melody, with all the devil that was burning in him, turn back to face her. I can see our Sandy as she must have been, and I can hear the agony and the grief and the dread and the horror in her voice, when she said to him: "If you go out, you'll find him . . . and if you find him, you'll fight . . . and if you fight, you'll break your word to all of us. Lew, there are only twenty days left."

Old Furnival, sitting in the corner, saying never a word, waited and watched and lifted neither voice nor hand to influence young Melody. I suppose there was enough in the gray eyes of Lew to keep the rancher dumb, and I suppose that it was at that moment that he made up his mind that this man could not be the husband of Sandy.

He saw Melody raise a hand to shut out the accusing face of the girl, and heard the youngster muttering: "I've got to go. I've got to find him, Sandy."

It made her frantic; she caught at his hand and dragged it down and made him look at her. "If you do it, you'll lose me!" she cried to him. "Do you understand? If you break your word like a rotten rope, I'll keep mine. I'll never see you again . . . I'll never speak your name. Lew, for God's sake, stay with me and I'll help you fight it out!"

He wavered, then, but I suppose that he heard her only dimly. For, as much as he loved her, the instinct was still too fresh and strong in him. He had fought once before that day, and his hands and his heart must have been tingling with the battle. It is the taste of whiskey in the throat of the drunkard that drives him on to call for yet another drink—that wakens him at night, half mad with a ravening thirst, and sends him stumbling out into the dark. So the tiger in Melody thrust the lover aside. He did not try to argue with her; he simply turned on his heel and fled out into the moonlight.

For the moon was high. I remember that night as well as I know this one on which I write. The sky was washed clean, and it was turned steel-gray by the brilliance of a moon three quarters full and shining with a wonderful brightness through the thin mountain air. That light guided Melody, I suppose, but I feel that there must have been something more—some instinct of which ordinary people have no knowledge whatever. The beast that had come up in his eyes when he heard Sandy's story, and which had filled her with such horror, was the same beast that still led him on to find Geary.

In the hollow behind the barn and the sheds, the men of the bunkhouse heard the sudden chattering of guns and rushed out to see what had happened. They did not need lanterns; the moon was so bright that it showed them, under the thick pattern of the shadow of the oak tree, the huge, outstretched body of Geary. How he appeared I have no wish to know, except that it was found that a bullet had struck him fairly between the eyes, on the very place where I had seen him lay his finger when he was talking with Joe Crockett.

You who believe in nothing weird and of another world intruding upon this sane existence of ours, explain that premonition in the brute soul of Stan Geary.

I suppose that when the bullet was fired and when that mighty hulk of a man fell forward on his battered face, the passion died out of poor Lew Melody as the life died out of his enemy. Yet he must have wandered through the hills, cursing his fate, wondering what demon haunted him, for a full hour. It was that length of time before he came once more to the house of Furnival.

I suppose that that grim old chap recognized the light, quick, stealthy tread of the killer as Melody came up on the verandah, for when he opened the door to the knock of Lew, Furnival had a sawed-off shotgun tucked under his arm, with a forefinger curled about the triggers. There was enough lead in that weapon to have washed the life out of ten strong men, and Furnival was quite prepared to use it all in one terrible blast against Melody.

But I suppose that a child could have controlled poor Lew Melody, after the fire had burned out in him. He leaned against the side of the door with a fallen head and a sick face, and, when he saw Furnival with the ready gun, he rubbed his hands across his eyes and looked again to make sure that he saw aright.

"I've come back to beg for one more chance," said Melody, pleading for the first time in his life.

"You've had your chance," said Furnival. "You get no more out of me."

"May I speak two words to Sandy?" Melody asked.

"You may not," said Furnival, with his finger more stiffly

pressed against the triggers. "It's time for you and me to say so long, Melody."

"Let me hear it out of her own mouth," groaned Lew. "I'll make no trouble, I swear it."

Furnival turned this idea in his mind for a moment, and then he called out, without taking his eyes from Melody: "Sandy, here he is! Will you talk to him?"

And the voice of Sandy came back, as cold and as clear as a bell—because sorrow will make a strong soul stronger and harder: "I've told him what it would mean to me, and I haven't changed my mind."

"I guess you hear her talk," said Furnival.

"Mister Furnival," said Lew Melody—although to me, who knew him so well, it seems incredible that he could have begged so—"let me have six months while things settle down. Then let me come back and see her."

Perhaps I have shown you Furnival as a matter-of-fact man; he was a grim man, also, and now he said: "I've seen your dead man, down under the oak. Well, Melody, I'd as soon have seen her married to him as to you."

And he struck the door shut in the face of Lew.

XIII

Furnival was not a talkative man, and, of course, Sandy and Lew Melody would never have spoken a syllable concerning what had happened, but such news could not be hidden. It was known, not only that young Melody had killed a man and broken his word to the Furnivals, but, also, every painful detail of the manner in which he had been refused the Furnival house after the crime was noised abroad and repeated with many decorations. Even the stalest imagination was able to think of a few ornaments for such a moving tale. I had to listen to at least twenty variants upon the truth before the sheriff called on me the next morning.

He gave me the confirmation of all the important points. And my miserable reflection when he had ended was simply: "We've crucified Melody, but, if it saves Sandy from him, it's worthwhile, I suppose. Yet there's something horrible, Crockett, in persecuting a youngster who has rid the world of such a vile rascal as that Geary."

The sheriff said with violence: "They had ought to give Lew Melody a medal in gold, with what he's done wrote down in gold across the face of it. I dunno that you and me, Travis, in our whole lives will ever do as much good in the world as this here boy has done in bumping off Stan Geary."

You will see by this that the sheriff was in the mood for using superlatives.

"But is it true?" I said. "Did Sandy really refuse to see him and to speak with him?"

The sheriff had fallen into a brown study. In place of answering me, he said: "Think of it! This young butcher that I thought I knowed so well . . . he stood by and let old Furnival shut the door in his face."

"A double-barreled shotgun might be the reason for that," I said.

Joe Crockett merely smiled at my ignorance in the large and tolerant manner of a man who knew more about such things. Joe was a plain-minded man who did not believe in miracles, and yet he said: "Shotgun? What's a shotgun to Lew Melody? No, that's not the reason. If he'd decided that he really wanted to get into the house and to the girl, he would have gone in spite of ten shotguns. But, afterward, he went back to the ranch, and he started to work this morning as though nothing had happened. What's in his mind?"

I saw instantly. "He is trusting to time to put him back on his old footing with her," I said. "The poor boy thinks that, if he lives steadily and quietly, he may be restored to her favor. That's why he's gone back."

"Do you think so?" mused Crockett. "Then will he be quiet, do you think, when I go out to arrest him?"

It staggered me. It popped me out of my chair and popped me back again with a groan. "Arrest him, Sheriff?"

He nodded.

"But," I cried, "what has he done that's worthy of arrest? Haven't you told me yourself that what he should have is a gold medal?"

"It ain't what he ought to get . . . not in the eyes of you and me and folks with sense. It's what the public wants, and the public wants to see him arrested."

"I know that," I could not help admitting. "But suppose that one of Furnival's cowpunchers had found Geary and killed him . . . why, that 'puncher would be one of the most popular men in the valley!"

The sheriff had an irritating way of talking down even to me, at times. Now he rolled a cigarette and lighted it before he seemed able to find words simple enough to explain his viewpoint to me. "If you or me," he said, "was to step out and kill a wild bull, we'd be heroes, I suppose?"

"I suppose so," I answered testily, "but what has that to do with it?"

"But when a professional bullfighter goes out and kills the bull in the ring, it's disgustin', ain't it?"

I could not help seeing the point, but that made me all the more angry.

But the sheriff went on: "I set up to have some sense, but I don't set up to have more sense than most folks. What the majority wants, that's what I'm here to do. Sometimes, maybe, they'd be wrong . . . like this case. But mostly they'd be right. When I know what they want, I shut my eyes and I go ahead and do it. I'm the servant of the county, Travis, and don't you never forget it . . . and if the county said to me . . . 'Go arrest Tom Travis,' . . . I'd go and do it quicker'n a wink."

It was very uncomfortable logic, and I told him so.

He merely said: "The main thing is . . . will this fool kid let me arrest him?"

"Certainly," I said, "because he knows perfectly well that, after he's arrested, he'll very quickly be turned loose."

"Does it seem that way to you?" said the sheriff. "Well, sir, I dunno. There's some that don't take very kind to the idea of a spell in jail. It looks sort of serious to 'em. And 'specially to them that stir around pretty free and active, like this here boy of ours, you might say. Will Lew Melody listen to reason, or will he start fighting? That's what I'm mighty interested in."

I began to grow afraid from that moment. I began to see, also, more clearly and deeply into the mind of poor young Melody.

"You can't be right," I said, "but, at any rate, you'll take several men with you to make that arrest?"

"I'd like to." Joe Crockett sighed. "Lord, how I hanker to take out three or four of the boys that are handy with their guns and don't make no fuss about usin' 'em. But it can't be done."

I was amazed and asked him why it could not be done.

"Because I'm the sheriff of this here county," said Joe Crockett. "Right now I wish that I'd never seen the job. But I've never been afraid to go out and arrest one man all by myself, and I ain't goin' to start taking water now. Not at my age. My habits are all fixed and settled on me."

I confess that it made the hair stand up on my head, and I told him so, but the sheriff's mind was indeed fixed. He bade me farewell and left, but very slowly. I never saw a man take so long in settling his hat upon his head or in opening and passing through the front door, or in arranging his stirrups, or in untethering his horse, or in dragging himself wearily into the saddle. A child could have guessed what was passing in his mind, and I was sick at heart—for Sandy, for Lew Melody, and for poor Sheriff Joe Crockett.

In the meantime, another man had ridden out to find Lew. Cordoba, the money-lender, who had never been missing from his place of business for the last twenty years, had saddled a fat-sided horse that saw service not more than once a month, and the Mexican had mounted and jogged through the twisting alleys where the dust was fetlock deep and every flick of the hoofs tossed a cupful of dirt into the air, where it hung, dissolving like a miniature rain cloud that is dropping a torrent upon the earth. He wound down to the danger line, he crossed the staggering bridge, and he rode at last slowly through the streets of the American quarter, and out the eastern road toward the hills. Lydia, who was working in the garden, called to me to let me know who had just passed. Then a sharp touch of intuition told me where the money-lender was bound, and I ran out onto the porch to stare after his form until it turned the next corner.

So he jogged on over the hills, until he came to the Marston Ranch, near to the Bert Harrison place, where Lew was employed. When he inquired at the ranch house, where only the cook was inside, he was directed toward the section of fence that Lew had ridden out to repair. Half an hour later he was drawing rein and looking down at Lew Melody, who had his mouth full of staples as he refastened a dropped length of barbed wire.

No matter what was in the mind of Melody, he was able to wave his hat to the money-lender and then come to take his hand.

"Come in and sit down and make yourself at home," said Lew. "Take the best chair, yonder," he said, pointing to a tree stump. "And, if you want, I'll let you play this game with me.

The one who gets in the most staples in an hour wins the game. What fun, eh?"

But the Mexican did not smile; he observed Lew for a sad moment, and then began to mop his fat face and raise his hat so that the wind could cool his head a little, for this was a blazing day and the sun was wearing high in the heavens. Barney River, in the center of the valley, looked no more than a larger heat wave springing from the burning ground, and the cattle were hunting even for the skeleton shade of Spanish daggers.

"I have not come to be gay," said Cordoba. "I have come to speak to you from my heart, my dear son."

I do not imagine that it was difficult for Lew to let the smile disappear from his own face. "Say whatever you wish," he said. "I'll listen to you about as soon as I'll listen to anyone in the world."

"It is many days since you have been at my house," said Cordoba.

"I have turned into a workingman," Lew Melody said cheerfully, "and at night I'm too tired to take a long ride . . . and then back again before midnight."

Cordoba shook his head. "I know everything," he said. "That is not the truth . . . it is the *Señorita* Furnival. All people know that."

You will observe that Cordoba had been a simple peon in the beginning, and he was not more than a peon in tact to the very end. I suppose that Lew winced a little under this direct thrust, and he winced still more under what followed.

"We are told," went on Cordoba, "that you came to see us so much not because you loved us, but because you wished that my girl should teach you to dance . . . and then you could go to the other. Is it true, *Don* Luis?"

The perspiration starts out on my forehead when I think of how I should have struggled to answer that question had I been in the boots of young Lew Melody, but, no matter how the words of the money-lender cut him, he answered with a frankness as great as the question itself: "It is true, *Señor* Cordoba."

The Mexican bowed his head for a time. I suppose that there was a great bitterness in his heart, but I suppose that there must have been a greater sorrow. He said at last: "I shall not say this to my wife, however, nor to my girl."

"Thank you," said Lew Melody simply. "I do not wish to have them despise me, my father."

The tears sprang into the eyes of Cordoba at this touch of gentleness, and he pressed his fat hands together and threw them apart again. "Ah, *Don* Luis, how dear you are to us," he said. "But it is no matter what has been in your mind toward us. We cannot harden our hearts against you. Besides, Juanita. . . ."

Here he could not go on, and he gazed wistfully at Melody as though begging him to understand. Melody set his teeth and wished that he had never been born, for he saw what was to come, but could not avoid hearing it.

"She loves you, *Don* Luis, with a great heart."

"No," said Melody. "But we have been like a brother and a sister . . . playing, *Señor* Cordoba . . . do you understand?"

The money-lender smiled sadly upon him. "We who are men, *Don* Luis," he said, "how can we know them? We have words for what we are and the things which move inside us. But they are like birds and like flowers. Love and care makes them beautiful, but, if they do not find love, they wither and grow ugly. Even I did not understand the heart of Juanita. But this morning very early, when the news first came to us of how you had killed the man and how you had lost the girl who you had chosen, she came into my arms and wept and wept.

" 'Now, Father,' she said, 'he will come back to us, perhaps.'

" 'Child,' I said, because it made me weak and trembling to

hear her cry so, 'do you wish something that another woman has thrown away?'

" 'I have tried to be proud,' she said to me, 'but I cannot. My heart is breaking, because I love him. I would go on my bare feet over the mountains to have one sight of him. I could say nothing, but now he is in trouble. They will go to arrest him because he has killed a man . . . perhaps they will kill *Don* Luis for what he has done. Who knows? They are cruel men. Go to him and save him, even if we never see him again.'

"So, Luis, I have come to you. If there is danger for you, I shall find a way to help you. I can do many more things than you know. I can make you disappear like magic and rise again like a river out of the ground far south in my Mexico, where men are free. You may have money to live as a king lives. You may have whatever you will have. No, no, I do not buy you for Juanita, but because we love you, and our hearts ache for you. Will you come with me, *Don* Luis?"

"If I could take help from any man," said Melody, "I would go to you first, my father. But if Juanita thinks that she is fond of me, I must never see her. Because I have hurt her, I am a dog . . . you should come to me with a whip. But as for running away, I cannot do it . . . it would mean leaving the other behind me. You have heard the truth. She has shut me out of her house. Still I cannot leave her. She is like my breath and my blood, a part of me. Do you see, my father, how I am punished for all my sins? I must go to her again and again, and still, like a dog, I must be driven away from her."

XIV

At noon, Melody rode in from the fence line, and he found Joe Crockett waiting for him, sitting on one end of the watering trough and whittling at a stick, with his hat pushed far back on his head to shade his neck as he slouched forward. The first impulse of Melody was the right one, for he reined in his horse at the first glimpse of the man of the law. But after an instant of thought he seemed to decide that his suspicion could not be right. He went on and spoke to the sheriff as he dismounted and jerked the bridle from the head of his pony so that it could drink. So that historic conversation began.

"How's things, Lew?" said the sheriff.

"Fair," said Melody. "How's things with you?"

"I've got a stitch of lumbago that's fetchin' me up pretty short," said Crockett. "That's a sign that I'm gettin' on."

"You ought to go to bed, then. Old Man Simmons is bothered a lot that way. He always goes to bed and beats it pretty quick."

"Simmons ain't the sheriff," said Crockett.

"Business keeps you stirring?"

"That's right."

"What sort of business brings you out this way?" asked Melody with a twinge of suspicion.

"Well," said Crockett, "there's a lot of things. I might come out this way to cut for sign of that cattle-killing grizzly. I ain't above hunting bear for the good of the county. Then there's old Charring. I got to talk to him about where that rascal of a son of his might've disappeared to. You see, there's always something to do. Besides," he added, "there's the case of that skunk, Geary, that you bumped off last night."

You will say that this approach was about as diplomatic as any you can imagine, yet Lew Melody was too highly strung to miss the first taint of suspicion in the air.

"And what about Geary?" he asked. "Do I get a pension from the county for that good job?"

The sheriff cast away the stick that he was whittling and began to make a cigarette. "Well," he said, "what spoils the pension idea is that Geary wasn't wanted for nothing particular."

"I might've brought him up for assault and battery," said

Lew Melody. "He jumped me for nothing in the town, yesterday morning."

"I've heard tell about that, which you thumped him pretty bad for what he tried, they say."

"I did what I could," answered Melody, grinning.

"But the main trouble about this thing," went on the sheriff, "is the fact that there ain't no charges ag'in' old Geary at all . . . not just right now. He was all cleared off and wiped up clean by turning state's evidence . . . the dog! So in the eyes of the law he's just the same as a newborn babe, pretty near."

"Look here," broke in Melody, "the chief business that brought you out here was on account of me and Geary. Is that right?"

"I ain't saying that it ain't the most important thing."

"What was wrong?" Melody asked. "It was a fair, stand-up fight . . . except that he started it by trying to pot me from behind a tree."

"Might you have any proof of that?"

"Sure. This!" He took off his hat. The crown, toward the peaked top of the sombrero, was neatly punctured by a half-inch hole. "This will save me from having air holes punched," Lew Melody said.

"Well, some folks might say that that hole was shot into the hat afterward."

"Some might," Lew admitted with a frown.

"And then, again . . . what might make some talk was the way that you started out rampaging after him."

"Crockett," said Melody, growing more and more excited as he saw the case against him turning black, "you know as well as I do that the fight was fair!"

"Oh, sure I do, Melody. But it ain't what I think . . . it's what other folks suspect. And the best way is always to clear up all of the suspicions."

"I suppose that's right, but what are the suspicions now? And whoever asked me questions like this or held me on such a short rope before? It isn't the first time that I've dropped a man, is it?"

"Not the first," said the sheriff. "No, that's one bad side of it . . . about the worst side. Folks know that you've been a killer since you was a kid. But every gent that you ever dropped before happened to be one that was on the wrong side of the book. It was always somebody that was wanted, and that was wanted bad. Most of them that travel transient through the west side of Barneytown are that sort, you know. But this time it's a man that the law ain't got a thing against . . . technically. And then there's the other part of it. Couldn't be said that this here fight was an accident, because there's folks that seen you grab a gun and run for the outdoors to get at him, even after you was stopped and argued with. Well, Melody, you see how the case sizes up."

Lew Melody dropped his hands on his hips and stared down at the sheriff for a long moment. "Is that the way that you see it?" he said.

"Me? It ain't what I see. And it ain't what the judge'll see. And it ain't what the jury'll see. But it's best all around for you to go in with me and stand your trial, and the whole thing will be dropped and never thought of afterward."

I know that the diplomacy of the sheriff has always been much celebrated because of the skillful manner in which he handled this affair, but I confess that I have always felt he laid an undue emphasis upon the case that the law might bring against Lew Melody. He wished with all his might to explain to Lew that he had a cause for arresting him; he succeeded so well that, before he finished, Lew was convinced that the state had a case against him good enough to land him in the penitentiary. I have heard that had it been a straight, unadulterated matter of trial for murder with a death penalty involved, Lew would have gone in and faced the music. But what he saw in this affair was not a death penalty, but the dreadful darkness of a long prison term closing over the prime of his life.

"So," said the sheriff, "that's why I've come out to ask you into town with me, Lew."

He said it very cheerfully, but Lew had heard too many reasons before this.

"I'm to go to Barneytown," said Lew, "and be tried by a jury of men who've known me for a troublemaker all the days of my life. They're going to try me for murder of a man with no crime charged against him right now. What do you think that my lot would be?"

"Why, Lew, you'd be acquitted, of course. I'd give you my rock-bottom word on that."

Melody shrugged his shoulders. "Every man can make a mistake," he said, "and I've an idea that this is your mistake, Crockett. No, I'm sorry to say that I'm not going in."

Crockett digested this remark with a wry face. And that face grew several shades lighter. "You won't do it, Lew?" he repeated.

"I won't do it. *Bah!* Don't I know that they'd railroad me if they had half a chance?"

The sheriff stood up slowly. "I want to make it plain to you, Lew, that I'm askin' you mighty polite to go to town with me. I ain't suggestin' no irons on your wrists. Nope, I'll go you better than that. I'm simply arrestin' you in the name of the law and askin' you to report at the jail . . . sometime today. I'm askin' you to promise to do that."

An odd manner of making an arrest, you will say, but the courage of the sheriff had been proved a hundred times; he could afford to use novel methods.

"I know that you're a white man, Crockett," said Lew Melody. "I've always tried to keep from stepping on your toes."

"I know you have, Lew," the sheriff said gently.

"I respect you, Crockett, and I like you a lot . . . and I ap-
preciate a lot the way you've showed me all the sides of this
thing, but I'm not. . . ."

"Wait a minute, Lew. For God's sake, remember that, if you
say no, I've got to try to make you come with me."

"I tell you, Crockett, I want no trouble with you. Give me
half a minute to get away from you, and then catch me if you
can. But don't try to put the irons on me by force. Because you
can't do it."

"Lew," said Joe Crockett, "I know that I can't. I know that
you're faster and a better shot than me, and a stronger and
quicker man and a better fighter every way from Sunday . . .
but I'm going to take you to Barneytown or die tryin'."

I cannot think of it without growing weak—those two honest-
hearted fighting men, standing face to face with nothing but the
greatest respect and gentleness in their souls for one another,
and yet forced to go on from one dangerous word to another
until nothing remained except a gun play.

Melody was greatly moved. It is said that he turned perfectly
white and begged Crockett with a trembling voice not to go any
further in the matter.

For answer, poor Crockett took the handcuffs out of his
pocket.

"I've served this county too many years," he said, "to be
afraid of dyin' for it now. Lew Melody, I arrest you in the name
of the law. Hold out your wrists for me."

Melody stepped lightly back.

"Then take what's coming to you!" shouted Crockett, and he
snatched at his gun.

You will understand that he was a famous warrior himself,
but yet he was so slow in comparison with Lew that the
youngster had time to select a special target, and that was what

saved the life of Crockett. For, instead of aiming at a vital spot, Melody had time to pick a less fatal target. He merely shot Crockett through the shoulder, and the gun of the sheriff dropped to the ground.

XV

People who have never seen a bullet fired into a human body have strange ideas about it, and, as a rule, they seem to think that the lead whisks through flesh as smoothly as a knife thrust. But I have seen a 200-pound man knocked flat on his face by the impact of a big, blunt-nosed .45-caliber slug from a long-barreled Colt, which shoots with almost the driving force of a rifle. And what the slug meets it usually tears or breaks in a shocking manner. But the bullet that Lew Melody sent through the body of the sheriff was so neatly placed that it went through the shoulder without smashing a single bone, yet the force of it twisted Joe Crockett around and made him slump against the watering trough. He would have fallen to the ground, had not Melody caught him in his sinewy arms.

There the sheriff lay, gasping with agony, as he saw the men running toward him from the bunkhouse.

"Lew," he said to Melody, "for heaven's sake, don't run away from them. Let them take you, and I'll never appear to press a charge for resisting arrest. Don't run, Lew. Stand fast, and. . . ."

It was about as honest and as kind a thing as any man of the law had ever said, I think, and particularly a Western sheriff with a bullet newly through his body from the hand of a criminal he had tried to arrest. But while he was speaking, the men from the bunkhouse, who had seen every happening in this affair, and who had heard part of it, were coming with a rush. They had been gathered together, washing up for noon dinner, and now they came in a compact group. Joe Crockett told me afterward that he thought Lew would have taken his advice,

even in that crisis, had it not been that some of the cowpunchers were already drawing their guns as they ran. They had a
foolish impression that, instead of supporting a wounded man,
Melody, with fiendish cruelty, was murdering a helpless man.
They were ready to shoot, and they did start shooting, in fact,
as soon as he allowed the body of Crockett to slip gently to the
ground.

It left nothing for Lew Melody to do except to flee, unless he
wished to stay and slaughter the whole crew of them. As perhaps
he could have done, for they were a wretched lot of marksmen,
as Crockett avouched later. Indeed, the average marksmanship
of cowpunchers with revolvers is strangely bad. I have gone into
a saloon after seven or eight score bullets from revolvers were
fired at pointblank range—result: windows, doors, floors, and
ceilings and glassware smashed all to bits, but in human casual-
ties not more than one dead and two or three slightly wounded.
One would think that even accident would cause a greater damage.

However, Lew did not pause to consider this. The moment
the sheriff was out of his arms, he heard the bullets *whizzing*
around him and he knew that he must run for his life. It was
then that he made a decision that was both wise and foolish. It
was wise because his own horse, which he had just ridden in off
the range, was a rather tired and very commonplace cow pony,
whereas the sheriff's horse was a handsome bay with a
thoroughbred's stride and something of thoroughbred blood in
it, also. But it was very foolish even in that emergency for Lew
to steal that same strong bay horse. It might save him for the
moment, but it made him something just a whit more detest-
able than a confessed murderer—a horse thief.

However, he was in the saddle and away in the split part of a
second. He was a natural horseman; in a trice he had gathered
that fine animal under him and pushed it to full speed. Another

second or two and he had swerved out of view behind the corner of the nearest shed.

They had sight of him after that, as they pursued, but with such a running start, and on such an animal, there was never a chance for them to capture him, unless he foolishly doubled back straight into their arms. In an hour he was out of hearing and out of sight, and, although they thrashed about the countryside all the rest of that day, with some score or two of other riders to help them out, they did not come upon any traces of the fugitive. He had wisely faded away toward the north, and toward the north the pursuit headed, while calls came back to us in Barneytown to make the telegraph buzz with the news and to carry the word to every little town on the line north and east and west of the valley. For somewhere in that direction was riding the criminal who had resisted arrest under the charge of murder, and who had shot down the famous sheriff, Joe Crockett.

It was spectacular tidings, and many and many a stalwart warrior of the cattle ranges, and many a shrewd, brown-faced farmer from the valleys, oiled his rifle and cleaned it and mounted his horse and struck in with some company of his fellows to haunt the probable paths by which Lew Melody might flee.

But what seemed most odd to everyone after the event was that no one had considered for an instant the trail that Lew did finally adopt, and that was the back trail down the eastern ridge of the hills and straight to the ranch and to the house of Furnival.

Yes, for there he went after the dark had fallen, and cached his horse in a stout thicket near the front of the rambling old house. Then he slipped up to the dwelling and climbed to the second story. A moment later and he was through the window and crouched in a corner of Sandy's room.

She went upstairs early that night—as soon as the after-dinner dishes were finished. She went upstairs, poor child, to weep from her eyes some of the tears that she had been striving to keep from showing since the news of this second crime of her lover's had come to her. And from her sad soul, I suppose, she would have tried to moan away some of the despair.

But the instant she turned up the flame of the lamp, carried it, and settled it on the table, she saw a tall shadow standing in a corner of the room, and shrank with a little gasp from Lew Melody.

I suppose that neither of those two wretched young people thought of it, at the time, but there was something childish in his desperate approach to her. He dropped on his knees in front of Sandy and reached for her hands and drew them down.

"Sandy, Sandy, Sandy dear," Lew Melody said. "I'm not trying to get you to talk to me, after you swore you never would. But I had to give myself one last sight of you before I started out."

What did Sandy do? She drew him to his feet and made him sit down in a chair, and she leaned behind that chair, with her breath beside his face, as she whispered: "Where are you going, Lew?"

"Outside the law," Lew Melody confessed.

"If you do that, you'll never come back."

"I'll never come back," he said.

"Ah, my dear!" she said and she began to cry—poor, broken-hearted girl—and the tears fell on the face and the hands of Lew Melody. "But can't you come back and take your chance? I know that they can't harm you for . . . the Geary man. And the sheriff is not badly wounded."

"I'm a horse thief," Lew Melody said, and that word was enough for both their Western minds until she cried to him: "But if the sheriff didn't really press that charge . . . and he wouldn't. . . ."

"What would I gain by it?" asked Lew Melody. "Sandy, could I come to you, if I won through all the danger of it?"

"No, no," said poor Sandy. "My father is a strange man, Lew. And now that he's made up his mind about you, you would have to kill him before you could have me. But beyond that, I've given an oath, Lew. Oh, what have I done that God should wish to torture me so?"

"You'll forget me in a month, Sandy," he said. "Because inside of that month I'll have done enough things to make you wish that you'd never seen me."

"Do you say that?" said this dear girl. "But I know, I've always guessed, that you could be terrible, but you could never be cruel or really wicked and low. I know that, Lewis."

The devil made Mr. Furnival miss his newspaper, and he came to the foot of the stairs to call Sandy.

"Will you kiss me once before you go down?" Melody asked.

"I cannot."

"It's the last time, Sandy. I'll never have to ask you again."

"I cannot," said poor Sandy. And then she hurried down the stairs and to her father.

As for Lew Melody, he stood there in the yellow of the lamplight, drinking in every bit of that room feverishly, hungrily. Whatever he saw was a part of her. That chair she sat in; the mark in that book her fingers had placed there. Before that mirror she had stood and looked at her smiling face this side and that before she went out on that very night that first gave her a sight of him. The toes of two slippers peeked out from beneath the bed. The very curtains that framed the two windows were gay things that Sandy must have found and chosen and hung there with her own hands.

He pressed their smooth silk folds against his face, and out of them came a ghostly thin fragrance of violets: Sandy. Two roses drooped out of a vase beside her bed: Sandy.

Then he pressed his hands across his eyes and prayed that he should not go mad, and so he slipped out the window as he had come, and down softly to the ground below, and so to the thicket of trees where he had left his horse, and then away on the strong-striding bay. This time to the north.

He stopped at the crest of the next hill. He could mark the house clearly and the light of every window, and, while he sat in the saddle there, waiting, like a signal to him he saw the window of her room go black, and by that he knew that she had come back and blown out the light to sit alone in the dark with her grief, because she could not bear the sight of the familiar things around her.

Then Melody turned his face to the north and jogged steadily away.

★ ★ ★ ★ ★

LEW AND SLIM

★ ★ ★ ★ ★

I

When the desert rat lay coiled on his straw pallet in the attic of the shack of Stan Geary and listened to the short and pleasant debate between his master and Bert Harrison, and when he gathered from that debate that Geary's services were being purchased for the killing of a man, the rat was not shocked. He had bits of conscience left to him, but they were scattered here and there and not readily available. He remained, to the very end, the strangest morsel of humanity that it has ever been my fortune to encounter, and I think that, if the rat thought very much about the journey of his master south to Barney Valley, it was with rather a pleasant anticipation of the end that was to be. He himself had felt the heavy hand of Geary so often, and those cruel fingers had so wrung and crushed his body, that the rat was glad to think that the mighty hands would be used upon another creature.

He prepared, in the meantime, to wait for the return and enjoy the absence of Geary. How long his master would be away, the rat could not tell. Geary had said: "A week." But that might mean anything from a day to a month or more. Geary in leaving had tossed the youngster $1 and told him to spend that present with care.

But it was indeed a present to the rat. He had no intention of spending a single cent out of the 100. For what did he need to sustain his life? There was Geary's old rifle in the corner, and an ample supply of powder and lead and shells. With those materials he could turn out bullets that were a delight to the eye, and Geary professionally and habitually preferred the handiwork of the boy to store bullets out of a machine.

"They got a sort of a nose to foller the right trail, the bullets that kid turns out," Stan Geary was fond of saying.

So with that rifle and with those bullets of his own manufacture, with a little cornmeal, baking powder, sugar, and salt, the youngster was prepared to face a stay of any length whatever in the desert. For he was a wonderfully skillful hunter—that is to say, he was a wonderfully patient one. Geary had not taught him; Geary could not teach him; instead, he was the provider of the food for the table as well as the cook and the dish washer.

Do you wonder, as I wondered when I first heard the story, why Slim, as he was called by the few who knew him, should have spent his time as the slave of Geary? I could not understand until it was explained to me that fear was the solution. Through bitterest fear, Geary had bought this boy and by the power of fear he kept the youngster.

But how could fear follow the boy into the desert? Why could he not take that rifle and some ammunition and salt in his pouch and plunge into the untracked desert? There was nothing for him to dread there. He could go bareheaded in the frightful sun, more recklessly than any Indian. He could go without water for a length of time, in comfort, that would have reduced a normal person to death, or nearly death. What if Geary pursued? The rat knew 1,000 holes to hide in, and, beyond all that, he could trust to his heels, which would jog him smoothly over the sands and the rocks at a rate that even the best horse and rider could not follow after a short period of days.

Yet the boy could not leave his master, and the reason was that he was as hypnotized with terror as the bird is said to be hypnotized by the presence of the snake's head. But, to understand how this thing could have been, we must go back a little.

Three years before, Stan Geary, in rambling through the hills, prospecting, or pretending to prospect, had chipped off a corner of a rock by accident and he found the gold in the rock glittering and staring at him. It was a foolish vein of ore that pinched out almost at once, but it lasted long enough for big Geary to sell it for $6,000 to a credulous rancher. The $6,000 made up a larger sum than Geary had ever had before, and he had gone as far as Denver to spend it. Not the Denver that you and I know, but the Denver of days that were pressed back nearer to the days and the ways of the mining camps. And while Stan Geary was blazing his trail with folly, right and left, tossing his money away as fast as he could, he caught sight of a little pickpocket at work in the crowd one night.

He was fascinated by what he saw. Surrounded by men who were armed to the teeth and nervously or joyously ready to use the very first occasion to whip out a gun or a knife, this boy of eleven was threading his way through the mob, working with consummate adroitness. It was only by the chance flash of his eye that Stan Geary had detected a theft. After that he trailed the youngster and kept his gaze so steadily on him that he was able to follow the deft, lightning-like swoop of the child's hand. For an hour Stan Geary watched the little knave at this work of deviltry, and he laughed and roared with delight as the boy played his tricks, until it occurred to Stan that this would be a good time for he himself to reap the benefits of the pickpocket's work. The boy's pockets were by this time bulging with his thefts. So the long arm of Geary fastened upon the neck of Slim.

It was like laying hold upon an eel, for Slim twisted quickly around and fired a revolver into the face of the big man. A finger's breath to the right, and that bullet would have knocked the brains of Stan Geary into the dust and ended his wicked life three years before Lew Melody found him and crushed him. But that bullet, unfortunately, did not go home.

My dear Lydia, leaning at my shoulder now, has exclaimed: "What a thing for a minister to put down in black and white! And besides, aren't you ashamed, Tom Travis? Isn't there an example for you to set in this town?"

Well, I suppose that there is. But even if it is not Christian to wish the guilt of murder on the head of a child, still when I think what mischief would have been left undone if Geary had never come to Barney Valley. . . .

However, I must go back to the facts. The bullet from the boy's gun merely grazed the skin of Stan Geary and drew out three drops of blood. Those drops were three prices that the big man paid for the soul and the body of Slim.

He picked up the boy and tucked him under his arm and carried him off where he could examine him. The boy struggled only once to slip away. For, at his first movement, Stan Geary, with the sting of the new wound in his temple, gripped furiously at the throat of the child. Another instant and Slim would have been dead, but Geary relaxed his hold just in time. As it was, he had to throw the boy down on the ground and wait for him to recover.

By the time Slim came slowly to himself, Geary had appropriated his entire possessions. What he found was quite unique. Besides the recent thefts that crowded the pockets of Slim, Geary discovered that the coat of the boy was lined with a complete kit of everything that a hobo could desire in the way of knives, needles, thread, patch cloth, and so forth. He realized that he had nipped in the bud the career of one of the youngest thieves and professional tramps in the world.

But it is needless to say that was not the reason that Stan Geary took the boy with him into the desert. It was because an immense malice had been stowed up in his heart by the resistance that Slim had made to him. A thousand times he remembered that a bullet fired by that child's hand had nearly ended his career of greatness, and a thousand times as he thought of it, he reached violently for Slim.

I presume that no one in the world could know all that he did to torment the boy in the first part of the time during which the rat was a prisoner, and kept close. But I shall put down one device. Stan Geary at length decided that he had amused himself enough, but, when he left the shack, he wished to make sure that the boy did not escape. So he deliberately starved Slim to a staggering weakness, and then he went away.

He was gone only ten hours, but, when he came back, Slim was gone, and it was only by chance that Geary was able to pick up the cunningly hidden trail and catch the youngster. Slim had stuck like a bulldog to his work, and he covered a full twenty miles before Geary gathered him in.

There was another regime of hell, and, when Geary departed the next time, he left behind him a boy too weak to more than crawl.

But Slim crawled. Horrible to relate, the dread of the unspeakable Geary forced the boy out like a dreadful nightmare, and he dragged himself up to the top of the next hill, and then down into the next hollow before his strength gave out. There Geary found him and carried him home by the nape of the neck, as a cat carries a kitten.

But after that, Slim had learned his lesson. Upon his mind there was formed the conviction that this man was irresistible in might, unsurpassable in cunning, and the king of all cruel devils. In the last assumption I think that Slim was probably right.

But the time came when big Geary could leave the shack freely and journey away as far and remain away as long as he chose. When he cared to return to the shack, he was sure to find there an obedient slave ready to cook, clean, catch and saddle horses, chop wood, and, in general, make lazy Stan Geary perfectly at home.

Slim did not hate Geary. His emotion passed beyond the bounds included in such a term. It was so great that it extended beyond all gnashings of the teeth, all mute ragings, even; it was a perfect detestation, and like all perfect things it was calm.

Geary was sure that the boy would murder him sooner or later, for he had enough animal wit to look beneath the quiet surface of Slim. The pleasure to Geary was in watching the silent suffering of this boy, and the pleasure, perversely, of keeping a poisonous serpent in his bosom.

II

So three years passed over the head of Slim, and during those three years, partly taught by Geary, and far more by gathering up through native wit and intimate contact, he came to know more of the desert than many a native who had spent his life in the land of little rain. And then Geary went on his expedition to murder young Lew Melody and earn $400.

A week, and then two weeks passed, but Slim was not alarmed. He was very much contented to remain there alone for an indefinite period. He was fourteen, now. His body was lithe and hard-muscled. He was not large, but he was as tough as whip leather. And in the hardships of the desert he found his recreations.

Then a stranger from the direction of town—Slim knew that direction, although Geary had never let him go to the place—came over the low, sandy hills under a blistering sun and drew rein at the door of the shack. Through that open door, without dismounting, he could see Slim sitting cross-legged on the floor, deftly sewing together rabbits' skins that he had dressed himself. The skin of the rabbit is not tough, but it possesses a soft and comfortable warmth, and all the long summer Slim was busy preparing himself against the ardors of the winter—laying up stores of dried or smoked meat, and laying up warm furs, and mining the long roots of the mesquite for fuel. The stranger looked in and wondered at this boy, more than half naked, and brown as a Mexican.

"Hello, kid," he said.

Slim did not reply; he merely made a covert gesture to bring the knife that lay on the floor, closer beside him.

"Are you deaf?" asked the traveler.

Slim, since his back was turned, could afford to smile with satisfaction. He was not yet able to wreak his vengeance upon huge Stan Geary, but it was no little satisfaction to annoy all other men in large ways or small ones.

The rider was sufficiently irritated and interested to dismount from his horse and step through the doorway. There he looked around upon the frightful poverty of that wretched shack. It was literally falling to pieces. The leaning, staggering walls had been braced up by the boy through a sort of clumsy masonry—rocks being built up in the corners to support the flimsy walls against the shock of the winds. And, to keep the walls themselves from disintegrating, because he had no nails, the boy had fastened the boards together with thongs of leather. The floor itself was bare. There had once been a boarding across it, but that boarding had been torn up by Stan Geary in an idle moment and thrust into the stove to make one winter's day cheerful.

The rider was one who had known poverty all of his days, but he had never seen a white man living in such conditions as these.

"Might your pa be around?" he asked.

Slim turned his head over his naked shoulder and regarded the other with a baleful calm. "You're standin' in my light," he said.

Take it all in all, it was about as perfectly satisfying an insult as one could imagine. The stranger, at least, felt it to be complete, and his hand made an instinctive gesture toward the neck of the seated boy. It was as though he had waved at a wildcat. Slim was away in a corner of the shack with a single bound, and there he stood with his teeth showing and the knife poised for the throw—lying flat in the palm of his hand.

"Holy, howlin' devils," said the cowpuncher. "What might be ailin' you, kid?"

"Get out and keep out," this ugly-tempered boy said. "Did I ask you to stay here? I didn't, and you'll budge, and budge *pronto* . . . don't make no move to grab that gun, or I'll stick this knife between your ribs up to the handle and make it sing a song for you!"

There was no doubting the savage energy and joy with which he expressed these things. But it happened that the cowpuncher was a man who had been through so many kinds of peril that his only emotion now was joy because he was face to face with a new thrill. Instead of leaping out through the door, as I am sure I should have done, and so would most other sensible people, the cowpuncher merely sat down on a stool beside the door and began to make his cigarette.

"Cover up your teeth, kid," he said. "And don't start acting like a girl in a tantrum."

I think it was a well-chosen speech. For there is nothing that a boy dreads so much as the least insinuation that there is a feminine touch about him. Slim was still in a temper, but that shrewd insinuation weakened him. He lowered the hand that held the knife and regarded the cowpuncher with a scowl.

I can testify that scowl of Slim's was one of the most unpleasant things that I have ever encountered in this rough world; it came close to the snarl of the beast Geary himself. However, that young cowpuncher merely smiled at the sullen fury of the child. He continued to make remarks about the place—not concerning its naked ugliness, but the adroitness with which it was supported and made to continue to be a shelter. And so he turned the current of his talk to the father of this odd boy.

"I had an idea that the trappers didn't pick out this part of the country no more to work?" said the cowpuncher. "Does your pa get on pretty good? Does he have any luck?"

"I've got no pa," said the boy.

It must have startled the other a little. "You live here all alone!" he exclaimed.

"Did I say that? I didn't. Stan Geary, he hangs out here a part of the time."

"Stan Geary!" cried the cowpuncher.

"Yes," said the savage boy, "and, if he heard you yap like that when you was namin' him, he'd bust you in two till the stuffings ran out of you."

The cowpuncher merely shook his head. "He'll do nobody no harm no more," he said. He looked more closely at the naked shoulders of the boy, and it seemed to the cowpuncher that he could distinguish the last traces of a diminishing criss-cross where the weal of a whiplash had been raised.

"Now, what might you mean by that?" asked Slim.

"What's your name?" asked the cowpuncher.

"I dunno that I got no name. Why?"

"Good Lord, youngster, d'you mean that you have no name at all?"

"I disremember bein' called nothing more'n Slim so far back as I can remember."

"Your mother is dead, too?" said the stranger.

"My mother? I dunno."

"You don't know!"

"Well, that's what I said. I never seen her. Now what's this about Geary doin' no harm no more?"

"I mean that."

"Have they stuck him in jail?"

"Kid," said the good-natured cowpuncher, "maybe Geary has stood by you and done you some good turns . . . and maybe again the turns he's done you ain't been as good as you think. Anyway, you better pack up your things and come along with me. I see that you got a pony pack yonder . . . and there's a saddle. . . ."

"What the devil are you talkin' about?" said the boy.

"Geary is dead," the cowpuncher said gently.

It had an astonishing effect upon Slim. He struck his hands together in a great fury. "You lie!" he yelled at the cowpuncher. "It ain't true. Because he's gonna be saved for me . . . and I'm gonna . . . he ain't dead! He can't be dead, and stole away from me!"

The cowpuncher made out vaguely that this unusual boy was lamenting not the sudden departure of Stan Geary from this world, but the bitter loss of an opportunity that he had himself long looked forward to. He merely groaned because the slaying of Geary had been stolen from his own hands.

The desert rat grew more calm after this. His next question concerned the slayer of the man who had tormented him so long.

"It's about the only man in the world that *could* have killed Stan Geary, I guess," said the cowpuncher. "It's Lew Melody, of Barney Valley. He's gone north . . . they ain't found his trail yet. And they've planked out a pretty neat reward for him, dead or alive."

"Hey?" cried Slim. "Reward? Reward on him for what?"

"Why, nothing but murder, hoss-stealin', resistin' arrest, and shootin' the sheriff and woundin' him. That's all he's done lately that's worth talkin' about."

"Murder of who?" asked the boy in the same sharp tone.

"Of Stan Geary, of course. I've just finished tellin' you that."

"Did he shoot him from behind?" Slim asked, keen with interest.

"I suppose it was a fair enough fight, though there wasn't no witnesses. Geary was found with a bullet. . . ."

"Between the eyes?" asked Slim.

"How did you guess that?"

"He always aimed to say that there was where the slug would hit him. He must've knowed. But if it was a fair fight, why ain't they offerin' a reward to this here Melody, because he killed a skunk like Geary? Why are they houndin' him down?"

"Because the fool wouldn't stand for an arrest," said the cowpuncher. "If he'd stood by his guns, he'd've been tried by the judge, and the jury would sure of set him free and give him a medal besides, most likely. But when the sheriff come for him, he put a bullet through his shoulder, grabbed the sheriff's own hoss, and beat it. Well, folks can't stand by and see one gent take the law into his hands like that." He added, as the boy was thoughtfully silent: "Now, kid . . . d'you aim to come along with me?"

"What way are you travelin'?" asked Slim.

"West to. . . ."

"I'm beatin' south to Barneytown. So long . . . and thanks for all the news."

III

You will have a somewhat clearer understanding of this son of the wilderness when I tell you that even after what he had heard from the cowpuncher, he was not half sure that Stan Geary was really dead. The dread of that monster with his long, thick, gorilla arms, and his vast, monkey face remained constantly in the heart of Slim, and, as he made his preparations for departure, he had a sense of guilt and fear, and constantly he was looking toward the southern hills, as though he half expected the familiar, bulky outline of Geary to loom above the horizon. What he intended, first of all, was to go to Barneytown and make sure of the great tidings that he had just heard. If he could see the grave with the name of Geary on the tombstone, then he would be moderately certain that his persecutor was indeed no more. What he would do after that, he hardly knew; the time would tell him as the occasion arose.

But it did not come into his mind that he possessed information vital to Lew Melody; Slim could prove that Geary had been hired to go to Barney Valley for the express purpose of murdering Melody, and that evidence would most certainly take the imputation of a murder from the shoulders of the fugitive. But there was no care for the welfare of others in the mind of Slim. I believe that in his entire life he had never met with real kindness. He looked upon the world as a sort of gigantic labyrinth, beset with poison and with traps, and his one thought was for his own comfort. Besides, the mere idea of going to an officer of the law, even to give testimony on behalf of another man, seemed to Slim little short of insanity. He had had enough experience with those gentry who defended the pocketbooks of stupid people. They had heavy clubs and heavy hands and heavy voices that more than once, during his career of petty crime, had descended cruelly upon him.

Yet he had a very sharp feeling about Lew Melody as he made up his small pack of necessaries and mounted the stunted mustang that was to carry him on the long southern trip. Trying to draw a mental image of this uncanny warrior who had beaten down Geary, he appeared to Slim in a thousand forms, but always as a giant. Perhaps it was for that reason that Slim had so little care to give his testimony in behalf of Melody. He who had crushed Geary could take care of himself, certainly.

So the desert rat trekked south. Sometimes he jogged the

mustang remorselessly along; sometimes in rough country he dropped from the saddle and ran ahead, with the little horse following like a dog at his heels—it saved the strength of the animal, and it gave Slim a chance to express in physical action some of his burning desire to get to Barneytown. It was a march made almost at railroad speed, and, when Slim came into Barneytown, he wasted no time, but made instant inquiries after the fate of the giant.

Everyone could tell him. In the churchyard the body of Geary had been buried, and to the churchyard went Slim.

I had finished an evening service; the people had left the church. As I went out wearily—for it had been a long, hot day—I saw the ragged form of Slim sitting on the new grave in the farthest corner of the burial ground.

No matter at how many burials I have officiated, death is never an old face to me, and the sting of it does not grow dulled by time. I felt a sudden stir of my heart as I looked toward that grave and the solitary youngster sitting on it. I had not heard that the dead man left behind him any dependents—certainly not a son—but then there were many chapters of the life of Geary that even Sheriff Joe Crockett—now flat on his back in his bedroom nursing his wounded shoulder—had not been able to tell me. So I went softly and reverently toward that pathetic-looking young waif.

He neither heard nor saw me, for his back was turned, and I was walking over the grass. Therefore I had an opportunity to see him unsheathe a long-bladed knife and suddenly bury it in the new turf with which the grave had been covered over.

It does not seem an extraordinary action, naming it as I have done, and I have no power to tell you with what a concentrated venom that knife was driven home and then the blade worked deeper still, like some venomous man making the weapon writhe home in the wound. An instant later he heard me and whirled to his feet with the knife in his hand.

I thought, at first, that he was about to bolt away, but then he changed his mind. My clerical collar showed him my profession, and in the same instant I could see relief and contempt come into his face. It was a little irritating, but what I had seen was too curious and too horrible not to make me want to have some words with this boy; I could not simply order him off the place for profaning a grave.

I said: "My young friend, you were not a friend to Stanley Geary, it seems?"

He was wiping the dirt carefully from the glistening blade of the knife while he kept his suspicious eyes upon me. "Look here, mister," he said as he put away the weapon, "d'you ever know anybody that *was* the friend of Geary? Lemme hear you say who."

He pointed this challenge by thrusting a grimy forefinger at me. I could not help pausing in amazement to examine him again. It was the bright afterglow of the sunset, for the sun being just down, its light was thrown up against some cloud masses in the west and these turned into crimson towers of fire, threw a red light across the world and across the brown face of Slim. He had the serious face of a philosopher. There was a great forehead, shaped magnificently: broad, high, and smooth, except for a whimsical little corrugation between the eyes. Beneath that forehead was a pair of big, intelligent eyes. The lower part of his face was much older than his age. There were deep lines of pain drawn beside the mouth, and the whole face was so pinched and drawn that he might have stood for a picture of a famine survivor. It was a look that never left the boy, although it was denied by the health of his sun-blackened skin and the brightness of his eyes. But he appeared so perfectly wild, so utterly savage, that he fascinated me.

1 admitted that I did not know of any intimate friends of

Geary, but I knew that there must be some who were fond of him. "Because," I said, "even the worst of men will do some kind things which other men will remember."

The boy merely grinned at me with greater contempt than before. "That's a lie," he said, while I started at such an abrupt contradiction. "There wasn't no good in him. He was crooked, and he was a measly skunk. That's all there was to him."

"You knew him very well?" I said.

"I got the marks of him on me," said Slim.

I was burning with curiosity. I found out that he had no particular place to spend the night—that he was without resources—and I straightway followed an impulse and invited him to come to my house and take a bed there.

He would not accept at first. He canted his wise head to one side and regarded me for a long moment as though he were trying to get at some hidden reason that must be behind my offer. But, at last, I marched off down the street with him. A downheaded mustang, which I had noticed standing in front of the church hitching rack without being tied, turned and followed at our heels like a pet dog. I was more interested than ever before. I could not help wondering at this savage youngster, this wild thing that had been able to train a dumb brute so well.

"How did you manage to do it?" I asked him.

"The hoss?" he said.

"Yes."

"Oh," said Slim, "that ain't nothin'. You see, a hoss is straight. There ain't no crooked hosses until some gent makes 'em crooked."

I thought of my fat mare, with her stupid habit of putting back her ears when I came near to her, and her way of flirting her heels in my direction; when I considered how little work I had given her to do and how well I had fed her, I could not agree with the youngster. However, I did not deny him. It is

113

always better to have a child talk right out from his heart rather than to have him argue. When a boy argues, he is too like a woman.

"But this seems a rather old horse to be trained," I suggested.

"Does he?" said Slim. "Well, he ain't so old. About nine, I guess. He looks old because he's got that fool look and that big head. But he trained pretty easy. Any hoss that was used to Geary would train pretty easy for a gent that treated him half decent. Sam, here, all he knowed about a currycomb was a club swatting him on the ribs . . . all he knowed about conversation was Geary's cussing. Did you ever hear Stan Geary cuss?"

I admitted that I had not.

"It was considerable cussing," said Slim. "It laid over pretty near anything that I ever heard."

"What is your name?" I asked.

"Slim."

"But your real name?"

"Ain't that real enough? Why should I pack around a lot of other names? One is good enough for me. They used to call me Denver Slim when I was on the road."

It gave me a flash of insight into what the poor boy had been through. I could understand, even then, something of what was behind the thrusting of the knife into the grave of Geary. But here we reached the house, and I was busy making explanations to my dear Lydia. She gave one glance at the dirty, naked feet of this boy and his tousled head of hair that had not known a comb for years and that had apparently been trimmed from time to time with a sheep shears. It had not been trimmed recently, however, for I could see the upper layers of hair sun-browned and faded, and beneath was jet black, like the eyes of the boy. I realized that I should have to have some private conversation with Lydia, so I drew her aside into the kitchen and told her what I had seen.

She was too angry to argue, which was a great relief. She could only say: "We'll have to have everything in the house cleaned from top to bottom after that brat gets out of it. Heaven alone can tell when he's had a bath!"

IV

The attitude of Slim was very much that of a wildcat that is feasting in a chicken yard—enjoying the tender morsels thoroughly, but with a watchful eye upon the house from which the scent of man and guns is issuing. So Slim sat at the table and ate his portions. I put that word in the plural advisedly. Never was there such a falling to. He ate as though he had not seen food for a month—and such food as my dear Lydia placed before him—with an upturned nose, I am ashamed to say—I presume he had never seen before. I would venture a guess that he put aboard provisions enough to last him many a day in the next of his camel-like marches.

The size of that meal defeated my purposes, for Slim, having eaten like a boa constrictor, went promptly to sleep in his chair while I was still at my coffee. I had to shake him by the shoulder in order to rouse him, and, when he was stirred, he gave one cat-like start, one wild glance at me—then made sure that there was no immediate danger and slumped in his chair again with dulled eyes. I got him to a room and shoved him in his bed. Then I went out to soothe Lydia, but she declared that the boy was simply a little wild animal and that no good would ever come of him. I was a bit downcast myself.

I went back onto the verandah and looked into his room half an hour later. He had tried the bed—the covers were thrown in a heap, but beds were not to the taste of this young savage. I saw him stretched on the rug with one corner of it thrown over his body, snoring loudly and contentedly. One would have thought that the hard floor was a downy couch.

I could not help smiling at this, but, before I could pursue any further reflections upon my strange young guest, Mrs. Cheswick arrived after her choir practice. She was full of news, full of excitement, full of tears. Of course I asked first of all if Sandy Furnival had come in for the rehearsal, and I was a happy man to hear Mrs. Cheswick say that she had. Since the day when she had broken with Lew Melody—the very night before he became a fugitive from justice by shooting down Sheriff Joe Crockett—Sandy had not come near the church or near the town. So I took Mrs. Cheswick by the arm as I met her at the door and heard this good news, and I rushed her into the house calling to Lydia: "Sandy has been at the choir practice, my dear! Sandy has come at last!"

My Lydia did not even stay to dry the dishwater from her hands and arms, and I forgave her for that neglect. She simply ran in agape.

"And how is she?" asked Lydia.

"And how does she look?" I said. "And what does she say? And did she seem happy to be singing again?"

Mrs. Cheswick shook her head in answer to everything. The good woman really had tears in her eyes, while she told us that Sandy was a ghost of her old self, with her face wan and her eyes spiritless.

"Like a poor, dying thing," said Mrs. Cheswick. "But she'd made up her mind to start in where she left off and carry through. And she did. She sang almost as well as ever, but the music brought no joy to her . . . a child could have seen that. And there was such a look in her face that no one dared to talk to her except that little fool, Susie Graham. I wish to heavens that we had never taken Susie into the choir!"

"What did the little idiot do?" gasped out my Lydia.

It appeared that Susie Graham, overcome by the sorrow in the face of our Sandy, had finally run up to the poor girl and thrown her arms around her and burst into tears.

"I don't care what the rest say!" declared this inspired young fool to our heartbroken Sandy. "*I* wish that you *had* Lew Melody, no matter how many men he's killed! I *do* wish it. Oh, Sandy, I'm afraid that you'll never smile again for us!"

Lydia and I were dumbfounded. It seemed impossible that even a Susie Graham could have done such a tactless thing, but Mrs. Cheswick declared that Sandy did not as much as change color—being pale enough already. She merely looked gravely at Susie and thanked her for her good wishes.

Lydia grew more excited than ever. "I don't like that," she said. "She should have broken into tears . . . how could she have kept her face in front of such talk as that? If she'd broken down . . . but who would have thought that there was so much strength in our Sandy? But, oh, Tom, isn't that the sort of strength which is brittle and makes people break at last?"

I was too sick at heart to answer. For another moment we sat silently looking at the floor and wishing, every one of us, that such a person as Lew Melody had never been born. Even I wished it, and yet I think that I was more a friend to him than any other person in the valley.

Mrs. Cheswick wiped her eyes. "But just as Susie had finished shocking us, the worst thing of all happened!"

"What could be worse?" groaned Mrs. Travis.

"It was old Missus Kingdon. She came running in to ask if we had heard the news. We asked her what she meant, and . . . of course the half-blind old thing didn't see Sandy. She blurted out the cream of the news in one breath. It was too much for Sandy. When she heard that the posse was getting ready to ride, and that Bill Granger and Doc Newton were going with it after him, she staggered up from her chair with a choked sort of a cry and left the church. I tried to stop her. I couldn't. She gave me one desperate look, and I couldn't say a word to her."

"But what news was it?" Mrs. Travis and I cried in one breath.

"What news? Why, it's been in town for more than half an hour! The posse is gathering as fast as it can. Deputy Sheriff Sid Marston had sent all over Barneytown for the best fighting men that he can get . . . and they're riding out at once."

"For what, Missus Cheswick? For what, in heaven's name?"

"Is it possible that you haven't heard!" she cried. "But Lew Melody has robbed the bank at Comanche Crossing!"

Just what story Mrs. Cheswick told us of that wild adventure, I forget. What I know now is the full story as I gathered it from a dozen different sources later on.

When Melody left the sheriff lying by the watering trough with a bullet hole through his right shoulder, he had ridden back that night to say a last good night to Sandy Furnival and try—vainly—to make her change her mind. Then he had turned north and held steadily to the rough upper hill country, probably killing his food as he went, for he was glimpsed only twice, and both times by hunters for game, not for man. Both reports represented him going steadily north and north.

But he had apparently wearied of this dull life, with nothing but the mountains to keep him company, and so he turned straight back and came out of the hills and down into the upper part of Barney Valley until he reached the old Indian ford where the rich little town of Comanche Crossing had grown up. It was not more than fifty miles from Barneytown itself, and I suppose that there must have been half a hundred men in Comanche Crossing—to put it mildly—who had seen Lew Melody face to face. Besides that, the description of him was everywhere, together with posters that showed an excellent likeness of him, taken the year before when he had won the bucking contest at the rodeo at Twin Rivers. In spite of all this, Lew Melody had dared to ride into Comanche Crossing in the middle of the day and straight down the street on the bay horse that he had taken from Sheriff Joe Crockett.

He had gone to the bank and dismounted and thrown the reins of his horse just in front of the main door of the little building from which half of the mining and the ranching of the valley was financed. Then he had sauntered in and gone to a bench at the side of the room. There he sat down and lighted a cigarette when the doorkeeper-janitor came to him and told him he would have to put it out, because there was a bank regulation against smoking in the building—which was of wood.

Lew Melody had answered so pleasantly, and put out the cigarette so obediently, that the janitor had fallen into conversation with him about the major topic of the day, so far as our mountains were concerned, and that was about Lew Melody himself. The janitor had a theory that Lew was striking toward Canada.

While they were chatting, the line in front of the cashier's window melted away and, when there was no one there, Lew Melody excused himself from the janitor and walked up to the window and asked for a blank check and a pen.

The cashier gave it to him and he wrote across the check: *Please pay me $10,000 in large bills and about $500 in small ones. Lewis Melody.*

This little note he shoved under the window to the cashier, and then dropped a significant right hand upon his hip and waited.

The cashier read that note and looked up with a grin, but the grin went out when he studied the grave eyes of Lew. He remembered the pictures that he had seen, and suddenly the surety came to him that this was the man—and not a joke at all.

I know that people have been fond of criticizing that poor cashier for cowardice. He had a revolver lying on the bench just beneath his window. All he had to do was to snatch it up and fire it into the breast of Lew Melody. That is to say, unless Lew

Melody was able to get his own weapon out first and plant his shot in time. And, considering that Lew's weapon was in its holster, that likelihood seemed very far distant. However, can one really blame the clerk? I put myself in his place, and honestly say that I cannot. If those steady gray eyes looked into mine and made such a demand upon me—why, I am sure that I would have done exactly what the cashier did—that is to say, I should have gone to the open safe and taken out a sufficient quantity of money and carried it back to the window. And there I should have passed it over to Lew Melody.

This, at least, is what the poor man did, and Melody backed toward the front door, chatting still with the janitor in a lively manner, but keeping his deadly eye fixed upon the cashier. So he reached the door and leaped out of it, just as the cashier yelled the bad news to the rest of the employees.

Of course they snatched up weapons and poured out onto the street, but all they saw of Lew was the flash of the tail of the bay horse as he jerked that animal around the next corner and fled for the hills again.

V

That story, or some part of it, was what Mrs. Cheswick told us as we sat agape in our parlor and wondered how much daring could exist in any mortal breast. Then something was heard boiling over on the stove in the kitchen, and my Lydia bolted toward it with a cry.

She came back almost at once. She stood in the doorway and said to me sternly: "Tom Travis, I found the side of bacon lying on the kitchen table, with a great chunk cut off from it. I think that you'd better go to see if your precious young vagabond is still in that room."

I hurried into the room to find out—and, sure enough, Slim had taken French leave with his chunk of bacon, some coffee, and a parcel of sugar together with a little flour. It was not a great theft, but it was a stinging one to me and made another black mark on the list that one cannot help keeping in one's heart of the misdeeds of those who we have trusted.

Of course it was not worthwhile raising a hue and cry. But I wished that I could give the young rascal a good hiding—not on account of the stolen stuff, to be sure, but because his little crime gave Lydia an immense superiority over me for whole days to come, and I was never able to answer back. And that is a sad thing even in a minister's household.

In the meantime, my precious imp had not chosen to flee directly from the town. Instead, he had gone straight to the jail, where Deputy Sheriff Sid Marston, taking the place of Joe Crockett while the sheriff was wounded, was gathering a select group of riders and fighters.

I have no doubt Slim, being awakened by the sound of our voices, had overheard enough of our conversation to stir his blood. At any rate, in front of the jail he found the posse mustering when he appeared there on the back of his lump-headed mustang. He discovered Sid Marston at once, in the center of the group, giving instructions. Marston was a man of some distinction, with a pair of well-trimmed, martial mustaches and bristling eyebrows, and a terse, commanding way about him. He was in no hurry in the organizing of this posse. What he wanted was the best material he could get into his hands—men who could ride hard and had horses that could stand hard riding, men who knew the country like a book, and, above all, men who could shoot straight and who would shoot straight.

He was about ready to make his start. He had with him only seven men and seven horses, but every man was an ideal frontiersman and every horse was an iron-limbed devourer of mileage. Sid Marston called them around him and made a speech.

He said: "Boys, we're not starting out to make a little dash upcountry, beat around a while, lose the trail, and come back with tired hosses and a pile of wasted time behind us. We've got to match up ag'in' a shifty lad who knows those mountains and the desert as well as any of us. He's got a hundred thousand square miles of hole-in-the-wall country to run around in . . . and we're gonna be beating around pretty much in the dark, most of the time. But he's got to be landed, and it's worthwhile landing him.

"He's got to be landed because he's gone all wrong. Ever since he was fourteen, he's been raising hell, but the hell he raised was mostly over in the greaser section of Barneytown with American yeggs and greaser gunmen. Well, boys, that was all right. It wasn't the sort of fun that you and me would want to fool around with. But it didn't bother us none while he was usin' up bullets on thugs. But now he's changed. He's got the blood taste. About the killing of Geary . . . well, I dunno that that was so bad. Geary had a record of his own. But anyway, that's a murder charge. And then comes the shooting of Joe Crockett. Well, that's different. After that, he swiped Crockett's hoss. Boys, a hoss thief is a skunk, as you all know. A hoss is a thing that a gent's life is apt to depend on. In this here country where it might be sixty miles to a water hole, the gent that swipes a hoss don't deserve no more kindness than we'd show to a rattlesnake. But that ain't enough for Lew Melody . . . things get dull for him. So he slides down out of the hills and takes ten thousand dollars out of a bank. I ain't saying nothing about the men up there in Comanche Crossing. I think, though, that he couldn't've got away with that in Barneytown."

There was a hearty cheer of assent at this point, and the deputy sheriff went on: "We got a duty in this job. It was Barneytown that raised this pest . . . this Lew Melody. It was Barneytown that let him get his practice. It was Barneytown that let him get rambunctious. It was right here in our valley that he killed Stan Geary. It was our own sheriff that he shot down. It was our own sheriff's hoss that he stole. And, by a way of speakin', you couldn't blame the folks up in Comanche Crossing if they was to put the credit of this here bank robbery up to us.

"We got a duty to get this Lew Melody, because we're sort of responsible for the things that he's done. On the other hand, it wouldn't be such a bad job to finish off. The bank is offering a two thousand dollar reward, besides a percentage of any of the bank's money that we should get back on him. And they's close to fifteen hundred put up by other gents in the valley. Before we nail him, you can lay to it that the reward will be around four or five thousand dollars, and, if you split that into eight chunks, it leaves a pretty good salary for each one of us. That's the money side of it.

"All right, I say that if we start out and plan to stick to this job, and not put in three days, but six weeks at it, we got a chance to land our friend Lew Melody. Them that don't want to make a good long campaign of it can step out now. The rest of us will go on."

No one fell out of the party on account of these remarks. It merely made them look upon the work before them more soberly, but Sid Marston had chosen these fellows with care and had known beforehand, quite accurately, what they would think and what they would do. He had finished his little address and they had signified their acceptance of the conditions with a murmur and then silence, when Marston added: "We'll travel light, with small packs. But if any of you hasn't along as much as he thinks he'll need for a six-week roughing trip through the mountains, go home and get the odds and ends."

There was no answer to this; each was prepared to start as he stood.

The little crowd that had gathered to see the posse start fell back to give them room to ride away when a voice said: "It ain't all right, Sheriff. You got eight men, and that ain't lucky."

Sid Marston, very well satisfied with everything that had gone before, looked with a grin upon the lithe form of Slim as that ragged youngster pushed his mustang forward.

"What might be a lucky number, son?" he said.

"Nine," said Slim.

"Might you be the ninth man for us?" asked the deputy sheriff, beginning to guess what was coming.

"I'm the man you want," said Slim with much assurance. For the news that he had heard about hundreds of dollars in reward for the capture of the criminal had filled his imagination completely. And from the grim, efficient look of this troop of fighters, he felt sure that even the giant who had destroyed Stan Geary must fall before them.

His suggestion was received with a chuckle from the posse and a roar of laughter from the bystanders.

"You got a hoss," said the deputy mildly, "that ain't got the looks of a speedster."

There was another laugh at that.

"Old Sam," said the boy, "will start you all laughin' on the other side of your face. He'll stay with you. He ain't got the looks, but he's got the stuff in him. Besides, I don't weigh as much as the rest of you."

"Suppose that you was to stay on the trail," said the deputy sheriff, "are you pretty much of a fightin' man, kid?"

"I'll show you," said the boy. He raised the old rifle and looked around him for a target, while the crowd nudged one another and chuckled expectantly. But what the boy chose was the staff of a weathervane that stood above the new jail. "That rooster up there," said Slim, "looks pretty sassy, so. . . ." He tucked the butt of the rifle into the hollow of his shoulder, steadied the heavy barrel with his sinewy hands, and drew his bead on the line of moonlight that ran along the gilded staff of the weather cock. Then he fired. But the rooster remained undaunted in his post. There was a loud yell of derision and amusement from the crowd.

Marston began: "The cocksure man or the cocksure kid ain't always. . . ." He stopped abruptly, for there was a shout of astonishment from all those people as they saw the weather cock sway and then sag forward and drop from his staff. The bullet from the boy's rifle had cut through the staff, but still the vane was supported by a few shreds of wood and the pressure of the first puff of wind was needed to tumble the cock down.

"There you are," Slim said, highly gratified by the surprise and the applause. "And that ain't all that I can do. I'll hit a mark no bigger'n that rooster with a knife, and I'll find you sage hens and mountain grouse where you don't find nothin' but sand and rocks, and I'll live on half what you big gents need. Does that sound to you, Mister Sheriff?"

Marston scratched his head. Of course he felt that he could not take this confident little imp along, but he also felt that it would be unfair to refuse him a place pointblank after he had passed such an entrance test. "We're beating north," he said. "If you're with us when sunup comes, you can stay along with us as long as your hoss lasts for the work. That's all I can do for you."

Slim regarded the other horses with a solemn eye, and then nodded. "That's easy," he said, and, when the eight men with Marston in the lead jogged with a *jingling* of bits and spurs and a *creaking* of saddle leather down the street, Slim brought up the rear on his nondescript pony.

VI

When it was found that Slim was still in the rear of the party and his ugly mustang traveling along without signs of very great effort, Marston passed the covert word among his men to increase the pace to a marked degree and let their horses out. He set the example, and for the next ten miles those fine animals worked hard up the valley. But at the end of ten miles, as Marston slackened the gait a little, the shadowy form of Slim came bobbing up from the rear.

The deputy sheriff was astonished, and I suppose that he had good reasons for feeling surprise. Nevertheless, it had to be taken into consideration that that pony was carrying fifty pounds, or nearly that, less than the other horses; besides, its rider relieved the mustang of even his trifling weight when they came to one of the steep hills that dropped down from the mountains toward the river through Barney Valley. Up those hills, the boy ran as swiftly and as lightly as a mountain goat and leaped into the saddle again at the crest to coast down the farther side. Therefore, at the end of the ten miles, Slim was panting as hard or harder than the mustang was breathing. But he was full of joy. For, with a little pushing, he felt that Sam could be up with the leaders of the party.

The problem of the boy became a more and more serious one. So, at length, Marston decided to have his party ride their horses out that night. A thorough rest would let them recuperate the next morning; besides, it would perhaps be as well to cover the first stages of the journey with a rush and get into the upper mountains toward which the bank robber had fled. In addition to all this, his primary object was to shake off that tenacious youngster. So he freshened the pace of the party again and through the night he drove them remorselessly onward to the dawn. But when the pink of the morning came, and the deputy sheriff turned in his saddle to look back over Barney

Valley, far beneath him, with the river curving in a pink ribbon through the midst, the first thing that he saw, over the top of the next hill below him, was the form of a slender boy running strongly up the steep slope, with a mustang jogging at his heels.

At that, Sid Marston understood how the ugly little pony had been able to keep up with the party, and his heart jumped a little in admiration of this persistent youngster. He was grave the next moment. It went against the grain to deny the boy after Slim had put forth such an effort and worked all night, but, obviously, the posse could not go into action with any such child in the ranks. If a bullet from the sure rifle of Lew Melody should strike down this boy, it would be a blot upon the repute of Marston that could never be rubbed out.

First he invited Slim to breakfast with them. On the shoulder of a hill, in a thick cluster of pines, the tired men made their bivouac and there Slim ate bread and bacon and drank black coffee with the rest, then they rolled themselves in their blankets.

It was late in the morning when they were wakened by the signal of Marston, telling them: "The hosses are rested, even if we ain't . . . and we sleep no more than the hosses do on this here trip. Turn out, boys!"

They rose, stifling their groans, for the ride of the night before had taxed the strength of the best of them. While they made ready to depart, Sid Marston called Slim to him and they sat down on the edge of a boulder that looked down on the dipping hills to the valley, a dizzy distance beneath them, with the Barney River, like silver, in the midst.

"Slim," said the deputy sheriff, "I've got to tell you something that takes the heart out of me. I've got to tell you that this here job that we got on our hands is all for men, and not for boys."

He expected an outburst of rage and perhaps tears at the end. But Slim, sitting slouched forward and with his chin in his brown palm, merely turned his head slowly to the side and regarded the deputy sheriff with a look of scorn and weariness in his dusty-black eyes.

"I knowed that something like that was coming," said Slim.

The deputy sheriff bit his lip. "After you knocked over the weathervane, kid," he said, "and after you showed so much nerve in you, I didn't have the heart to turn you down flat. But when I looked at the stumpy legs of that mustang of yours, I figgered that you wouldn't have a chance to keep up with the party. And that's why I told you that, if you were with us in the morning, I'd let you keep along with the party. Y'understand?"

"*Aw*, the devil," said Slim, "I understand, right enough."

"Now, I ain't gonna send you back with nothing for your work. Here's twenty dollars, kid. You take that. It ain't bad for a day's work, like you've had."

Slim regarded the bill blankly. It was more money than he had seen in his life before, with a chance to call it his own, but now it meant nothing to him. All night he had lain awake by fits and starts, or fallen asleep to dream of himself standing among the dead of the posse, leveling his rifle and firing the shot that brought the dreadful Lew Melody to his death. And after that—he had seen himself acclaimed as a hero by the thousands. He had looked at his picture in newspapers. And he had spent a long time translating $600 into other terms. There was almost nothing that $600 would not do. It would clothe one from head to foot. It would give one underwear, to begin with—Slim had almost forgotten what that term meant. It would gird him with a cartridge belt supporting the finest of revolvers. It would seat him on a glorious horse—one that floated over the ground, rather than pounded along upon it, as poor Sam did. It would put upon his head a sombrero enriched with Mexican gold and silver work, and it would mount him on a rich saddle, glittering with metal, and in the long holster beneath his knee would be the shining length of the finest repeating rifle. And in the pack behind his saddle he would have a little hand axe of the truest steel; the knife in his belt would be a razor-edged minister of death; he would have a true wool blanket; his boots would be shop-made of bright leather.

When all this was accomplished, would there not still be very much of the $600 left? Slim felt that there would—certainly enough to last him until he came on the trail of another man that needed catching. And with such a rifle, and such a revolver and knife, and with such a horse beneath him, what human being could escape from him?

So he dropped his glance from this glorious vision to a wretched $20 bill. "What's this for?" he said.

"For you and your work and the nerve you have, son," said the deputy sheriff kindly.

"I don't want it," said Slim.

"It's yours," said Marston, and, putting it down on the rock beside Slim, he stood up.

"Wait a minute," said Slim. "Are you pretty sure that you don't want this no more?"

"It ain't mine," said Marston.

"Then I can do what I want with it?"

"Sure," said Marston. "A kid like you ought to find plenty of spending in twenty dollars, I guess."

"*Aw*, well," Slim said, "I s'pose that you figger it that way. This is the way I spend chicken feed like that." He wrapped the bill around a rock and flung it far and true down the slope until stone and money splashed in the foaming waters of a little creek.

"Why . . . you little fool!" cried Marston.

"The devil," Slim said. "A cheap guy like you ain't got a right to talk to me. But I'll tell you what . . . when you catch Lew Melody, I'll be a dog-gone' old man. Hell will be froze over before you catch him, and you'll be wearin' skates on the ice. Stay with you? Why should I want to stay with you? You and your bunch of bums, they couldn't catch rabbits if they were all greyhounds, which they ain't. Stay with you, naw . . . I'm sick of you!"

The deputy sheriff, biting his lip with anger, endured all of this reproof, because he felt that he had earned it; he held his tongue and watched Slim stalk in dignity to the despised mustang, Sam, and then ride slowly down the slope toward the hollow where the gray roof of a house appeared among the trees. Marston, taking note, bit his lip and groaned again, for he saw that the boy was not taking the back trail to Barneytown.

But once Slim was out of sight of the deputy sheriff and the rest of the men, he flung himself onto the ground and burst into a wildcat fury, tearing at his hair, beating the ground with naked heels and brown fists, spitting and cursing and moaning in a frenzy of rage. He even started at a run, stealthily, up through the trees, swinging his rifle at the trail beside him. But as he ran, he heard the noise of hoofs start off down the slope of the mountain, heading still north and west.

Then Slim paused and leaned his hand against a tree, a boy very sick at heart and very weak of spirit, hanging his head, and wishing heartily that he had never been born into such a world of liars, sneaks, and scoundrels. Compared with such conduct as this, even Stan Geary had qualities worthy of some admiration!

So thought Slim, and sat down for a moment with his head in his hands.

But who could sink down on the trail and surrender to gloom when there had been such golden visions to cheer him only the night before? He started up again and ran back toward poor Sam. For he told himself, that if the sheriff and his clan had a chance to capture Lew Melody, so did he. And $4,000. . . .

He waved his hands above his head and laughed with joy. Now he could bless the fate that he had been cursing the moment before. $4,000—for himself—riches—riches beyond calculation. For, if he attempted to list the very articles on which such a vast sum could be spent, how could he do it? He tried, and his brain failed him. If a stout pocket knife cost 37¢, how many pocket knives could be purchased for $4,000?

Confusion, but the confusion of a heavenly bliss.

He, too, rode north and west.

VII

The next bulletin that we had concerning the activities of Lew Melody was brought to us by a special messenger from the fighting front. He came down the valley riding on the bay horse of Sheriff Joe Crockett, which Lew had in the first place stolen. And he brought with him a letter to the sheriff. It read:

Dear Sheriff Crockett: The bearer is being paid for riding the bay back to you. I apologize for running away with the horse, but the boys seemed pretty much set to blow me to bits when they came at me out of the bunkhouse. So I thought that my own pony, which was pretty fagged, wouldn't have a chance to make a fast getaway. I borrowed the bay, and here it is back again. He may be a little thin, but I haven't had to press him hard at any time. He's a wonder, and, if I last long enough at this new job of mine, maybe you'll catch me on him!

If that luck comes to anybody, I hope that it comes to you. Because of all the square sheriffs that ever threw a leg over a saddle, you're the squarest and the whitest. And if I had the thing to do over again, I'd stand still and let you put the irons on me. But I couldn't that day. I thought of jail, and being tried for murder—that's a black word! And if I got away from hanging, I thought that it would mean a

131

good many years in the penitentiary, and so here I am, up to my neck in it.

Not that I really repent. No, you can tell the boys that I'm having the time of my life.

I've had to have another horse, and the one I've taken is the Gray Pacer. I suppose you know all about it.

Best luck to you on all trails—even on mine!

Lew Melody

This odd letter was received with a transport of enthusiasm by the entire population of Barneytown. There was something jovially daredevil and carefree about it that appealed to all Western hearts. Besides this appeal, the letter was brought by a man who carried back the bay horse to the sheriff. And then, to turn the matter into a greater jest than ever—while returning one horse and liberally paying a man to make the trip back with it, he had stolen another and far more valuable one.

I hastened to Joe Crockett to get his reactions to that letter, and I found that honest man thoroughly stricken.

"All I wish is this," said Crockett. "That Stan Geary had dropped into the middle of the earth before he ever come to Barney Valley to raise hell here."

"Aside from the swearing," I said, for it always annoyed me to have the sheriff speak as though my profession were as vulgar a one as his own, "aside from the swearing, I'm tempted to agree with you . . . but the more I think of the thing, the more I see that it had to come about. In one way or another, Lew Melody was sure to break the law before the end. He had too much strength and he plunged too much to be kept in any harness ever made by the law."

"D'you think so?" said the sheriff. "Well, I dunno. But now the good he's done is forgot, and nothing but the last things he's done is remembered."

"The good he has done?" I could not help crying. "If you

please, what has that boy ever done except kill with a knife or kill with a gun? And kill human beings, Joe Crockett!"

At that, the sheriff looked at me with a flush of real anger. "A gent in your line of work," he said, "ain't expected to know about such things."

"Come, come, Crockett," I said. "You must not talk down to me, but tell me what you actually think."

"You and your kind," said Crockett, "would be for going out among the crooks and the grafters, the murderers and the gunmen, and playing the fairy godmother . . . the devil!"

"Your language, Crockett," I said with dignity.

"My language is my own!" exclaimed the sheriff. "What I'm askin' you to think about is what would've happened in Barney Valley if it hadn't been for the kid? What was the jail like? Always full of gamblers, and sneaks and hired man-getters, and hobos and knife experts. And what was life in Barneytown like? When could you go out of a house without lockin' all of the doors and the windows? And I ask you whoever thinks about locks any more?"

It was rather convincingly put, and I confess that I had never thought of it so clearly before. "Surely, Crockett," I said, "surely you cannot attribute all of this change to one twenty-two year old boy."

"Can't I?" said the sheriff with a sneer of superiority. "And only twenty-two, is he? Look here, Tom Travis, how old is the average man in gunfightin' or knife plays? How many fights do they have? How many have you had?"

"A ridiculous question," I said. "Is that my business?"

"No, it ain't. But how many does the average gent have? About a third of one fight. Or less. Of sixty growed-up men in the town, d'you think that there have been twenty gunfights among the lot of 'em? No, there ain't. Well, old son, I ask you to look at the facts and see for yourself that no matter how old or

how wise a gent may be, it ain't likely that he's had much fighting experience. But this here Lew Melody had been near killed
when he was only fourteen, and he's been fighting ever since. I
ain't counting fists and wrestling matches, or beer bottles heaved
around, or a chair thrown at his head, or somebody trying to
stamp his face in when he's down, or them that tried to brain
him with a club because they figgered that a knife or a gun
wasn't no good ag'in' him . . . him having a sort of charmed
life. I ain't countin' none of those little things, but outside of
them, I tell you that Melody has fought a hundred times with
knives and with guns . . . fought for his life!"

I threw up my hands in real horror. "Do you mean that he
has killed a hundred men?" I cried at Crockett.

The sheriff sighed, a man really in despair. "Certainly not,"
he said. "For about four years, he was being licked about every
third time, and half of the times in between the fights was a
draw . . . somebody broke in and stopped 'em before the finish. But I want you to remember that he's got the print of them
fights marked all over his body. He's a mass of scars that would
make a trail puzzle for a grizzly to puzzle its head over. But in
the last four years, Travis, since he got dressed up in his real
manhood, he ain't never been beat, and the number he's killed,
nobody knows. The river has taken a lot of 'em. And a lot of
'em have dropped in the desert where he chased 'em down and
the wolves and the buzzards finished 'em. But even them that I
know about for sure would make a list that would stagger you. I
ain't telling you how many. It's a number that I don't name
even to myself. But I'll tell you this . . . that while a lot of the
folks have been praisin' me for keepin' good order around these
parts, it's been the work of Lew Melody that's kept the crooks
down. It's his work, and nobody gives him no credit for it. Why
don't the gunfighters come this way no more on the Mexico
trail? Why don't the greasers drift along the valley on their way

up from Mexico? It's because the word has gone up and down the line that Barney Valley is bad medicine. They've had brothers and fathers and cousins and sons that've got this far and disappeared. Well, most of 'em don't know it . . . but Lew Melody is the main reason."

I had heard a little of this before; of course, everyone in Barneytown had heard it, but it was startling to get such a complete confirmation from the lips of the sheriff himself.

"Sheriff!" I exclaimed. "What can we do to get this boy back to the town and make him become a good citizen?"

"That's easy," he said. "Just work a miracle. You being a churchman, it ought to be in your line."

What can one say to such a man? I left him more irritated than ever, and rode out to make some parish calls. That ride took me within a mile of the Furnival house, and I went to it. I found the broad, powerful form of Mr. Furnival seated on the front verandah, smoking a pipe. He nodded to me in his unenthusiastic way.

"How is Sandy?" I asked him.

"Fair to middling," said Furnival. "Is it something important?"

"Why, not particularly, I suppose," I said.

He took his pipe from his mouth and looked at me in a thoughtful way. "Then I guess you'd better not see her," he said. "I guess that nobody had better see her."

It filled me, of course, with a cold fear for her. "What's wrong, Furnival?" I asked him.

He merely said in his stolid way: "Womenfolks are queer."

I wanted to ask more questions; I wanted to stay and insist on seeing her, but there was something about the manner of Furnival that distinctly discouraged more questions. So I withdrew and got on my horse again.

I was turning the horse's head up the road when the rear

door of the house slammed, and I looked back and saw Sandy herself carrying a bucket of chicken feed toward the hen yards. But what Sandy was this? Her walk had been the tread of something disdaining the ground; her head was always high; there was always a trail of song behind her. But now she went slowly. Her head was fallen. Her step was heavy. Once she paused to put the bucket down and pick it up with the other hand, as though the weight of it bothered her. Sandy, whose strength was like the strength of a boy.

Then I rode suddenly back to the verandah. "Furnival, is she sick?" I asked him.

He removed his pipe again and considered the question and me for a moment that made me thoroughly uncomfortable.

"I guess that you know as much about it as I do," he said, "or maybe a mite more, Mister Travis."

It was an uncomfortable answer, and it sent me hurrying up the road, a very sick man at heart. She was sick indeed, and the cause of her sickness was Lew Melody. What a frightful world it seemed on that day.

VIII

When I reached Barneytown again, I heard the complete story of the stealing of the Gray Pacer, which I had overlooked in the excitement. It had seemed no more than a small incident, compared with the return of the bay horse to Crockett and the letter to the sheriff that accompanied the return of the animal. But now I learned that it was something more—a great deal more.

I had heard of the Gray Pacer, of course. I suppose that everyone in the entire country knew about it at the time of his capture; it made the sort of a story that newspapers like because of its color. The Gray Pacer was a mustang stallion—big, fierce, wise, and incredibly swift. Three years before he had made his appearance on the range—he was probably two or three at that time. Then his age at the moment of his capture was from five to six. He was no dwarfed thing, but a splendid creature of more than 1,200 pounds, with all of that weight so beautifully distributed over his body that he did not appear to stand within 150 pounds of his real weight.

His career was a costly one to the horse breeders in the mountain valleys. This cunning devil seemed to know by instinct exactly how to open corral gates, and, once he had a gate open, he knew how to lure the mares out after him. Again and again he built up formidable bands of the finest horse stock on the range and again and again the ranchers organized hunting parties that ran the bands down. They could recapture those of the mares that had not been killed by accident or ruined by overhard running. But they could not hurry the Gray Pacer. It was said that he had never broken his pace at any time. I suppose that one reason for this was that he kept very much to broken country, and up hill and down a gallop is not so good as a smoother gait. But even across the open country, his four legs of iron, stockinged with shining black silk, carried him away from all pursuit.

The damage he had done mounted into thousands and thousands of dollars, not only on account of horses that were swept off in his band and that were lost there, but also on account of the vast efforts that were made to capture the equine rascal. Bands of a dozen men and more laid elaborate traps for him, took out strings of their best horses, and worked a month at a time to get the fleet-footed beauty. It began to seem probable that no one would ever be able to put a rope upon this shining flash of a horse, and finally men were sent out to kill the brute.

But even in this more dangerous game—a hopeless game for the horse, you would say—he continued to win. It was said that when a man got that animal well in the sights and drew a bead on it, the beauty of the stallion was too much for the hardest heart, or else the hand of the marksman began to shake with something far more violent than deer fever, and so the great beauty was away again, rolling across the plains at his matchless gait. Jap Tucker brought out a string of four thoroughbreds. They had more foot across perfectly level tracks, of course, but, when it came to traveling through desert sand fetlock deep, they could not compete with the tremendous strength of the stallion; neither were they inured to the hardship of mountain travel. The Gray Pacer was like a mountain sheep, flying up rocky steeps and hounding down precipitous cliffs like a rubber ball. So he still escaped.

But there is usually a great rival for any great master. If a Pompey appears, presently Cæsar looms; if Hannibal marches halfway around the world, at last a Scipio stops him. And so, if I may be allowed to descend from great things to small ones, when all the rest had failed and for a space of three years the Gray Pacer had left a streak of disaster behind him, Ches Logan, hunter extraordinary, appeared on the scene.

Ches was a man who did not know the points of a horse from the points of a cow. He had never used anything but mules and burros in his profession—which was trapping. But the skill of Logan was concentrated for the perfection of one art. He had arms of steel and an eye as sure as the eye of an eagle; with a rifle he was a master.

So, with a burro behind him to pack his food, and with a rope coiled on top of the pack, and with his rifle slung across his back, and with a fat reward of more than $1,000—I believe— hung up by the ranchers to encourage him, Ches Logan started forth to capture the Gray Pacer. Luck brought him within fair range of the big horse in ten days, and the rifle did the rest. A bullet, aimed with a skill beyond praise, nicked the spinal column of the stallion high up on the neck toward the head, where the cord is close to the surface of the flesh. The Gray Pacer dropped, and, before its senses cleared, Ches Logan had secured it with hobbles.

He drove it back to Elkhorn, collected the reward, and immediately found himself the cynosure of all eyes. But Ches, having captured the stallion, knew how to make the most of his prize. He understood that curiosity can be capitalized. And everyone in the mountains was curious about this beautiful monster. They were willing to travel scores of miles for a close view of it, so Ches made them pay dearly for those views. He drove the horse out of Elkhorn to a little shack half a mile from the edge of the town, There he closed in a corral with a lofty board fence, and put the Gray Pacer inside. Thereafter, whoever chose could look as long as he pleased at the stallion, but for every visit the charge to pay was $1. It was said that $100 came the first day, and thereafter, although the numbers diminished, Ches Logan ran a very profitable little show that beat trapping in ten ways. He had only to sit down and enjoy his pipe, look at the mountains, which tumble up to the sky around Elkhorn, and cook his meals. Money rolled into his hands without his labor.

Then, on a warm evening, a man stood in the open door of his shack, and he found himself looking into the face of none other than Lew Melody. There was no chance to reach his rifle; besides, at close quarters, what chance had a rifle against the revolver that was sure to come like lightning into the hand of Melody. The trapper merely nodded and said: "Come in, Lew, and rest your feet. How's things?"

So Lew came in and sat down. He wasted no time. "I want the Gray Pacer," he said. "What's the price?"

Ches Logan looked at the holstered gun of Melody and answered: "I suppose the price of one slug is about all you'll have to pay for him."

"You have the wrong idea," answered Melody. "I've come to buy that horse."

"Money," said Logan, "is all I'm making out of him."

"You've taken the cream already," said Melody. "You're not making very much now. There were only five people here today, and, before the winter comes, that'll dwindle to two or three."

"Two or three dollars is wages for me," said Logan. "I ain't one of these here proud gents. I live pretty simple."

"There's a price on everything," said Melody. "I'm not offering a hundred or two hundred. I'll give you five hundred dollars in cash."

"Look here," said Logan, "if you want that hoss, why don't you take it?"

"I don't rob poor men," said Melody.

"If I was to take your money, wouldn't the bank at Comanche Crossing take it back again?" asked Logan.

"That money I got from them wasn't marked," said Lew. "They could never touch it. Besides," went on Melody, "there was never a saddle on that stallion. I have to break him in. And every time I have to make a trip down to him, at night, you'll collect a hundred dollars."

"Is that a go?" said Logan. "D'you think that you can break him in five tries?"

"I think so."

"Well, son, you shake on that with me," said Logan. "You pay me a hundred dollars a trip and I'll sell the hoss to you as soon as he's broke."

"You think he's unbreakable?" asked Melody.

"I don't think, I know," said Logan. "He ain't a hoss . . . he's a tiger."

"Well," said Melody, "I'm ready to start the payments before I've seen him. Here's a hundred now."

So Logan took that money and they went out where Melody could get at the Gray Pacer and Logan could sit by to smoke his pipe and watch. What they both saw was worth seeing. Melody found a devil disguised as a horse, and maddened by the blind confinement behind those tall walls of the fence. It is not hard to imagine what the Gray Pacer was at that time. I have seen 600-pound mustangs with more life than a wildcat and more venom than a rattlesnake. But those were ratty little geldings; even so, it took a mighty skillful rider to keep in the saddle for half a minute. But here was 1,200 pounds of shapely stallion, with the freedom and the kingship of the open range behind him and a thorough conviction that his one grand purpose in life was to set his teeth in the first man that he could reach, or drive his heels through the body of a victim.

But Lew Melody started his work, and he did it without haste. He was paying $100 for every try, and that rate was enough to make most men anxious. However, the nerves of Melody were adjusted perfectly for just such trials. He went calmly to work and acted as though time was nothing in his estimation. That first night he tamed the stallion only sufficiently to take an apple from his hand—and try to eat the hand as well as the apple. But Melody was not discouraged.

He came down a second time and paid another $100, and on that night he appeared to have lost ground. The third night he made greater progress. The fourth night, the stallion was wilder than at first, and Melody, looking along the glimmering flanks of the beautiful beast in the starlight, saw a shadow that looked like the long welt of a whip.

He said to Logan: "You've been out here tormenting this stallion. Logan, tonight's money goes for tomorrow night besides."

That was the beginning of hard feeling between them, but Logan saw that it would be dangerous to try to trick the outlaw any more. He sat still and continued to collect his $100 for each visit from Lew Melody.

IX

I have often thought of the oddity of that bargain between the trapper and the outlaw. Both were as nearly lawless as could be imagined, and yet I suppose that the nearest approach to a law-loving spirit was in Melody and not in Logan. If Ches had not broken the law, it was merely because a trapper does not often have a chance to invade the rights of other men.

But it was a delightful experience for him. He had proved that his judgment was right in one respect, at least. Five visits had not tamed the wild spirit of the Gray Pacer, although each visit from Melody lasted from dark until dawn, when he withdrew toward the rough mountains. For he had come to this region not primarily because it was the place where he could get the Gray Pacer, but because it was an ideal hole-in-the-wall country. The mountains swelled all around the valley in which the little town of Elkhorn lay. They were difficult, but not impassible, those mountain trails. A man who had a close knowledge of those trails had an immense advantage over those who did not know. And it was said that Melody, befriending a widow living in the hills, learned from her son as much about those trails as the mountain goats themselves could have told him.

It was a very broken country, indeed. There was not only the jumble of the rocks and the steep cliffs, but there was the manifold problem presented by many little streams that raced down from the snows and choked the Elkhorn River with their burdens of mud and of pebbles and rolled stones. Some of those arrowy little currents could be leaped by a fine horse, but no horse in the world could wade through the raging currents. There were places where the waters pooled a little, running over flats, and these could be swum or forded. But these places were continually changing as the furious waters hewed new destinies for themselves through soil or hard rock. To combine with all of this was the heavy foresting of mighty trees in the lower valleys shading to marching ranks of lodgepole pines that walked away over the crests—except for those summits that lifted above timberline and carried their naked heads into the white region of snows. A stranger would never have found ground, except by accident, on which a horse could raise a gallop. But one familiar with the district could dip onto good ground for a comfortable percentage of the traveling. And all the backcountry around Elkhorn was of a similar nature. It was no wonder that other criminals before Lew Melody had fled to this district; it was no wonder that Lew himself had found it.

But what he primarily needed, in such a region, was a horse with the endurance of a mule and the sure footing of a mountain goat. Otherwise it was really better to travel on foot. As for the big, lumbering bay of the sheriff, so excellent to stretch away across level going, it was of very little use here. One must have an animal that moved upon springs, and that had been educated to mountain work—one that could tell what slope must be coasted down on braced legs, because the soil was loose, and what slope could bear the weight of driving hoofs and a heavy body. He needed a horse that could leap the narrow streams without being frightened by their great voices, that could walk along a rock ledge a foot wide without growing dizzy at the 1,000 feet of nothingness that dropped on either side or the other; a horse with limbs of steel and a heart of steel, also. And here was wild Gray Pacer made to his hand. No wonder he was willing to risk his life itself in order to gain such a mount. It was as though he were adding wings to himself and leaving earth dwellers, to find safety among the birds.

The excellent Ches Logan appreciated this very well. Sometimes he cursed himself because he had not set the price at $200 a visit, instead of $100. However, the bargain had been made, and he saw that he would have to stick to it unless he wished to have a bullet from an unerring Colt crash among his ribs, or unless he could devise some cunning expedient.

The expedient at last came to him. It was not an honorable one, but what Ches Logan wanted, after a life of hard labor, was plenty of money and plenty of ease. What he decided to do, finally, was to betray Lew Melody to the men of the law who resided in the town of Elkhorn. He made a trip to the town, therefore, and in very vague and general terms suggested that, with good luck, he hoped one day to be able to lead them to Lew Melody. He wanted to know what his share of the reward would be, if he took no actual hand in the danger of the capture. The answer was that one half would come to him.

It was enough. The thought of $2,000 in addition to the $1,000 he had made from the capture of Gray Pacer, the extra hundreds that had been poured into his coffer by the show that he had conducted, and the additional money that he had received from the hand of Lew Melody himself—these items all united to form a fund that was well above contempt. With some little management and moderation in his scheme of living, he could exist for the rest of his days upon that sum. Ches Logan decided that the time had come for him to seize opportunity by the forelock and retire while the way was opened before him.

He made his visit to the town after the fifth night trip of Melody to the shack, but still he could not make up his will to betray Melody at once. Every additional trip that the outlaw made added another $100 to the coffers of wise Ches Logan. And $100 is the price of how many coyote furs, gained by how many miles of hard trudging, and how many hours of dirty, disagreeable work?

The sixth visit from Melody saw him bring down his saddle and actually succeed in fastening it upon the back of Gray

Pacer. But still he had not sat in the saddle as yet, and the trapper scratched his chin and bided his time. The seventh visit, however, saw Melody sitting in that saddle, and, although it was with an uneasy seat, and although Gray Pacer was as uneasy as a wild colt under this strange burden, yet he did actually answer the reins a little. And Logan saw that the time had come.

Dawn was not bright on the next day, and Melody was not gone an hour, when Logan started from his shack and walked hastily into the town. There he told his story. Which was, simply, that Lew Melody, tired of his lonely life in the mountains, had formed the habit of slipping down from the mountains and chatting for an hour or so in the evening at the house of the trapper.

The very next evening he had promised to pay his host a visit, and therefore Ches Logan invited the officers of the law to come to his shack and secret themselves there. Who could have resisted such an invitation? No matter how much they despised the treachery of Ches Logan, all men know that it takes a rascal to catch a rascal,

They made their plans with care, and they gathered eight good men and true to march out to the shack. Four were to hide in the brush outside the cabin. Four more were to wait quietly indoors, to provide an unexpected reception committee for the desperado. With this plan arranged, they started out from the town at noon and walked to the shack.

But when they came in view of the little house, they were surprised to find a tall bay horse tethered outside the door to a sapling at which it was contentedly chewing, raking off the tender bark.

"It looks," said someone, "a devilish lot like the hoss of that Sheriff Joe Crockett, away down in Barneytown."

So they scattered like Indians in a circle around the shack. It seemed incredible that Lew Melody should have risked a daylight visit to the shack, but there stood the bay horse, answering point for point the description with which they were all so familiar, and of which many of them had dreamed by night.

They stole up on the shack on their hands and knees, taking advantage of every bit of covert. When they were close, they charged the front door with a yell, struck it, burst it from its hinges, and rushed in upon an empty room.

No, not quite empty. There was no Lew Melody there, but upon the little deal table in the center of the apartment were two $100 bills, nailed down into the wood. There was a message beneath each one, and on top of one there was secured a letter addressed to Joe Crockett.

Beneath the first bill was this penciled message: *This money is for the man who will take this letter and ride the bay horse back to Barneytown and give both the horse and the letter to Sheriff Joe Crockett.*

Beneath the second bill was a note for the eyes of Ches Logan, and it ran as follows:

Dear Ches Logan: You've been figuring me away in the mountains, but, as a matter of fact, I've made my camp in those pines on the hill not 500 feet from your shack. I saw you start for town, and, if that trip means any good for me, I admit that I'm a fool.

But, in case my guess is wrong, I leave the last payment for the Gray Pacer. He's taken to me at last. I would have worked a couple of more nights with him, but I suppose that I'd better risk a trip on him now rather than wait to see what you might bring back with you from Elkhorn.

If I'm wrong about you, I give you my apologies now.

If I'm right about you, and you really meant to double-cross me, then all I have to say is that Elkhorn and every other place in the mountains is bad medicine for you. Take

my advice and go East—far East! They have healthier air
out that way!

Lew Melody

The first rush was to the enclosure where the Gray Pacer had
been kept. But the corral was empty. When they searched the
ground nearby, they saw not far away a patch of soft earth that
told of a deadly struggle between the half-tamed horse and the
half-wild master. The ground had been torn up by plunging
heel, and here and there were broad marks where the big animal
had flung itself down in an effort to escape from the clinging
rider. However, in the end, the man must have won, for suddenly the trail stretched away in long gaps, showing how Gray
Pacer had bolted off toward the mountains.

But the cruel part of it all, from my viewpoint, was that
although Lew had paid for Gray Pacer, it needed only a flat
denial from the trapper to put Melody down as a horse thief
once more.

X

I begin to feel a great sympathy for historians who have anything
other than the simplest narrative to express. For here am I with
all the threads of my account scattered far and wide across the
mountains. Perhaps someone with a keener eye for good order-
ing of material would be able to bring all of these threads
together in a smoothly working description. But just how it can
be done, I cannot tell.

For yonder is silent Furnival, smoking his pipe, never changing his expression, and always watching his daughter, feeling
that she is dying on his hands and that he can do nothing to
help her. And there with him is Sandy Furnival, breaking her
heart for Lew Melody, and yet determined with an iron will
never to weaken and never to admit her love for a breaker of the

law—more than that—a man who had broken his word to her.

Then look to the figure of Melody himself, grown greater in the imaginings of everyone through the ranges by this last exploit in taming an untamable horse; there is Lew Melody living like a hawk among the peaks, and laughing at the pursuit. And there is the pursuit, counting in the lists of those who ride and walk to find Lew Melody—hundreds of hard fighters. They have swarmed up out of Barneytown, out of Comanche Crossing, and in particular out of Elkhorn itself, for the men of each of those towns feel that the long freedom of Melody is a matchless insult to them. They are working patiently, hungrily, these sharp-eyed prospectors, these strong-armed lumbermen, these infinitely wily trappers, these bold and reckless cowpunchers, these professional hunters who know the ways of rifle and bullet and all their hidden mysteries. They are following trail by trail as they work the mountains in a honeycomb pursuit.

How I should like to have the space or the power to take up those men, one by one, and tell of the thousand labors, the privations, the sharp hungers, the long thirsts, the weary feet, the stumbling horses, the emptied canteens, the sun-wearied eyes—but this would be an Iliad all in itself, and to tell it would be to attempt a canvas greater than the skill of a humble minister in a small Western town can possibly compass. But, sooner or later, these hundreds are sure to win. The wit and the daring and the invention of one fugitive will hold them at bay for a time, but in the end numbers plus patience, skill, and courage are sure to win. Lew Melody is condemned and lost as surely as though a bullet were at this minute lodged in his brain.

Yet that is not all the picture, not all of it by any means. I could call you back to little Barneytown itself and show you many new aspects. I could show you the stream that had so long been turned away from the town—the stream of malefactors, American and Mexican, beginning to seep silently into the town once more on their long trails to Mexico and away from it. I could tell you the story of the little pilferings that began, and then of hold-ups in the streets at night, and then grim stories of carnival, riot, bloodshed across the danger line of the Barney River where Lew Melody's dreadful right hand had once kept all things quiet, and where the prowling of that lion had sent jackal and coyote and panther scurrying away for shelter. So that Lew Melody, according to the sheriff's prophecy, began to appear to us in a new light and grew greater and greater among us—as the shadow of a man, toward the sunset of his day, streams like the outline of a giant behind him. So did the thought of Lew Melody grow among us. People no longer damned him carelessly. They began to speak of him with reverence, almost. And yet they spoke of him as a lost soul.

But there were our men, our chosen men under Deputy Sheriff Sid Marston, still working away among the mountains near Elkhorn, and there among those mountains was a much neglected and little-seen form skulking along on a ragged cow pony—little Slim, working on the blood trail with a heart full of fire and a soul as ardent for the great battle as any among all the scores who strove to crush Lew Melody—for the sake of money and for the sake of the glory that is greater than gold.

But nowhere in all the mountains, not even among the young boys to whom the stirring adventures and the prowess of Lew had made him appear as a young Achilles—nowhere was there such a burning of the heart and such a great outpouring of sympathy for the hero as in the home of the money-lender, Cordoba, in his house beyond the danger line, on the farther side of the river.

No, I myself, who had always loved the boy in a certain way, know that I never had the great passion of love for him that lived in the three hearts under that roof.

Each day while Cordoba sat in his counting room, with the

steel bars across the windows and a shotgun at his side—each day in this manner between his business dealings he gathered in the latest news. You will imagine what the news consisted of. For the whole mountains had to talk of Lew Melody. If there were no facts to deal with, there were always rumors. No crime could be committed within 500 miles without tying it to his name in some manner, and, if one expressed doubt that he could be in so many places at once, there was always the convincing answer: "He has wings, now . . . he has the Gray Pacer."

So, every night, when Cordoba went wearily up the stairs to his living rooms, he took out this parcel of news and distributed it. Not all at once. He told only the cheerful news in the presence of Juanita, for when she heard of peril for Lew Melody, her face turned pale. But, when he was alone with his wife, he told her all the things that he had gathered, and they wrung their hands over him, and every night the three dropped upon their knees and prayed for the safety of the adventurer. Or if Juanita did not pray, it was only because her throat was closed with weeping. The next day, with infinite teasing, infinite coaxing, Juanita was always able to worm the full story of the day before from her unwilling mother, until at last they would throw themselves into the arms of each other and cry over the wild story.

But when the news came of the stealing of Gray Pacer, and the second escape of Lew, Cordoba was blank and silent.

"They will never be able to get him!" cried Juanita.

"Ah, girl," said her father. "Can you say that? Such things as he has done are always punished in the end."

"How punished?" Juanita asked, trembling. "And what has he done that is so bad? Was not *Señor* Geary a famous devil? Did he not deserve to die?"

"The law is the law," Cordoba responded sadly. "Sometimes

it is gentle as a lamb, and sometimes it is a hungry bear that tears out the hearts of men without any pity. So it will be with *Don* Luis, poor boy."

This speech left a grave silence in the room, the *señora* looking anxiously at her daughter, and Juanita looking in blank terror straight before her.

Cordoba took out a pendant of three emeralds, held by a chain of gold.

"And yet," he said, "this little thing . . . this little bit of bright glass, you might say . . . could save his life and give him back to us."

"Ah?" cried Juanita. "Can you mean that?"

"Do you not see, child? The price of this is far more than the ten thousand dollars which he stole."

"But horse thefts . . . and murder. . . ."

"Well, I have enough money to stop the mouths of the ones who might talk of horse stealing. As for the murder of that *Señor* Geary, I think that even if *Don* Luis came to trial for it at this minute, when the minds of all men are so hot with him, he would be acquitted. He would be saved by such lawyers as I should hire for him. Ah, we would fight for him, would we not?"

Juanita ran to him and slipped onto his lap. She was trembling with joy.

If he loved her, he would give that little trio of stones to poor *Don* Luis. What was such a sum to her father, and was it not life to *Don* Luis? Besides, she, Juanita, would love her father twice as hard all her life if he did this one little good thing.

"So?" said Cordoba, smiling sadly at her. "Do you wish it so much? But do you not see, child, that it cannot be taken to him? And even if it were brought to him, he would refuse it."

"It can be taken to him," said Juanita. "Ah, it can be done."

"Why, girl," said the money-lender, "are there not hundreds of brave, wise men, trying to come even close enough to him to send a bullet through his heart?"

This was too much for the poor girl. She ran to throw herself on a couch and there broke into a passion of tears.

"What have I done?" Cordoba asked, expanding his hands toward his wife.

The *señora* looked upon him with eyes of fire. "Nothing . . . nothing," she said. "Speak to her one more thing like this, and all her troubles will end. You will kill her, and she will not be here to bother you any more."

Cordoba cast a glance of anguish at his wife, and then he went to sit beside Juanita.

"Look, child," he said, fumbling with a desperate mind for something that would soothe her. "Here are these. They are for you, Juanita. They are yours, my dear girl. Take them and forgive your stupid father."

The small, soft hand of Juanita closed over the three emeralds. The fine chain of gold that bore them coiled like a bright little yellow snake across the transparent olive skin of her wrist. Presently her sobbing ceased, and she gathered the trinket to her heart.

"See," whispered the money-lender, delighted, to his wife. "She is only a child, still. She has taken the toy . . . now she will forget."

But the *señora* merely stared at him and sighed in despair. "You are always so far from her," she said. "Do you call her a child? She is old enough to be a mother even now."

XI

Now, when the next day dawned, it seemed that Juanita had recovered her spirits wonderfully. The color was returning to her cheeks, and two or three times during the day her mother was transfixed by hearing the voice of the girl raised in a snatch of song.

It was noted, too, that Juanita went out to the stable behind the house and spent much time caressing the little pinto mare that Lew Melody had given to her because she taught him to dance. That beautiful little creature she had not been able to look upon since Melody disappeared. But now it seemed to fit into her mood at once.

She asked for money. What she asked for in that house was never questioned; she took what she would, but her mother had not more than a few dollars at the moment, and so she sent Juanita down to her father's counting room. There, sitting on his table and thereby throwing a pile of important papers into hopeless confusion, she teased his wallet from him and extracted from it a whole handful of bills.

"Merciful heaven!" cried Cordoba. "You have taken hundreds! I shall be a pauper." And he laughed at her, delighted. There was no pleasure in his life so keen as the joy of filling her hands with whatever her heart desired.

She took this money on a strange shopping tour that carried her, first of all, to the big store, which was an emporium where everything the Mexican heart delighted in, from chiles to gold lace, could be bought. But her purchases made the storekeeper stare.

"It's a present," Juanita explained. "Also, it is a secret." And, paying him ten *pesos* above the price, she laid her finger on her lips and smiled. The storekeeper was enchanted.

"There is a steel lock on my lips," he said. "I cannot speak. *Señorita,* you have not entered my store this day."

"That is enough," Juanita Cordoba said, and took her bundle home. She smuggled it up the back stairway to her room, and after that her merriment increased. Who could have said that she was now in a fit of deepest melancholy such as had lain upon her during all these days? The *señora* made a special trip to the office of her husband where she had never appeared before.

"Something has happened to our dear," she said. "She is singing like a bird. She stops every five minutes to run to me and to kiss me. Could it have been the gift you gave her last night? Is she such a child as that?"

Cordoba was enchanted. "Ah, well," he said, "you still put me down as a fool, but I know the heart of my own daughter, if you please."

That evening they were both convinced. For Juanita could hardly be still for a moment. Dancing and singing and chattering, she filled their eyes with light.

"It is true," whispered the *señora,* "that she has dropped the thought of *Don* Luis from her heart."

"Is she not my child? Do I not know her?" said the money-lender, more enchanted than ever. For he felt that he was about to conquer the admiration of his wife, even as he had won her love long before this day.

There was only one shadow on the evening, when Juanita ran to her father and took his burly head in her arms and whispered in his ear: "Whatever I do, will you always love me?"

"There is a question, foolish girl."

"Tell me, though."

"But could I help it?" said Cordoba. Afterward, to the *señora,* he said: "What could that mean?"

"Heaven only knows," answered his wife. "But there is something in her mind. It is not hard to guess that."

What was in that mind they were far from dreaming. But when their voices had been stilled in their room for half an hour after dark, Juanita was up from her bed again. The bundle of her purchases was raised and opened—stealthily, stealthily. For how much noise, like a crashing of feet over dead leaves, the unfolding of stiff paper will make. And all must be done with the light of the lamp turned very low indeed.

She drew out from the package, finally, shining riding boots of the finest leather, and socks, and trousers, and a gay silk shirt, and a broad-brimmed sombrero, bright with metal work, and a broad belt of white goat skin with cartridge holders running around it, and a quirt, and a pair of golden spurs, and, strangest of all, a black leather holster with a neat .32-caliber revolver in it.

She took out this weapon and held it with both hands, and, standing before the mirror, she leveled it at her image and made a face at the grim result. Then back went the revolver into the holster, and she was working at the clothes.

There were myriads of buttons, it seemed, to the unaccustomed fingers of Juanita, but, when her slim body was clad in the new outfit, she ventured to turn up the flame of her lamp and view herself more fully. All was well, she thought, except for her head. Even when she had crushed the sombrero well down, there was sure to be a curling lock in sight.

It needed a great heart, but she was determined. She tossed the sombrero on the bed, took out the pins, and allowed the shining weight of her hair to tumble to her waist. Then, with a scissors, she began to cut steadily. One glistening lock fell beside another on the floor as the steel cut through the masses. At last, the damage was done. And what a change it was. Half the woman seemed to have been stolen from her face by that stroke. And when the hat was replaced, she felt a little tingling shock of surprise. For here was a boy indeed, smiling back at her from the glass.

So, squinting sidewise judicially, at her image in the glass, she made a few strides up and down the room, as long as she could stretch them, and, when she was ended, she decided that the impression was as masculine as anything she had ever seen.

Her confidence, which had been a badly shaken thing before,

now seemed much restored. She gave one look and one sigh to the black and gleaming strands of hair upon the floor. So ended, she felt, her old life.

Then she scribbled on a piece of paper:

Dear Ones: I am going to take the emeralds to *Don* Luis. Forgive me and love me still if you can. I should have died if I had had to stay here, hearing every day of the troubles he lived in. Do not doubt that I shall find him and that I shall come back safely. You know that we have been in Elkhorn, and I remember the country around it very well.

Juanita

So she gathered the last of her pack and rolled it in the slicker that she had not forgotten to buy with the rest. Then out with the light, while the blanketing darkness swept closely around her, a pause to make sure of her bearings—then through the door. Ah, how slowly, slowly she opened it. There seemed to be a coiled spring resisting her, but it was only the rust upon the hinges, and, if she pressed too hard, a *squeak* began to develop. But the door was open at last.

Yet that was only the beginning of the dangers. *Señor* Cordoba could be depended upon to sleep heavily through all noises. Her mother, by the same token, could be depended upon to waken at the first stir, with all her faculties aroused. And here was a creaking floor to be crossed—how strange it was that she had never noticed the weakness of the floor before.

In spite of all her care and her time, there was a stealthy murmur from the floor and instantly a voice from the room of her mother: "Is it you, Juanita?"

"It is I, Mother."

"Why are you up, child?"

"For a book."

"You must not stay awake to read. Go back to bed."

"Yes, Mother." She rested a hand against the wall for a moment, to enable the blood to ebb out of her brain, for a dark mist of excitement was swirling there. Then she hurried down the stairs—but not too fast for fear—ah, there it was again—just before she reached the bottom of the flight, with the rear door of the house before her hand, a loud and heavy *creaking* sounded beneath the pressure of her foot.

And, from above: "Juanita!"

She did not answer. Desperate with haste, she opened the door and hurried out into the barnyard, and straight across it, running lightly on her toes, toward the stall of the pinto mare.

The devil possessed that fiery little creature. Fine feed and little exercise had made her like a frolicsome puppy. And it was a great task to settle the saddle on her back, and put the bit of the bridle between her teeth. When that was done, there was still the pack to be strapped on behind the saddle. But at this instant, she heard a loud scream from the house and she knew that the worst had come upon her. Her mother had grown suspicious, at last, and in the room of her daughter she had found the message of farewell.

After that, blinded with fear, she struggled with pack and straps, but, at last, the thing was somehow in place, while windows were opening, and the voice of her mother was crying into the night: "Help! Help!" And yonder heavy thunder was the footfall of her father racing down the stairs of the house.

She was in the saddle and out of the barn in a flash, and, as the rear door of the house opened upon her father, lantern in hand, she swept past him, with the spurs glued to the sides of the pinto mare.

No main roads for Juanita. Instead, she swerved down dusty alleys and by-streets. When the pursuit started, it would rush north, according to the directions in her letter, but Juanita was riding south with might and main, and the little mare was flying with flattened ears and stretching neck through the night.

XII

It was not such a difficult trip. Not a sight or a sound of the pursuit that raged after her came to Juanita, but she drifted north and north, after her first southern detour, keeping always to the rough going of the mountain, and seeing hardly a living soul, except once a cowpuncher, who merely waved his hand from far off and jogged his horse on along the trail. But even that casual greeting gave heart to the girl, for she felt that it was an earnest of the success of her disguise.

As the sun browned her face and the backs of her hands more every day, she felt that she was fitting more accurately into her rôle. So she came to the rugged mountain heads from which she could look down upon the rough valley in which lay Elkhorn—itself as rough as the mountains around it. It had seemed fairly simple to the girl up to this time. The long, easy rides and the pleasant campfires in the chill, pure air of the mountains had made her almost love the life as she found it. At least, she was not sitting idle in the house in Barney Valley, eating her heart out with despair as she drank in the ill tidings from the mountains.

But when she sat the saddle and looked out over the mountain heads, with whole upper country tossed up like the ocean under the blast of a sharp gale, and when she saw the many white, twisting streams that streaked the mountainsides, and the dark masses of forest, the cliffs, the rolling ground, the thousand perfect coverts in every square mile of that wilderness, her spirits began to fail her and she turned instinctively and looked back toward the south.

It was the mid-afternoon. Now that she was come upon the ground where her search must begin, what should she do first? She rode aimlessly until she came to the banks of a thundering stream; so great was the noise, and so heavily was it magnified in the damp, dark throat of the ravine that Juanita expected to come out into view of the real river. But what she found was no more than a large brook, given such a roaring voice because of the narrow steepness of the course it kept. It was impossible for the pinto to leap that stream, and, when she urged the little beast down to attempt a fording, the pinto whirled with an angry snort and such sudden violence that the girl was nearly thrown.

She let the pinto wander up the bank of the stream for some distance, but it did not seem to diminish, and, as the evening was coming, she determined to pitch her camp in a pleasant clearing that she reached not far from the voice of the water.

There she built her fire, cooked her supper from the diminishing contents of her food pack, and rolled herself in her blanket. Pinto would be her guardian, and in an instant her eyes were closed.

It was, in fact, the snort of the mare that roused her, and made her sit up, blinking in the dying red of the firelight. She made out, before her, a shadowy form and the ray of light that traveled down the barrel of a rifle, leveled at her breast. The courage of Juanita ran like cold water out at her fingertips, and she threw her arms across her face.

"*Aw*, the devil," said a boy's voice. "It's nothin' but a kid."

Juanita uncovered her face and found that the shadow in front of her, holding the rifle, was only a ragged imp—a veritable young wild man of the mountains with legs clad in bagging man's trousers that had been cut off, or frayed away to strings at the knees, while a very consummately dirty shirt covered the rest of the body of the boy. There was no covering upon his head except a dense thatch of sun-bleached hair. And the wild, bright eyes watched Juanita with the curiosity of an animal. Now the youngster lowered his rifle and leaned upon it. As he came closer to the light, she could see that there was a revolver strapped around his waist, and behind him loomed dimly the form of a pony-like horse with a ragged forelock hanging far down on its face. She was reminded of a picture of some wild young Tartar about to leap on an enemy.

"What might you be doing up here?" asked the little savage.

"I'm looking for Lew Melody," she said.

"What?" barked out the other. "You lookin' for Lew Melody? And what would you do if you found him? Let him eat you?" With this, his bare foot kicked onto the embers of the fire a dried branch of pine, full of resin, that flared up high at once and cast a wild yellow light over the clearing. By this light, which half blinded her, she saw the glittering eyes of the little satyr shining forth at her beneath a forelock as ragged as that of his horse.

"All right," said the boy, "you're gonna get this here Melody and bring him in by the nose, ain't you?"

"I didn't say that," Juanita said, repenting her frankness bitterly.

"Well," said the boy tyrannically, "I'm glad that you got some sense, because I'll tell you what you look like to me . . . you want to know?" He did not wait for her answer, but he continued with a savage heat: "You look like a softy to me! Y'understand?"

He came a fierce step nearer, and Juanita began to grow terrified in earnest. She remembered her revolver, in an unlucky moment, and dropped her hand on the butt of it as she rose to her feet. "Keep away from me," she said, with as much energy as she could summon. "Keep away from me, and don't . . . !"

"Why should I keep away?" said the young savage, his eyes beginning to flare more brilliantly than ever. "Why should I keep away from you?"

"It will be safer for you," said Juanita, trembling violently. "If you come another step. . . ."

"Here's the other step."

He came with a leer, but as she snatched out her revolver, he leaped in and gripped her wrist with fingers that ground through her soft flesh and bit against the bone. Juanita, with a cry, let the gun fall to the ground and cowered away from him. At this, in an ecstasy of brutal joy, the boy swayed back and forth and shook her limp hand and arm with a savage energy.

"You're a devil of a sort to go after Melody," he said. "Where you belong is home in bed . . . you mamma's boy!" He cast her hand away from him and dropped his rifle; he slipped off his cartridge belt and the revolver with it and tossed them to the ground. "You hear what I called you?" he demanded.

"I heard," murmured Juanita.

"I called you a mamma's boy," Slim said, rolling this frightful insult over his tongue. "I called you a sneakin' softy and a mamma's boy with a pretty face. A girl's face! *Aw*, the devil, won't you even fight for that? Look here . . . I'll give you the first punch." He extended his arms magnificently and offered her the first blow at his wiry young body. But Juanita was shrinking farther and farther away.

"Hey," yelled Slim, "you're just a sneaking coward! Are you?"

"I'm afraid that I am," said the girl.

At this hideous admission, Slim's strength gave way. He slumped down upon a fallen log and stared at her with his mouth agape. "Oh, my Lord," Slim said, "I'd ruther've died than have said that to anybody. I'd've took more'n Stan Geary ever give me before I'd've said that. Tell me, what'll you ever do if you was to see this here Melody?"

"I don't know," said Juanita.

"Nor me neither," he said with immense contempt. "I dunno what you'd do. But I tell you what . . . you'd better leave off wearin' guns, till you learn how to handle 'em. Why, if I'd had that gun and been where you was, and you where I was, why, I'd've blowed your belly clean out before you budged a step at me. But I could see by the way that you laid your whole hand on that butt, instead of just the fingers, that you didn't know how to get it out fast. Otherwise I'd've finished you off quick and not waited to take it out of your hand. But it's a pretty slick gun, ain't it?"

"I don't know," shuddered Juanita. "You may have it, if you want it."

The blood rushed to the face of Slim. He scooped up the revolver and examined it with a glistening eye. It was perfect. It had a caliber large enough to kill a man, of course, and yet it was lighter than the tremendous Colt that might be toys in the hands of giants like big Stan Geary, but which were an arm load for him. That weapon fitted into the heart of the boy more than anything he had ever seen. With this revolver in his hands, he felt suddenly that even Lew Melody would not be able to stand before him, so greatly was his power multiplied. Now he looked upon Juanita with new eyes.

"Would you be giving it to me?" he asked in a hushed voice.

"Yes, yes," said the girl.

"Well," said Slim, burning with emotion, "I . . . I'd aim to pay you back for it . . . someday . . . when I got a chance . . . someday. . . ."

"I don't want you to pay me back," said Juanita.

"The devil you don't!" Slim exclaimed, completely downed again with astonishment. For that so much cowardice and so much generosity could exist at the same moment and in the same breast seemed to him an incredible thing. "Why," Slim said, "that's sort of generous . . . that's sort of . . . what made you give it to me?"

"Because you look as if you could use it," Juanita said truthfully, and she added with a touch of flattery, as some of her courage began to return, "and because I hope that you'll be able to get me a sight of Lew Melody."

For a burning instant he studied her, and then a broad grin began to form on his face; he stretched out a dirty hand. "Shake," he said. He took the hand of Juanita and frowned as the fingers gave way and the soft palm folded under the pressure of his iron grip. He weighed that hand in wonder, and then released it. "It's sort of mushy," Slim said, regarding with curiosity and some disgust the loveliest hand that ever wore a ring. "It's sort of . . . different. But," he added, firing with a new enthusiasm, "no matter about you and fighting, and no matter about the way that you handle a gun . . . lemme tell you, kid, that if anybody tries to get fresh with you while I'm around, I'll punch his face for him too darn' quick. And I'm the gent that can do it. Feel here!"

He pointed to his biceps, and, while she laid an obedient hand on the dirty shirt, he doubled his arm slowly, quivering with the intense effort. She felt a hard little knot of muscle rise and tremble on his arm.

"Wonderful," Juanita said, beginning to be amused now that her fear was leaving her.

"It's work that done it," said Slim in explanation. "Look at my hands. Them calluses mean work, too. *Aw*, I've worked most of my life . . . worked hard. That's why I'm strong. And because I'm strong, that's why you come to the right gent when you ask me to give you a sight of Lew Melody. I'm gonna give you a sight of him, right enough. You're lookin' on the gent that's gonna kill that big sucker . . . and get the reward."

"Kill him?" cried Juanita.

"Sure! Why not? I can shoot as straight as any man you ever seen. And I've worked out the thing that'll get him for me. I've worked it all out and done it this evening. Tomorrow I'm gonna get him sure!"

"How can you possibly do it?" asked the girl.

"I'll tell you, because I guess that you ain't gonna steal none of my fire. The other bums have been tryin' to find *him*, but I'm gonna make him try to find *me*. Y'understand? I'm gonna fetch him to me, and, when we meet, let the best man win!"

XIII

The scheme of Slim was not without a considerable measure of ingenuity. According to his own code, a fairly rendered challenge was a thing that must perforce be recognized and accepted, and for that reason it was necessary that Lew Melody should meet in an equal fight with the readiness of any man of honor. Therefore, he had worked out his plan.

He knew that, from the ready ease with which Melody had avoided many of the efforts to capture him, he must be receiving occasional word from friends of the movements that were being made against him. Accordingly, that evening, the boy had gone down to Elkhorn and on the bulletin board of the post office he had placed a large sheet of paper on which was scrawled the following message in large letters:

Lew Melody, lissen to me:

Ime gonna ride down the Culver Cut tomorrer on a roan hoss. Ther ain't gonna be nobody but me along. Meet me ther and may the best man win.

Slim

If this missive were misspelled, the spelling was not much worse than most of the mountaineers would have been capable of. And if the letters were formed with a shaking hand, they were at least large and perfectly legible. Most of Elkhorn gathered to read this challenge and guess the reaction of Lew Melody when the news of it came to his ears, and great was the speculation as to the identity of Slim. But, while they foregathered, Slim was helping himself to certain articles in the general merchandise store, to which he made his entrance through a rear window. He got safely away with his bundle of loot, and with that bundle strapped behind his saddle he had stolen hopefully up on the solitary campfire that he found among the trees. In the morning he proposed to make himself into as close a semblance as possible of a man, and ride down the deepest and the narrowest of the passes that drove through the mountains leading to Elkhorn—through the Culver Cut, in other words. As he explained to the girl, he could thus give the outlaw a fair chance to make sure that he rode alone, and he would also give Lew Melody a chance to come out and fight him at any point of the valley that he preferred.

"But if he knows that you're just a boy . . . ," Juanita began unluckily.

"Only a boy? Whatcha mean?" snapped out Slim. "Ain't I fifteen years old? And don't I look a pile older? And can't I ride, and can't I shoot? And what more can a man do?"

She said no more, and indeed the face of the youngster was so filled with savagery that, when she had rolled herself in her blanket that night, she could not sleep for a long time, but lay awake wondering if there would truly be an encounter on the next day. Slim, curled up on the far side of the fire, was asleep long before her.

In the dawn, he was first awake, also.

"Hey, kid!" he sang out to her, and, when she sat up, startled, he added: "You ain't told me your name?"

"Juan," she said. "And yours?"

"Me? I'm Slim. Folks'll know my name after today. Look here, kid, the best way to start a day is to take a swim. The water ain't so cold as it looks. Come on along with me, will you?"

"No, no!" said Juanita. "I . . . I *hate* cold water baths."

"Gee," said Slim, "you *are* soft, ain't you?"

In another instant he was at the brook and had plunged into the roiling water, while Juanita with a discreet face turned the other way, and started the breakfast fire. He came back half purple with cold and half red with high spirits, and all through breakfast he kept up a running fire of comment. But, when breakfast was over, he donned his new clothes.

He had not had a chance to pick well in the obscure light of the store when he robbed it. His boots and his trousers were much too large. So was his coat. And yet, when he was equipped, and a felt hat slouched over his head, he did indeed look more like a man—all except the invincible youth of his face.

"But I got the way to fix that," declared Slim. He combed out a bit of hemp rope of a fine weave, and finally produced two tufts that he affixed upon either side of his upper lip with daubs of glue. Juanita could not help smiling when she was close, but, at a little distance, the effect was startlingly real. It added many a vital year to the boy's appearance.

So they started off for the Culver Cut. It was a strange experience for Juanita, but her reasoning was not without sense—it might indeed be that Lew Melody would answer the challenge that the boy had posted in the town. But when he arrived at the cut, it seemed hardly probable to her that Melody could fail to see that Slim was none other than a young boy.

However, when, as Slim had instructed her, she followed him down the cut at a safe distance in the rear, her heart began to misgive her. For, from the rear at least, he made a very convincing appearance of a mature man, and in the heat of a sudden meeting, with those ridiculous mustaches to help out the appearance, it was more than likely that, if Lew Melody appeared suddenly out of the mouth of one of the many cross ravines that pierced the sides of the cut, there probably would be a gun play before there had been a chance for any close examination of one another.

She had reached the decision and decided to hurry her mare ahead and try to dissuade the boy from his foolish attempt, when Slim with his roan mustang disappeared around the next curve of the cut, and the next instant she heard a double report—the first a deep barking gun and the second the familiar, sharp, rifle-like *clang* of the little .32 that Slim had been practicing with all the morning.

She gave the pinto the spurs then, and whirled around the next elbow of the valley wall in time to see Slim, poor man, stretched flat on his back while above him leaned the man she loved, and behind Lew Melody stood the most glorious horse that the girl had ever seen, a thing of silver, flaming beyond belief in the slant light of the morning.

Melody was on his knees, now, and he looked up from the prostrate body of the boy with a raised gun and a piercing look to meet this next enemy. The waved hand of the girl warned him first, and then he recognized the pinto that he had given to her, and by that help he knew the girl herself.

But he gave her not a glance after that. She arrived and threw herself from the saddle in time to be received with curt, quick commands to hold this—to pull there—to help here. For Melody, his face whiter than the face of his victim, was slashing the body of Slim out of its clothes, and presently the scrawny torso of Slim appeared with a small purple blotch in the chest. Melody raised and turned the body gently—in the rear of the body, below the shoulder blades, there was a great gaping hole through which the bullet had torn its way out.

Juanita, turning sick, braced herself against a rock, but harsh orders came barking at her ears. Melody was working in desperate haste to make a bandage. Out of his shirt and that of the boy he constructed it, passing it around and around the slender chest, and Juanita, presently, was working swiftly beside him. When that was done, he gave a small swallow of brandy to Slim, and the eyes of the youngster fluttered open for an instant of recognition.

"Oh, Lord, Melody," he said, with a smile of admiration, "you're fast. But next time . . . I'll get you . . . sure. . . ."

His voice trailed away. His eyes closed again, and Melody, still supporting the meager body in his arms, looked sternly across to the girl.

"And you," he snapped out. "What are you doing here?"

Oh, to ride those many weary leagues, to make an effort so great with all one's heart, and then to be greeted in such a fashion.

She looked down for a moment, biting her lip, then she swallowed her grief and drew out the three emeralds and showed them to him with a look of hope.

"Do you see, Luis? They are worth more than all the money you took from the bank. When that is paid, my father says that you can come back and face all of the other charges. Do you understand that, Luis? And why do you look at me with such a black face? What have I done?"

He pointed mutely to her clothes.

"How else could I dare to come . . . alone?" she asked.

At this, he made a gesture to the sky. "Do you know how they'll handle you in their talk?" he asked her fiercely. "Do you know how they'll mark you with soot? But we can't talk about it now. There's something more important, and that's the life of this little fool . . . or hero . . . God knows which he is. Juanita, he's dying, I think, unless he can have better care than I can give him. Ride, girl. Ride as though your horse were on wings. I've got to stay here with him and do what I can. Take the Gray Pacer. He's like a lamb, now. Only don't touch him with the spurs. He'll fly with you all the way. Here . . . I'll shorten the stirrups. Now go! And go fast! Never draw the rein on him. Hills are nothing to him, but kill him to get to Elkhorn. Find a doctor . . . keep my name away from him if you can . . . and bring him back on the fastest horse he can get. Do you understand?"

She was in the saddle. "But if they recognize Gray Pacer . . . if they follow . . . if they take you, Luis . . . ?"

"What does that matter? But I'm not taken until. . . ."

"I shall not go!" cried the girl. "Not until I have your word to make no fight if they come in on you . . . not until I have your word to surrender, Luis . . . and to take these things to pay. . . ." She forced the emeralds into his hand.

"Take your father's charity? Great heavens, Juanita, do you think I'm such a begging cur? No. . . ."

A groan from the wounded boy cut him short and was echoed by another cry from Lew Melody: "I'll promise everything. But ride now. If he dies, I'm damned forever. There's no place in hell hot enough for me."

XIV

No sooner had Dr. Loren Kennedy closed his office door and settled himself to a cigar that was rather above the price he usually afforded, than he heard a *clattering* of hoofs in the street and then a small whirlwind of a boy darted through the door—a wonderfully handsome, graceful boy, crying out: "Are you Doctor Kennedy?"

"There's an accident . . . a gun . . . ," said Kennedy with gloomy foreboding.

"There's a dying boy in the hills!" Juanita cried. "And. . . ."

But here, through the open door, he saw the glorious form of the Gray Pacer, now darkened and shining with sweat.

"The Gray Pacer," breathed the honest doctor. "Youngster,

169

what has Lew Melody to do with this?"

"Nothing," Juanita said, twisting her hands together in an ecstasy of haste. "But hurry . . . he's shot through the body. . . ."

"By Lew Melody?" insisted the doctor. "Tell me the truth, or I don't stir a foot."

"God forgive you if a harm comes to him," Juanita said. "Yes, it is Lew Melody."

Loren Kennedy lost himself for a single instant in thought, but then he knew the thing that he must do. He told her to remount the horse, and then he ran for his own horse shed, but on the way he waved to his man of all work, who was digging in the vegetable garden. It brought the fellow thumping after him, and, while the doctor saddled his best horse, he gasped out instructions.

"I'm riding into the hills to take care of a man who Lew Melody has wounded. Lew himself will probably be there. The moment we've started on, get out into the street and stop every man you find to tell them the news. Tell them to trail us. Tell them to ride hard. I don't know, but I think that this day may be the last free day for Melody, and, if it is, I'll see that you share my part of the reward."

I have used that instance 100 times since, in my sermons, to prove the power of money, which works silently and unrelentingly to accomplish the work of its possessor. I have no doubt that Dr. Kennedy was as moral and as just a man as most, but, nevertheless, the pressure of the eternal dollar carried him off his feet at just the right moment to bring peril to Lew Melody.

But, indeed, it hardly needed his warning to bring other riders instantly behind them. For when they started down the street, half a dozen had already gathered to see the Gray Pacer. Even with this seeming boy on his back, the horse was too well known and too much talked about to go unnoticed or unrecognized. The whir of comment went like lightning through the town. An unknown boy, riding the Gray Pacer, had come into the village and gone off with Dr. Kennedy, both riding as if they were possessed. What could be the meaning of that, unless Lew Melody lay wounded or ill among the mountains, in such a desperate need that he had sent this youngster in on the famous horse to rush out succor to him?

The two rushed their mounts through the rough trails by which the girl had come down to the town, and, as they galloped over down slopes and level, and as they struggled up sharper ascents, the doctor ever and anon turned his head and pried at his companion with a piercing glance. Before they reached the Culver Cut, his suspicions were running very high. When she saw what was in his face, the first blush was enough to confirm them. It was a wretched ride for Juanita Cordoba, on this day, and shame was hot in her, and anger at the cold impertinence of this doctor. Truly he must have been a man without many of the graces and without much kindness in his heart.

However that might be, he was a man of worth in his own profession, and, when they swept into view of the wounded boy, the doctor was already loosening the strap that secured his medical kit.

As another might be said to land running, so the doctor truly landed working, and he was instantly upon his knees and laboring over the prostrate boy.

"Is there hope," was the first question of the outlaw, as he instinctively obeyed the directions of the doctor in lifting and turning the body of the boy.

"I don't know," said Kennedy.

Then: "Doctor, if you don't need me, I shall have to ride on. You will understand why."

Of course the doctor understood why, and of course that was

the reason that he lied broadly but smoothly enough, because he wished to detain Melody until his capture might be sure. For the reward had been pushed to $7,500, since the taking of the Gray Pacer.

"Man," he said to Lew, "I'm helpless without you. Do as you think best, but, if you leave me, I shall not answer for the life of this boy."

Lew, with a groan, and one longing look up the Culver Cut, where he knew he should be riding for life by this time, submitted. He added with a sudden thought: "Doctor Kennedy, I want you to know the *Señorita* Juanita Cordoba!"

The doctor turned upon her with a broad grin and a bold eye. "I had my own idea," he said.

But the sharp voice of Lew Melody—how well I know that voice—brought him up as with a jerk on the curb: "I have a hope that this lady is to be my wife, Doctor."

The tone and the message both were enough to make the doctor bite his lip and turn crimson, and he nodded to the girl, then he went back to his work. He was so busy that Lew Melody could turn to the girl with a gesture as much as to say: "If not this . . . you are hopelessly compromised. Am I right?"

And she, throwing out her hands to him behind the doctor's back, was saying with her trembling lips: "Do you love me, *Don* Luis?"

"With all my heart," lied Lew Melody, like a gentleman.

Here the eyes of the boy popped open. "I heard the whole thing." he muttered faintly. "Jimminy. Lew, you don't mean it, though. He ain't a girl!"

"*He* is," Lew Melody said, smiling.

"Oh, Lord," said the boy. "What have I said to her . . . and how've I treated her . . . oh, Lord. What'll she think of me?"

"Nothing but good," said Lew Melody. "Nothing but good."

"*Aw,*" said Slim, "when I think. . . ."

"Hush," said the doctor. "You must not talk."

"Steady, partner," said the more gently warning voice of Melody.

"Shut up, Doc," answered the irrepressible Slim. "Look here, old-timer," he added to Melody, "I ain't gonna bump out. I ain't gonna go dark. I could carry around ten slugs like them. Only. . . ." Here he closed his eyes and his face wrinkled with a spasm of pain. But after that, he looked up eagerly toward Melody. "I pretty near sneezed," he said, full of anxious apology for this contortion of the face. "Ground kind of damp, maybe."

"Maybe," Lew said gravely.

"And they's another thing, Lew. Maybe this here bone-sawer will be follered along by some of his pals. Beat it, Lew, will you? For Lord's sake, beat it before they nab you. . . ."

"Will you shut your mouth!" snarled out the doctor. "Before that wound starts bleeding again. . . ."

But it was too late to give a warning to Lew Melody. He looked up and down the valley now, and he saw with one sweep of his eyes that his fate was coming upon him. They had not ridden out of Elkhorn in the form of a few stragglers. Two score hardy men had pushed into the hills, and ten had been outridden by their more luckily mounted companions. Now, spreading out like a fan and converging rapidly toward the mouth of the little ravine in which the boy was lying with Lew near, they spurred along at full speed.

For an instant Lew thought of the last great chance and started to his feet. But the ravine walls before him were almost as sheer as masonry, and his foes were coming fast. He merely unbuckled his belt and laid it beside Slim.

"Keep that, Slim," he said. "Because you're the chief winner."

And Slim, cocking up his head with an agonizing effort, saw the approaching horsemen and lay back with a groan. "*Aw,* what a coyote I am, Lew," he said.

XV

The men of Deputy Sheriff Marston's party were at least useful for bringing back the fugitive, and there were additions to the escort. It was felt that eight men were hardly enough to form a safe bodyguard for such a desperado as Lew Melody. In fact, had I been in Marston's place, I know that I should have welcomed an escort of 100.

On the whole, I suppose that it was one of the greatest days in the history of Barneytown. Sheriff Joe Crockett was around with his right arm out of a sling, but although it was useless, the holster that he wore upon his left hip was significant enough, for that hardy fighter was almost equally sure with either hand. The town, therefore, sent out a dozen or so riders to meet the escort as it passed down the valley, and then the whole cavalcade came in together. Deputy Sheriff Marston, riding in the lead, with his prisoner handcuffed beside him, looked as proud and as happy as though he had been the captor in person.

I shall never forget the face of Lew Melody as he came in this fashion back to his hometown. One might have thought, from his appearance, that he was returning from a pleasure jaunt—unless it were because of the shackles on his hands, and the manner in which his horse was tethered to the horse of Marston. But he carried his head as high as ever, and turned it from side to side to view the staring faces that lined the street and crowded the porches. There was perfect calm and perfect contempt in his manner, so that Mrs. Cheswick, although she was not a harsh-minded woman, burst out to me: "Doesn't he look like a killer?"

Although I would not admit it aloud, I could not help admitting it to myself. For such demonical pride must ride to the ruin of others, I felt.

We crowded like sheep after the procession and saw the cavalcade stop in front of the jail and saw the heavy doors opened, and saw Lew Melody march up the steps with Joe Crockett beside him and Marston behind.

The meeting between Crockett and Lew became famous.

"Well, Lew," said Crockett, "I'm glad to see you back. But I ain't gonna forgive you for turnin' down my hoss for another nag."

"I'll tell you what, Joe," said the desperado, "after they string me up, I'm going to give you that gray, and you'll agree with me."

I have left out the most spectacular element in the whole parade, next to Lew Melody, and that was the horse he rode on. For it was the Gray Pacer himself. You will understand that Ches Logan had taken the sound advice of Lew and departed for regions unknown. In fact, he was never heard of again, and, when Lew swore that he had paid the required price for the animal and Ches was not present to debate the point, there was nothing to do except declare the stallion the property of Melody, as, indeed, it had a right to be called. But it was on the back of this silver-coated beauty that Lew made his appearance, with the Gray Pacer dancing along as though he were bearing his master to a coronation ceremony instead of to the jail.

The great horse furnished a little touch of pathos, too, for that occasion. For when the jail doors closed behind his master, he plunged halfway up the steps, whinnying after Melody, before he could be controlled and dragged down again. It brought a tear to my eye, and to other eyes, for I think that no one in Barneytown expected that Lew Melody would ever mount the gray stallion again.

I went to Joe Crockett at once and asked him if I might see the prisoner, but, before I had half finished my request, there was a sudden silence among the people who had been chatter-

ing outside the door, and then in came none other than Sandy
Furnival. She was pale, but there was a spot of excitement in
each cheek, and, if she were changed a little in outward appearance, the spirit of Sandy could never change, and that was
beautiful to the last. She spoke to me with a smile, and then to
Joe Crockett: "I wonder if you will let me see Lew Melody,
Sheriff Crockett."

I can answer that, I, for one, grew weak and faint, and Joe
Crockett had to clear his throat twice before he could speak.

"Right this minute, Sandy," he said. "Come along with me."
So he led her into the nest of cells and brought her to Lew
Melody.

Half a hundred people heard what was said, for voices carried loudly in that barn of a place and through the thin walls;
neither did either of them care to speak in whispers.

She said to him instantly: "Lew, I've come to tell you that
I've changed my mind. I used to be very proud, I think. But I
have no pride left. I love you, and I want you . . . and, if I've
been cold to you, Lew, it was only because my heart was breaking. Will you believe me?"

Who could have heard her without belief? Not the sheriff and
not I, as we leaned shamelessly against the door of his office to
hear what we could. We gripped one another. The sheriff was
whispering: "Lord, Lord, will you listen to that? Will you listen
to that?"

Then he heard Melody say in such a voice as I have never
heard before or since, there was such an agony in it: "I've asked
Juanita Cordoba to be my wife, if I come alive out of this thing,
Sandy."

A little breath of silence after that; only the sheriff's whispered
curses could I hear.

But Melody added: "But I'll never come out of it, Sandy . . .
and I hope to heaven that I don't. I'm weary of living."

"Hush," said Sandy. "Isn't that a weak, silly thing to say? But you will come out of it, Lew. Besides, you'll be happy with. . . ."

"Sandy!"

"I won't say it, then," she said.

"Sandy, will you tell me that you'll try to understand?"

"I do understand," she said with never a quaver of her voice. "It's the only right thing, and the just thing. It was she who went to you."

What a dying note of bitterness in her tone as she said that.

"But always, and now, and ever after, if I live . . . there's nothing under God to me except your love, Sandy."

Ah, if the proud women and the stilted and cruel and vain girls could have heard her answer: "I know that, Lew. Nothing could take that away from me. Then tell me what I can bring you to make you comfortable here. Or will she do all of that?"

"You can do one thing for me, and that's never to let me see you again. Because I can't stand it. Ah, how beautiful you are, and how dear to me."

"I'll do as you wish," she said. "Good bye, then."

"Only for this time . . . it's the last time, Sandy . . . will you kiss me?"

"Yes, dear," she said.

Ah, well. Ah, well. Joe Crockett was the sheriff and I the minister of the town, and therefore both of us were inured to sad things, but when poor Sandy came out of the cell chamber and passed through the office, she found Joe Crockett bent behind his roll-top desk apparently inclining his head to scrutinize a difficult page of script. And she found me with my back turned to her, looking out a corner window and seeing nothing.

But she? To this day the wonder of her and the scorn of myself and all other men burns up in me when I remember it.

She said in a clear voice as she paused at the outer door:

177

"Will you tell Missus Cheswick that I'll be in again for the next choir rehearsal, Mister Travis?"

I tried to speak. I suppose that I did say something, but it was not intelligible to my own ear, and then we heard the *click* of the door that told us that she was gone.

The sheriff turned in his chair and looked suddenly at me, and I looked at the sheriff and turned away as quickly as he. But, after all, why should we have been so ashamed? When I went out of the jail, I found that the crowd that had gathered in front of the building had dispersed; there were only a few small boys, and even these had an awed, frightened look.

I went home, stumbling, and there I found Lydia in tears. The whole town knew everything, and she among the rest.

"I don't care what is law!" cried Lydia. "Something has to be done! Something will be done! They . . . they can't lay a hand on him . . . they dare not!"

"What do you know about it?" I thundered at her. "What do women know about anything, except to make confusion and ruin wherever they go and whatever they do!"

Lydia listened with a meek face. I have noticed that it is only in times of great trouble that I can override Lydia. These times I believe that I could number upon the fingers of one hand.

XVI

The trial had to hang fire for some weeks, because the star witness was not able to appear—that star witness being, of course, Slim. In the meantime, opinion in the valley was divided under two heads. Before the return of Lewis Melody, there had been only the one camp, and this was crowded with his wholehearted enemies. But now there were two great parties, and the majority were those who upheld the cause of Lew with a sentimental violence. I do not blush to state that I was one of the leaders of this faction. I rejoice to say that Joe Crockett was next to me in the violence with which he upheld the side of the outlaw. On the other side, the minority was a little more compactly organized than ours, I must admit. But I think it is generally true that benevolent emotions are usually dissipated in talk, whereas malice works with edged tools,

Upon this occasion, Bert Harrison came in from his ranch and got himself a great deal of notoriety by strongly advocating the prosecution of Lewis Melody in the bitterest fashion. He led the way in subscribing a large fund with which to hire a brilliant assistant to our district attorney.

Between the pair of them they did a nut-brown turn on that investigation; their chief difficulty was with the jury—because a Western jury is usually a compact body, when it comes to senti-ment. For instance, what it believes to be right, it believes with a tremendous conviction, and what it believes to be wrong, it hates with all its heart. And what stuck in the crops of the twelve good men and true, who were hearing the trial of Lewis Melody for the murder of Stan Geary, was a fact that had not the slight-est thing to do with the case in point—it was the fact that everyone knew and willingly admitted—that Lew Melody had permitted himself to be captured in order that he might remain and give his best help to a foolish little daredevil of a masquer-ading boy who had challenged him and been shot through the body.

As for the defense, it was baffling to discover that while rich Cordoba was breaking his heart with eagerness to spend tens of thousands to get the finest lawyer in the land for this case, Lew Melody himself refused to retain special counsel and insisted that a young lawyer who the judge appointed was quite good enough to represent his affairs.

Nothing could be made of such conduct as this except a fool-ish and perverse pride. However, that young lawyer intended to make a stirring peroration, at some time in his summing up of the defense, pointing out how Lew Melody had worked for the life of Slim; to gain more evidence, he took a special trip to the north and visited the bedside of Slim. When he came back, he had the case put off from week to week until Slim himself could be brought down, although everyone wondered what evidence Slim could present that had to do with the murder of Geary.

Meanwhile, the other charges had fallen by the boards. Joe Crockett refused to prosecute any charges of resisting arrest or assault on an officer of the law, and thereby Crockett gained an almost unanimous election the next time that he ran. As for the bank robbery, old Cordoba took a trip north and saw the bank officials at Comanche Crossing, with the result that that charge was squelched. There remained only the Geary affair. Yet that was really the one great thundercloud that would have made all of the other charges seem ridiculous in comparison.

Well, to come to an end to this portion of the narrative, the trial began. In the beginning, the evidence for the prosecution seemed very damning. For the gold of Bert Harrison had placed a very competent lawyer at the elbow of the district attorney, and the cross-questioning to which they subjected Lew Melody was very severe and pointed.

He was a poor witness for himself. He answered any question and answered it almost at random; indeed, he began to contradict himself on small points. It went to such an extent that the impression suddenly gathered head through the courtroom and through the mind of the judge and of the twelve jurors that Lew Melody did not greatly care whether or not he lived or died.

This, from a lad of twenty-two, was very odd. Yet there was a confirmatory and explanatory rumor. The whole town knew the pitiful details of the last interview between Sandy and Lew—the whole town except the Cordoba family, I dare say. And every day there were the Cordobas, sitting, all three in a pale, anxious

row, worshiping Lew Melody with their eyes, and Juanita growing whiter and more staring from day to day. But, on the other
hand, when people looked for the face of the other girl, they
found only the grim, set features of Mr. Furnival, who sat always
in the same place, seeing and hearing everything and watching
with a sort of remorseless scorn everything that went on.

When the defense began, it had very little to go upon. The
testimony of Lew Melody on his own behalf was extremely
poor. He merely would say that he had met Geary under the
shadow of a great oak and that they had fought it out. He freely
admitted that he had rushed out of the Furnival house with the
announced intention of finding and killing Stan Geary.

When all of this had been established, to the comfort of the
prosecution and the utter confusion of Lew's young lawyer,
there was a call for Slim.

Never had such a witness taken the stand.

"What other name?" asked the clerk. "What real name, your
honor, if you please?"

"What real name?" said the judge to Slim.

"The devil," said Slim. "How do I know?"

Which brought a roar, and made the court turn purple to
keep from exploding. He had already struck a snag when, in
swearing the witness and asking him if he would swear. . . .

"Sure," broke in Slim, "I'm an old hand at it."

If the proceedings were almost broken up by these replies, it
was certain that the impression that Slim made upon the jurors
was immensely favorable. They beheld him with twelve
enormous grins, nudging one another freely and even whispering behind their hands. For Slim, after all, was known as the
boy who had masqueraded as a man for the sake of Lew
Melody. And having gone out to kill, and having been nearly
killed instead, was it not remarkable to see him turn with a
broad smile of welcome to the prisoner at the bar and sing out

most informally: "Hello, Lew. I'm gonna help get you out of the mess!"

I skip the first questions. They were not of importance until Slim began to detail events of his life with Geary. In spite of objections, Slim was able to rattle out certain details of the manner in which Geary had treated him and every man in the courtroom grew fighting mad, and every woman grew rosy with anger.

So, when the stage was set, the young lawyer for the defense began to snap out questions concerning a certain night on which Slim had gone to bed early—"because Geary kicked me in the ribs and it sort of tired me." And he had fallen asleep in the dirty, dark attic, when he was awakened by the sound of voices below.

At this point, a person of no less importance than Bert Harrison was seen to rise with a pale face and hurry out of the courtroom.

"And whose voices were they?" asked the lawyer.

"One was Geary, of course, and the other was a gent that called himself Bert Harrison."

Considering the sudden exit of Bert Harrison, this brought everyone up erect.

"And what did they talk about?"

"Harrison was offering two hundred dollars to Geary for the murderin' of my partner, yonder . . . Lew Melody. But Geary, he held out for four hundred, and he got it."

The prosecution, in vulgar language, curled up and died upon the spot, There remained of it hardly more than a dust streak on the face of the world. And, since all the other charges had been dropped, Lew Melody was set free in fairly record time, and had his hand wrung by twelve good men and true, and by the judge in person, and by all of Barneytown that could get near enough to do it.

But it seemed to please him no more than if they had been wooden images. He was engulfed by the Cordobas and taken away by them, through the town, and over the rickety bridge, past the danger line, and to their house.

As for Bert Harrison, he disappeared for some time. There was no pressure of the charge against him, but life would not have been agreeable to him in our community after that, and perhaps he was wise to leave his affairs altogether in the hands of lawyers.

★ ★ ★ ★ ★

IN THE RIVER BOTTOM'S GRIP

★ ★ ★ ★ ★

I

Look first into the office of Cordoba, money-lender of Barney-town; let me show him to you in his office, seated on a broad bench with his back to the wall and his table in front of him. But why should the rich man sit on a bench? Because he changed his position from time to time. Sometimes he sat erect upon the bench, but that was not the posture that pleased him most. He was erect now; in fact, there was a dent in his fat back, he was so erect. His black eyes, ordinarily dull and not overly large, were glancing brightly into the face of his visitor.

It was *Señor Don* Mateo Valdez who lounged in the other chair, son of the rich Valdez who owned the great cattle ranch at the mouth of Barney Valley. Outside the house, hitched to the light buggy in which young Valdez had driven to town, stood two fine-limbed horses, still sweating and trembling from the merciless fury of their trip north. He was dressed in full Mexican regalia, was *Don* Mateo, and his delicate fingers held the cigarette gracefully and waved away the smoke that dribbled from his lips.

"It is only last month that you came to me last," said the money-lender.

"A month is a long time," said the spendthrift, "because it has thirty days, and money leaves me on every day."

"That is true, then," admitted Cordoba. "However . . . five thousand dollars. . . ."

"What is that to me?" said *Don* Mateo. "Considering what

187

security I have to offer. . . ."

"Ah, but what security have you?"

"*¡Señor!*" cried Mateo, lifting his handsome, languid eyes.

"What security?" repeated the money-lender.

"My father's ranch. . . ."

"The ranch is your father's, however . . . pardon me . . . and not yours."

"It will soon be mine."

"God forbid!" exclaimed Cordoba.

"*¿Señor?*"

"I trust that your father has a long life before him."

"He is ill."

"That I know."

"Then read this." He offered a letter signed by a doctor. It read: *My Dear* Don *Mateo: It is true that your father has not a month to live. However, this news must be kept secret. No one must know it. For if it comes to his ears, the shock will surely kill him at once.*

The money-lender lifted his eyes slowly. "He has been a great man." He sighed. "And this letter is to be kept a secret?"

"To a man like you . . . full of honor . . . tight-mouthed . . . what harm is there in showing it?"

"Well," answered the money-lender, "we each have different ways of thought. If this seems good to you, it is good. And I admit that it makes you good security. What sum will you have?"

"Ten thousand," *Don* Mateo said, his eyes snapping with pleasure.

"You must be careful," said Cordoba with an odd smile, "that your entire estate does not run into my hands . . . at this rate."

"I? Careful? I shall be careful in time. But one must have money . . . to live like a gentleman."

"This will cost you twelve percent."

"Ha? That is a double rate, Cordoba!"

"That is true, but it is a double risk."

"In what way, then?"

"Suppose that your father should change his will and leave you nothing."

"*Tush!* He loves me! Besides, what could make him?"

"The knowledge that you are showing me this letter, perhaps."

"Well," *Don* Mateo said, "let me have the money at any rate. I have no time."

What does it cost to scratch one's name upon a piece of paper? And behold, the fat money-lender waddled across his office, taking with him a short-barreled shotgun of large bore. He opened his safe. From a drawer he selected a parcel of money and returned with it.

"How much does that safe contain, then?" asked Mateo, his eyes glistening with hunger.

"You have almost exhausted the contents," Cordoba stated.

"Shall I believe that? *Adiós, señor.*"

Don Mateo was gone, but there was another instantly in his place—an old man with a rigid back that crumpled over as he sat down in the chair. He was bent so that his chin was thrust out, and he peered earnestly at Cordoba through his spectacles. Cordoba, straightway, leaned back and tucked his feet beneath him. He sat cross-legged to do business with this customer.

"The interest was due me yesterday," said Cordoba.

"Ah, yes, God knows," said the old man.

"And *I* know," said Cordoba sternly. "What has happened?"

"I have brought you in . . . only half the money."

"So?"

"Ah, *Señor* Cordoba . . . you are great in wisdom," said the old Mexican. "You know how the blackleg struck on my little ranch, and the cattle died like flies. I have been stripped. I have been beggared. I bring you this money. You may take a larger mortgage on my ranch for the rest of your money."

"You have three sons," Cordoba stated more coldly than ever.

"By the mercy of God, I have three sons. It is true."

"They have left you, I suppose, now that your little ranch is like a poorhouse?"

"Left me? No, no, no! They stand beside me . . . they work like three dogs. My eldest boy said this morning . . . 'You shall not be shamed by going to confess to Cordoba. Let me go and take the brunt of his tongue.' "

"Ha!" said Cordoba. "Did he say that?"

"Ten thousand, thousand pardons. You are angry, then?"

"I am very angry . . . that people should think I would use my tongue like a whip. Well, my friend, cattle are cheap, now, since the drought has made them so lean."

"They are like dirt. One names a price . . . the cow is yours. But mine are not lean. I have pasture enough."

"That is true. How many could you fatten of those lean ones? Ah, three hundred, at least. Here is a note from me. Show it where you please. Go buy . . . and send them to Cordoba for their money. When you have bought two hundred, come back to me and I shall take your note for the money that I have loaned you. As for this other interest money . . . it is forgotten. Take it back to your three sons, Santiago, and tell them that you surely will not starve for this winter."

Then he jumped from his bench and rushed Santiago from the room before the rancher could shower him with thanks. He had barely returned to his bench—with the shotgun beside him—when a third man entered, very different from the other two, a broad-shouldered, brown-faced Yankee, wreathed in an immense smile.

"Well, Fatty," he said, "I knew that I could not lose if I got you into the game with me, and I was right. I hit it quick. It come off like cream off the top of the bottle. Then a sucker of-fered me twelve thousand for the claim. I'd taken out three thousand. I grabbed the twelve . . . and here I am with the hard cash. Well, Fatty, your grubstake gives you seventy-five hundred. Count it out!" And he slammed down a potbellied wallet on the table.

The Mexican opened it without a word. He counted out a thin sheaf of bills. "The horse, the tools . . . everything, cost me only five hundred," he said. "I shall take two thousand. And the rest is yours."

"Hey!" barked out the American. "Are you gonna cheat yourself out of fifty-five hundred that belongs to you?"

"I have four hundred percent. It is very much," said Cordoba. "*Adiós*, friend."

"Is that all? Why, Cordoba, this ain't right . . . and. . . ."

A panting youth ran through the door. "*Don* Luis" he gasped out in a trembling voice.

Cordoba rolled with surprising rapidity to his feet. "What of *Don* Luis?" he cried. "*¡Adiós, adiós, señor!* I am very busy, as you see!"

The prospector, feeling that he had just been in the midst of a happy dream, hurried out into the day to make sure that this generosity was not in fact the stuff that dreams are made of.

"Now you speak of my son, of *Don* Luis?" cried the money-lender to the youngster. "What is there to say of him?"

"May he always be fortunate," gasped out the boy, recovering his breath as fast as he might. "But I have just heard through my cousin that Miguel and Cristobal Azatlán. . . ."

"What are they?"

"It was a year ago, *señor*, that *Don* Luis met with their brother, a very famous fighter from Mexico. . . ."

"And killed that man?"

"Yes."

"Quick, boy! And tell me if they have come to revenge his death?"

"It is that . . . yes!"

Cordoba wrung his fat hands. "The Lord bring them to a wicked end!" he cried. "But now, boy, do not let a word of this come to the ears of *Señor Don* Luis Melody."

"¡*Señor* Cordoba! Will you not warn him?"

"Warn him?" echoed Cordoba. "Name of heaven, no."

"But they are dreadful fighters. Miguel Azatlán on a day in Juárez. . . ."

"Do not tell me. Do not tell me. Foolish boy, do you not know that the more dreadful they are, the more my son will wish to meet them?"

II

Cordoba straightway locked his office securely and mounted a horse strong enough to bear up his weight, but passive enough to suit his rather timorous temper; it was a sort of rough plow horse that jogged with him through the twisting alleys of the Mexican quarter, and over the rickety bridge, which was known as the danger line, and so arching above the waters of the yellow Barney River into the American section of the village on the eastern bank. He went straight to the jail, and there he found Sheriff Joe Crockett. He tumbled at once into his story.

"*Señor* Crockett, you are a good friend to my *Don* Luis."

"D'you mean Lew Melody?" barked out the sheriff, who was in a rough humor. "And why in the devil should I be a good friend to him . . . me with my right arm workin' like a rusty gate since he sent that slug of lead through my shoulder?"

Cordoba blinked at him, and then made out the note of friendly raillery that had underlain the speech. "A bullet or two will not make a difference between two American friends," he said, grinning. "But you pour out a little blood as we would pour out a little wine. Is it not so?"

"*Aw*," said the sheriff, "I dunno about that. What's eating you today?"

"Your good friend, and my son, *Don* Luis. . . ."

"Hey! Has he married Juanita?"

"Not yet . . . the next week. . . ."

"Then don't call him your son until after the marriage. Go on."

"Two cruel fighting demons have come up from Mexico. It happens that they had a wicked brother who met *Señor* Melody a year ago, and they have kept a vengeance in their hearts all this time. Now they have come to Barneytown . . . they have arrived today. . . ."

"Well," said Joe Crockett, "what of that?"

"What of that, *señor?* You do not wish the murder of your friend?"

Joe Crockett merely smiled, and there was a great deal of sourness in it. "I could go to that pair . . . what's their name?"

"Miguel and Cristobal Azatlán."

"I could go to 'em if they'd listen to reason and give 'em some ripping good advice to get back to Mexico while they still got whole skins. But if they've come all this way, it'll take more'n talk to turn 'em back. There ain't a thing that I can do except to let Lew Melody go ahead and put on his specialty show . . . which is outshooting the shooters, you might say. That's all I can do, Cordoba. How's other things on the far side of the river?"

"The drought has been a sad thing to my poor people."

"But it'll bring coin into the Cordoba pockets, eh?"

"What is a little money to me, compared with the sorrows of my friends?" said Cordoba.

Joe Crockett did not smile. I think that if there was one man in the valley whose honesty and simplicity could be trusted without cavil, it was none other than this old Mexican money-

lender. But Cordoba went back across the river with his wor-
ries, and Joe Crockett came to tell me the news.

"They ain't had their lesson yet," was his way of phrasing it.
"They're still drifting up the valley to get Lew Melody. Well, in
a couple of days there'll be another funeral on the far side of
the danger line."

I asked him what he meant, and he explained. I was shocked,
naturally.

"Can't you do something?" I asked him. "Isn't it your duty to
do something?"

"The trouble with all of you ministers," said Crockett, "is
that you figger all men ought to do their business the way you
do yours, and that we ought to have the same kind of business.
But my job is different. Besides, I can't protect Melody unless I
put him in jail. He ain't the kind that wants protecting . . . he's
the kind that lives on trouble."

"He is about to settle down," I said, speaking my hopes rather
than my beliefs. "After he has settled down, there will be no
more trouble. When he is the father of a family. . . .

"The devil!" Joe Crockett cried. "How come you talk
nonsense like that?"

I tried to stare him down, being very much offended, but the
sheriff was in a stubborn mood.

"Marriage is about the only thing that would save him, I
admit," he said, "but not a marriage with a girl that he doesn't
love."

I tried my best to defend Lew Melody. "What else could he
do?" I said. "Juanita had risked her life and her reputation to
take help to him . . . he had to offer to marry her to keep fools
from talking about the poor girl, and they've been talking about
her in spite of the marriage that's to take place. Besides, old
Cordoba has treated him like a son. It was Cordoba who settled
the bank robbery trouble, as you very well know."

"Why, man," said the sheriff, "I don't say that Lew could have done anything else. I don't see how he could, bein' an honorable boy. Besides, that ain't my business. If I was a minister," he added with bitter point, "and had my hands mixed up in things like that all of the time, maybe I'd have been able to work out something different for him. But the way it is, he done the only straight thing. He had to offer to marry the girl."

"And why shouldn't he, for every reason?" I asked.

"She's a Mexican," he said.

"She's a lovely and a charming and a simple girl," I said with heat. "Besides, there are Mexicans as good as any people in the world."

"I ain't arguin'," said Joe Crockett in some disgust, "I'm just sayin'."

"Can you deny that she's lovely?"

"I deny that she's lovely like Sandy Furnival," he said.

I stamped. "Can you deny that she's wildly in love with Lew?" I asked him.

"I don't deny that. But she ain't no more wilder about him than Sandy is."

"They will have a magnificent establishment from Cordoba," I said, still talking against my better reason.

The sheriff raised his full height above me and laid a hand upon my shoulder. For the thousandth time I hated him because of his superior size.

"Look here, Tom," he said. "You know that this here is wrong. You know that he loves Sandy, and that Sandy loves him. You know that it's wrong for him to marry Juanita, no matter how much looks and how much money she's got."

"There is reason behind everything," I said. "I would never jump at conclusions, because on the whole. . . ."

"*Aw,* the devil," said Joe Crockett. "You argue like a woman." And he turned on his heel, rudely, and strode away from me.

I was too speechless with indignation to make the least retort. I was all the more angry because I knew that he was right, and because in my heart of hearts I understood that it would have been better for me to have had his side of the argument while he took mine, as a practical man. However, there was nothing to be done about it.

I had turned this question back and forth through my mind so many times, that I ached at the mere rising of it into my thoughts. As for the rest of Barneytown, the matter had been so well known for so many days, that most of the talk had subsided. There was only a quiet expectation—I might say, an evil expectation. On the one hand, was Juanita, darkly beautiful, filled with grace, and burning with love for Lew Melody. On the other hand was Sandy, growing quieter, growing paler as the time for the marriage came nearer, but never losing her courage or her ability to keep smiling. We had made the amazing discovery that, having decided that Lew owed a great deal to the Mexican girl and that he had no other way of repaying her other than through marriage, Sandy had reconciled herself completely to the affair and looked upon Juanita without the slightest bitterness.

Now, between these two was the wildest, the strongest, and the freest spirit that ever stepped in shoe leather in Barney Valley—or in the whole world, for all I know of it. Between them was Lew Melody. And the vital question was: Will Lew Melody go through with the marriage? Or will he smash through everything, scoop Sandy up in his arms at the last minute, turn his back upon the Cordobas, and ride away to marry the girl he loves?

It was a very uneasy question to solve or to answer in any way, for the possibilities of Lew were the possibilities of a thunderbolt. Indeed, although I searched my mind a thousand times, I did not know which way he ought to move. On the one hand, his love was for Sandy, as the whole valley, with the exception of the Cordobas, very well knew. On the other hand, his duty and his promise was to Juanita. And the Lord in heaven alone could tell what that passionate girl would do if he deserted her—particularly after the matter had gone so far as this.

For my part, I would have been unable to advise him. I felt simply helpless, and so did everyone else. But the suspense grew more tremendous every day, for, by a common concurrence of opinion, everyone agreed that something was sure to happen before the marriage took place—and now the marriage was less than a week away.

I had barely turned from the gate where the sheriff had spoken to me, when I saw, coming up the street, the man who had filled most of my thoughts for so many weeks. It was Lew Melody himself, but so changed in his costume that I could hardly recognize him at first, in spite of the fact that Lew and only Lew could be riding on the back of the Gray Pacer.

But as that glorious creature, made of modeled silver and shining light, came gliding up the street, turning his beautiful head from side to side to observe and scorn the people he passed, I saw that his rider had transformed himself, in all respects, into a typical Mexican gallant. And I knew that the first chapter of the final drama had been already written.

III

No one other than Lew Melody would have had the courage to conceive of such a thing, let alone the daring and the sublime scorn of public opinion to execute it. He had been famous through most of his life for the ragamuffin carelessness with which he dressed. A hat or no hat, old rusty boots, blue jeans, a flannel shirt with half the buttons missing, open at the throat, and a ragged pair of gloves—such had been the attire of the Lew Melody who had grown up terrible and careless and gay and wonderful in Barney Valley.

But behold him now, clad in the peaked sombrero of a Mexican youth, with a great band of glittering open gold work surrounding the crown—an open jacket that blazed with gold and silver lace—a shirt of brilliant blue silk—a great crimson sash with great hanging fringes about his waist, and tight trousers buttoned down his leg with immense silver conchas to ornament them. The saddle was a mass of heavy metal work, a staggering cost—the bridle was a jeweler's masterpiece.

But, oh, how my heart sank when I saw it. For I could see, I thought, something of the things that had passed in the mind of poor Lew Melody before he made this decision.

When he saw me, he waved his hand to me and dismounted. Gray Pacer followed behind his master and stood looking over the shoulder of Lew at me with glittering eyes such as only a stallion, of all the Lord's creatures, possesses.

But here was Lew Melody, not so greatly changed that he would not do as he had always done out of respect to me—that is, take off his sombrero and stand with it in his hand while he talked. It was a little thing, I suppose, but from this famous youth it caused a tingle to pass through my blood without fail.

I could not help saying, at once: "Ah, Lew, you are going masquerading, are you?"

"I look like it, don't I?" said Melody. "But no . . . I'm simply stepping into a new name."

"A new name?" I said.

"Yes, of course. You used to know a devil-may-care fellow called Lew Melody. I think his front name may really have been Lewis. I'm not sure. At any rate, you see another creature, now. I am a *don*, sir." And he tilted back his head and looked at me with that familiar smile—the mirth about the lips only, and the eyes made grave by the scar between his eyes that drew the flesh a little.

"Will you tell me what in the world you mean, Lewis?" I asked, trying to smile in turn and making a sad job of it.

"*Don* Luis, if you please," he said. "*Don* Luis Melody . . . the names go with a sort of hitch, though, don't they?" He laughed. It was an ugly sound, I thought.

"It makes no difference to me," I said. "I am your friend always, my dear boy. But other people will talk, you know."

"Other people have always talked about me," said Lew Melody. "I wouldn't take that pleasure away from them. That's one reason I'm glad to do it. It gives them a better chance to talk. They can say that I've turned greaser now."

"They will not dare do that," I said.

"Oh, I'm peaceful now," he said. "I make no more trouble. You can put me down now as one of the people who keep the law by force of habit. Besides, I'm afraid. When a man has been in trouble and then has to be bought out of it . . . it makes him afraid, you see. And Cordoba had to buy me out."

I didn't like this sort of talk; the bitterness was too close to the surface in spite of his smiling.

He rambled on, talking rather loudly, as though he invited my neighbors to hear, and, in fact, I espied the shadow of Mrs. Cheswick near her window, drinking it all in greedily.

"But I couldn't go on being plain Lew Melody," he said. "Not while my father-in-law to be is spending so much money to set me up as a gentleman. I suppose that you've heard about the ranch he's bought for me?"

"Of course I've heard that. It's a splendid place, I understand. I congratulate you, Lewis."

"*Don* Luis," he corrected again. "Or Luis, at least. Well, it's a very fine place, of course. How many hundreds of acres there are in it, I don't know. And how much the timber alone is worth is hard to calculate. But there are three little streams running through it, so that we'll never be bothered by droughts such as this year. I'll be entirely secure there."

There was an undercurrent of scorn and self-contempt in all of this that I pretended not to see.

"It must have cost a great deal," I said.

"More money than I dare to guess," said Lew Melody. "But *Señor* Cordoba seems to think nothing of it. The fortune of that man seems to be a staggering thing. He has rivers of gold running into his coffers every day. He simply emptied a few gallons out of his reservoir, and the place was his. But that's not the end of his spending. It's hardly the beginning of it, as a matter of fact. There is the house, too. Nothing but hewn stone for that house, sir!"

"So I have heard."

"The architect is plundering him for a small fortune. He suggests nothing that does not please my father. Beautiful furniture . . . and a floor plan that looks like a castle. Every day twenty more men are added to work on the place. It is a great sorrow to *Señor* Cordoba that the house will not be ready when the marriage takes place. But by the time we have come back from the honeymoon, the house will be open."

"And where do you go for a honeymoon?" I asked rather faintly.

"Where could the son of a rich man like Cordoba go? To Paris, of course. You surely will have guessed that, sir."

"I suppose so," I said. "I suppose so. Why are you so infernally snappy, Lewis?"

"Ah," he said, "I don't know. Forgive me."

It was too much for me. I could see, in this real glance at his heart, how thoroughly the boy was broken up by the whole affair. And I could not help crying: "If you feel in this way about the whole thing, in the name of heaven, break it off, Lewis!"

"Break away from Cordoba . . . after he has bought the ranch and built the house and after his wife has planned the wedding? Of course, I don't know what you mean."

The misery of it closed like a wave over my head. I could understand the set and sneering expression that he wore. It was the sheerest agony.

"Juanita is to be like the fairy princess out of the storybook," he went on. "There are so many yards of lace that it seems to me all the hands in the world, working forever, could never have contrived the stuff. But that's not all. The jewels, sir! It blinds me only to think of them. It really does. Emeralds . . . rubies . . . diamonds . . . what would a marriage be without jewels? And then the pearls. Oh, ropes and strings and heaps of them. Why, I could talk to you about these things through the entire day."

"I wish you would, Lewis," I said gravely. "I wish you would. Because it might ease your heart a little to talk . . . but not out here . . . and not so loudly.

He laughed in my face. "Why should I care if the whole world knows about my happiness? Let the whole town gather, and I'll make a speech to them about it. The church is to be one blaze of candles . . . a fortune spent in the purest wax. Every saint on the calendar will have an offering. There will be so much incense that I expect to sneeze for a month afterward. And there will be flowers . . . yes, expect to see Barneytown drenched with flowers for that occasion."

"I'm glad it's to be such a grand affair," I commented. "But not so loudly, Lewis."

"I want the people to know what is coming. The fairy princess will be the center of the show, you see. Then I step out as the prince. Don't I look like a fairy prince, sir? Give me your honest opinion." He stepped back a little so that I could survey him from head to foot. He turned slowly around so that I could see the heavy brocading on the back of his short jacket.

"Yes," I said slowly, "you will be like a prince, Lewis."

"Or a bullfighter," he said with equal gravity. "I can't tell which. However, it will be a great show. I am parading a little today so that people may know what to expect. I hope that you'll spread the news around a little."

I could not answer.

"Or tell everything to Missus Travis," he said. "I'm sure that she'd be glad to do a little talking."

I bit my lip. This shaft of irony had indeed struck home at the most vital spot of weakness in my dear Lydia. But the next word from him was a sudden whisper.

"Have you seen her lately, sir?"

I did not have to ask who he meant. "I've seen her," I said.

"Is she well?" Lew Melody asked huskily.

"I think . . . quite well," I managed to stammer.

"I rode out like a thief in the night," said Melody, "and I peeked through the window at her. I thought she was a little pale. But she is not ill?"

"No, Lewis, not ill."

"Sometimes I wonder . . . ," he began, and then stopped.

I did not ask him to continue, but, as quickly as I could, I changed the subject back to himself.

"A year ago you fought with a Mexican named Azatlán."

"Did I?" he asked carelessly. "Yes, I think I did. A dog who tried to knife me in the back."

"You killed him, Lewis."

"I'm glad I was lucky enough to."

"Two of his brothers are across the danger line, waiting to find you. Will you promise me to be careful?"

"Careful of the life of the son-in-law of *Señor* Cordoba, the rich money-lender?" he said. "Can you ask me such a question? If I did not trouble about myself, I should at least have to take care of such clothes as these, should I not?"

But when he leaped onto the back of Gray Pacer, the direction in which he rode was straight back toward the river, and I knew, then, how well he would heed my warning.

IV

He was not two blocks down the street when a rider on a foaming horse rushed up to him.

"¡*Don* Luis!"

"Well?"

"I come from *Señor* Cordoba."

"Heaven be with him," Lew Melody said in solemn mockery.

"He sends me to warn you that two men. . . ."

"Are playing mumble-the-peg?"

"Are in Barneytown hunting for you . . . brothers of. . . ."

"I know them," Melody said, "if they look like their third brother."

"You have heard, then?" said the fellow, much disappointed.

"I am glad to hear it over again, however," Melody said, and he gave the man a piece of gold.

"You are to ride straight back to the house of *Señor* Cordoba," said the messenger.

"I am? Is that the order?" Melody asked, swallowing a lump of scorn in his throat.

"The *señor* begs you to come at once."

"I shall do my best," said Luis. "But tell *Señor* Cordoba that the Gray Pacer has turned lame and that I may have to go slowly on the way home."

The other eyed the flawless beauty of the stallion. "Ah, well, *señor*," he said, flashing a glance of admiration at the calm face of Melody, "I trust that fortune will be with you again. But they are known men, both of them."

"Which means that they are known scoundrels, eh?"

"By all means!"

"Where were they last seen?"

"In a place where . . . you must not go, señor. Those are my orders."

"You are not telling me . . . it is a bird in the air," said Melody, and gave him another heavy yellow coin.

The other bit his lip, looked guiltily askance, and then: "In the old saloon. . . ."

"Which *Señora* Alicia keeps?"

"Yes."

"A thousand thanks."

The Gray Pacer turned into a flash of silver as it shot down the street, and carried Lew Melody over the staggering bridge that arched the Barney River, and across the danger line into the disheveled Mexican quarter. There he still shot forward at a round gait—the swimming pace that only a race horse could follow at full gallop. The dust cloud that he raised was towering far behind when the Pacer was stopped in front of a low-fronted adobe building that was set back behind an open shed in which horses could be tethered in the shade and where they could be watered. Here Melody left his animal and stalked straight to the door of the *cantina*.

At the door, he paused. The very suddenness of his approach had made it impossible for two or three ragged peons, who were watching him askance with eyes of awe and suspicion, to carry warning of his coming into the interior. As he listened, he could hear a quick humming of gay voices. But there was no conversation that he found important, so he threw open the door and stepped in. He found half a dozen men seated at tables in the big room. At the back of the room, *Señora* Alicia's assistant was keeping bank while two men shook dice against the house. Prohibition had not fallen heavily upon this *cantina*. For although the good lady's husband had been shot down, yet she chose to open the same place, and it was said that there was more evil connected with the place during her regime than there had ever been in the days of her fat husband.

She was behind the bar, and it was from her that a warning *hiss* came the instant that Lew Melody appeared. He remained by the door, for a moment, looking calmly from one face to another. At the *hiss* of the *señora*, every eye had glanced up with a sharp flash at him, and every eye had looked down again with an equal haste, as though each feared a discovery.

So he went to the bar. It was after the American style, with a great mirror extending down the wall. Melody turned his back upon the room and leaned an elbow on the bar. He asked for soda water, and, while the *señora* opened the bottle, she said: "You are drinking with care today, *Señor* Melody."

"I always drink with care in hot weather," said Melody. "It is a wise man's way. Liquor heats the brain . . . and makes a shaky hand. It is one thing to stumble with the tongue, is it not, and quite another to stumble with the hand?"

She smiled with hate as she put glass and bottle before him; a certain dear cousin of the *señora*'s had fallen with the accurately flung knife of Melody's sticking in his throat. That was a full five years before, but it was not hard for her to remember. There had been other actions since that time to keep her memory refreshed.

Now one of the men at the tables stealthily rose, reaching a hand behind him as he did so, until he saw his clear image rising, also, in the broad, polished surface of the mirror behind the bar. *Señor* Melody could see that reflection, if he were not blind, and no one had ever suspected him of dull eyes. The man sat down again, with suddenness.

"I saw the pretty *señorita* this morning," muttered old Alicia with a malicious side glance at Melody.

"But have you seen no handsome men?" Melody asked casually. "I have heard that two fine fellows came to Barneytown this morning. You have not seen them, of course?"

"I cannot tell what you mean," she said, looking down steadfastly, nevertheless.

"You could not, of course," he answered smilingly. He turned his back upon her suddenly and faced the rest of the room.

Señora Alicia took advantage of this respite to allow her face to wrinkle with hate until her yellow fangs showed.

"Do you hear me, my dear friends?" said Melody.

Not a head was lifted in response.

"I speak to you, among the rest," said Melody. "I speak to you with the black mustaches . . . not much of them . . . like the whiskers of a Chinaman. Do you hear me?"

I do not excuse the language of Lew Melody, but other things must be taken into consideration—all that was burning in his mind on this day, and a thousand agonies in his heart—and, in addition, the frightful odds that he was facing at this moment. For who could tell, for instance, if the old witch behind the bar might not have the courage to make her strength equal her hate and catch up a knife to plunge it in the back of Melody as he turned from her? Perhaps that very thought was in her mind, helping to wrinkle her face into a caricature of humanity. Yet his easy poise disconcerted her. He seemed so sure of himself that I presume she felt the young demon had eyes in the back of his head, capable of watching her every moment of the time.

The Mexican who had been addressed in this cruel manner lifted his head, perforce. He was an ugly chap of middle age, with a heavily marked face, and mustaches that consisted of a few black bristles, just as Melody had described them. He stared at Melody now with a brutal fury, but, although he set his teeth, he did not speak a word.

"Good," Melody said. "Now continue to look at me, if you please. This gold-laced jacket is worth a glance, is it not? In the meantime, I wish to speak, and I wish you, and the others, to hear."

No other heads were turned toward him, but a little shudder ran through that room. They pretended to go on with their card game, and with their dicing, but not a sound was made, and those bent heads were attending with a religious ardor to every syllable that Lew Melody had to say.

"I have learned," he said, "of two brave men who have come to our town from Mexico, the land of warriors." He paused to tilt back his head and smile as he said this. Then he repeated, turning the words slowly over his tongue: "From Mexico . . . the nation of warriors . . . two brave hearts have ridden up the north trail until they have come to Barneytown. And they carry the name of Azatlán." Here he paused and leaned forward a little, scanning every face in that room with a tigerish intentness; every man started, and one no more than another. A shadow of disappointment passed over the face of Melody, and he went on: "They came to inquire after another gentleman who rode to this town a year ago. His name, also, was Azatlán. He was, in fact, their brother. And it occurs to me that perhaps they may be hunting for this man. Do you not think so, *señor?*"

The man with the bristling mustaches made no answer.

"Speak, rat!" Melody commanded.

It brought a savage convulsion of rage to the features of him of the meager mustaches, and, for an instant, it seemed that he would leap from his chair and fling himself at the throat of his tormentor. But he recovered himself at once.

"I cannot tell," he muttered in an almost inaudible voice.

"You cannot tell?" echoed Melody. "Ah, well, still I believe that that is why they have come. And that is why I have ridden down to the *cantina* of my dear friend, the *Señora* Alicia. We are old friends, are we not, *señora?*"

A gasping snarl was her only answer.

"I have come to my friend's house in the hope that I might find them here, because I wish to tell them what became of the other Azatlán. Is there no one among you by that name?"

Not a head stirred, not a voice spoke.

"Then hear me and repeat it to the two good brothers . . . Pedro Azatlán has left this weary world. Do you understand? I, who tell you, know. Because it was my privilege to open the door for him. And I showed him through into his new life. I know that the two brave brothers will be interested. Tell them, also, that I called here in the hope of having a pleasant word with them . . . about their brother's journey." He tossed off his soda, and then backed to the door. *"¡Adiós, amigos!"*

And he was gone.

V

If you think that Lew Melody was exceedingly brutal in this matter, I must explain a little. First, that he had recognized one of the precious pair by a resemblance to the brute face of the man he had killed the year before. For, the moment he had left the *cantina,* there was a great bustle and stir behind him, and the middle-aged man with the bristling mustaches, who was none other than Cristobal Azatlán, rushed from his chair toward the door like a bull. A taller and younger man sprang after him, overtook him, and dragged him back.

"No, Brother," he said. "You were wise not to draw a knife or a gun. It was far better to let him go. We have not come here to fight like two fools, eager to throw our lives away. We have come here only to exact a vengeance, which is a holy thing, is it not?"

"Ah," gasped out Cristobal, well-nigh strangled with rage and with shame, "God must have sustained me, for otherwise I should not have been able to control myself. I should have rushed at him and torn him to pieces. Ah, Miguel, did you not hear it? It was he who opened the door, and sent our brother out of this life. Ah, dog of a *gringo!* Ah, the devil take and burn him little by little, forever. It must be today, Miguel . . . or I shall die. There is a fire in me. I shall die of hate if I do not kill him today!"

They led him back to a chair. *Señora* Alicia, full of solicitude, brought wine.

"Do not think, *Señor* Azatlán, that we suspect your brave heart. But is the bull as wise as the wildcat? No, no. It is fatal to rush at this *Don* Luis. He is a devil with ten hands, and each hand strikes deadly blows. I . . . your friend, who stands now before you . . . I have seen three bold and strong men rush upon him in this place. And that was in long years ago, when he was still a boy. Two of those men we kept in bed until their wounds healed slowly. And the third man was buried. It was sad and terrible. But all the men of the valley know that what I say is only the truth. It is the small shadow of the truth. Believe me, there is no shame for you. Tell him, *amigos,* if I have lied?"

Others came around Cristobal. It was to congratulate him for the patience with which he had endured the dreadful baiting of *Don* Luis.

"But it delivers him into your hands," they said. "Before, he thought he knew your face, and he was right. But now he cannot be sure that you are Pedro's brother. He is already a dead man, and you and Miguel will succeed where so many have failed. But do not meet him face to face. It is deadly and unescapable. It is better to face poison. He works by enchantment."

In this manner they soothed the injured pride of Cristobal, and more wine was poured for them, but not too much. For the advice of Melody himself was still in their ears—a stumbling tongue is bad, but a stumbling hand is a fatal disaster.

Lew Melody had ridden slowly away from the *cantina,* with his head turned over his shoulder, for he half expected that some

maddened man might lurch out through the door, in the hope
of putting a bullet in the back of the rider; for such an eager
enemy, Melody was prepared. I myself have seen him whirl in
the saddle while galloping at full speed and split the head of a
jack rabbit with his bullet.

However, his skill had been known for eight years in the valley; men shunned him as they were fabled to have shunned the
swords of Tristram and Lamorak and Lancelot in the old days
of King Arthur. I have often wondered if the heroes of the days
of armor were not much like this man? Not bulky giants, as we
are so apt to imagine them, but graceful, agile, sure-handed
men, with quick feet and unerring eyes. For it is not hard for
my imagination to dress Lew Melody from head to foot in
complete mail and set in his hand a long lance with a pennon
fluttering from the base of its point.

At any rate, having made sure that there was to be no sudden
rushing out against him, he let the Gray Pacer glide away
through the dusty streets until he came to the house of the
money-lender. There he rode into the court and gave the reins
of the stallion to a servant. He entered by the back stairs—
down which Juanita had told him she had gone when she stole
out through the night to carry him a wealth of jewels and so
buy his safety from the hand of the law. Melody, going slowly
up the stairs, could picture her descending, frightened of every
whisper through the old house, clad in her man's clothes, with
her hair shorn to disguise her the better. Well, she was a soul of
fire. How little he had expected such a strength in this girl.
How little he knew her—or any woman, for that matter.

But, in the meantime, the adventure that was just behind him
had so soothed his soul, and the thought of the courage of Juanita had so raised his heart, that he came into the living rooms
of the old house with the vital picture of Sandy, which had
never left his mind, now grown dim and pale. As for *Señor*

Cordoba and his wife, I don't suppose that they were able to notice anything except the prime fact that *Don* Luis had come back to them, and that he was safe in body. But Juanita saw something more. A haunted look had begun to come upon the face of this girl in the last days—almost since a date for her wedding with Lew Melody was announced. Not that she suspected the feeling of Lew toward Sandy, for, although she had known about that affair, she considered it more or less as a sort of foolish fling on the part of Lew Melody. His real love was for her, and for her only, she told herself. Yet she knew that there was a shadow in the soul of Melody. She tried with all her might to find what that shadow might be, but she could not. And she had no one with whom she could talk this thing over.

At last, she struck upon a solution, and, with the passing of every day, she felt that she must indeed have struck the truth. The shadow in the mind of Lew Melody was old Cordoba himself. For was not Melody the fiery soul of pride, and was not this father of hers no more than a peon? This, she told herself sadly, was the cause behind the gloom that she felt in Melody, although her mother and father seemed unable to detect anything wrong in him.

At this very moment, as he came in, singing and tossing his hat at a chair, she found his eye so lighted and his head so high that she could have cried out with joy. It was like the Lew Melody she had known of old.

"Did no messenger come to you from me?" cried Cordoba, when he saw the young American.

"Yes."

"Ah, you were so long . . . I had a fear that . . . well, here you are . . . and you are safe. Luis, you must not move from the house for a few days, until I have found a way of disposing of . . . never mind."

"Of Miguel and Cristobal Azatlán? Do you mean them?"

Lew Melody asked.

"The devil has told you their names!" poor Cordoba cried. "How have you learned?"

"I have been to see them."

"You!" cried all three, frozen with astonishment and with dread.

"But I could only find one," Melody explained, hastening to relieve their minds of all dread. "I found only one . . . that is, only one that I could recognize, and there was no bloodshed . . . nothing but words. I scolded him, my dear friends, and then I came back to you."

"Were there others there?" asked Cordoba.

"There were . . . and that's why I tell you about it, because I know that you'd hear very soon whether I spoke or not. But there is no harm done."

"Except that you have insulted one of them in public. And now he cannot exist in happiness until he has . . . ah, well, Luis, if you were not so terrible, we would not love you so much, I suppose. But now you must not stir out of the house. Promise me that, until I have had a chance to find these men and deal with them?"

"But how would you deal with them?" Lew Melody asked.

The money-lender winked broadly at him. "There are ways," he said.

"You will bribe him to leave the valley?" Lew asked. "But they would come back again. You cannot handle such nettles with a light touch . . . you must crush them. Leave them to me. It is all in the knack of the thing . . . very simple, and no danger. I only talk of it today, because I know that you will worry."

He was stopped by the expression of Cordoba. The poor man was in a complete panic. It had been one thing to hear of the fierce exploits of this youth, when he was no more than a gay visitor in the house of Cordoba now and again, but as the future husband of Juanita—yes, with that marriage barely around the corner of tomorrow, so to speak, it was absolutely necessary that they should find some means of curbing this creature of fire. But how put a harness on a comet? With despair, then, and with love, and with a sort of futile rage, the money-lender gazed at the youngster. Then he turned to his wife.

"Speak to him!" he entreated.

The *señora* had watched all of this scene with a keen and patient eye, with an interest neither feminine nor masculine; nothing existed in her except the mother afraid for her daughter's happiness, and in this moment she was seeing terrible ordeals in the long years that stretched ahead for Juanita if she married such a man. And, by a sort of premonition, a foreknowledge, she knew that this marriage should not be. So she made no answer to her frantic husband.

It was Juanita who spoke, and in such a tone as neither her father nor her mother had ever heard from her before. She simply said: "We have talked too much of what Luis should do. I suppose that he'll decide for himself in the end." It was as though she had said: "What are we, that we should prescribe?"

So that matter ended for the moment, but a strange chill had come over the household and would not leave them. They sat about fumbling for something to say, or something to do, conscious that the silence was more tense every instant, but unable to murmur a word. And Lew Melody? For the first time, really, he saw that in marrying Juanita he would be marrying her father and her mother, also. They would become a part of his family and of his life, and he would be held by three anchors, and not one.

But three anchors make a moveless ship—and he was Lew Melody.

VI

It was Cordoba himself who, at last, broke the silence that had gathered so heavily in the room. It seemed as though serious thoughts rolled very easily off his fat, round back—or perhaps it was the sense of his own trouble that brought to his mind the trouble of another.

He said suddenly: "It is the end of that poor *Señor* Furnival."

The glance of Juanita flashed whip-like to the face of Lew Melody; if she spoke never of the passion that had taken her lover from her side to that of Sandy Furnival, not so many weeks before, it was not because she did not think of it constantly. Think she did, and now her look probed at the face of Lew Melody. If it had been I, she would have surprised me, I know, in the midst of an expression of dismay that would have told a great deal. But I have noticed that men who are quick with their hands are, also, usually quick with their minds. So that the instant that Lew heard that word, he felt the prick of the spur, and then banished all semblance of pain from his face and presented an unruffled brow to Juanita's searching eyes. The *señora*, too, had looked askance at him, but she discovered no more than did her daughter.

"What's happened to Furnival?" asked Melody in a matter-of-fact voice.

"He is sick?" Juanita asked.

"He is sick in the purse," said the money-lender, and he could not help smiling a little when he thought of his own comfortable thousands in the bank.

"That's odd," Melody said cheerfully, "because he seemed to be a thrifty man."

"Ah, yes, very thrifty," said the money-lender. "But these thrifty men sometimes forget one little thing . . . cash, cash, cash. That is it." He rubbed his hands together and chuckled with self-satisfaction.

"But he has a good ranch," said Lew.

"So-so. It is a good ranch, stocked with good cattle. But there is a mortgage, eh?"

"It is worth more than the mortgage, surely," said the *señora*. "I have seen that place. It is good."

"Buying and selling," said the man of money, "is a beautiful thing. Do you know what the generals say? There is a time to fight and a time not to fight. And there is also a time to sell and a time to buy. Well, my children, this is not the time for *Señor* Furnival to sell. It is very wrong. But he needs cash . . . cash . . . cash."

"The bank . . . ," began the *señora*.

"It is the bank that holds the mortgage. It is the bank that wants the ranch. You see how beautiful it is?"

"Is the Barneytown bank the only one in the valley?"

"They are all allies," said Cordoba. "And the Barneytown bank has said to the others . . . let us alone. We want this thing. Another time, we will keep our hands off when you wish a thing. So it goes, do you see? *Señor* Furnival gets no money . . . he must sell . . . and the bank is the buyer . . . oh, very cheap. Because no one outside of the banks have the cash . . . not one except Cordoba."

"Then why does he not come to you?" asked the wife.

"Who can tell?" Cordoba said with a grin of satisfaction. "To some, I am only a greaser dog."

"Father!" Juanita cried, turning crimson.

"Oh, do not look at Luis," said the money-lender. "He knows what fools say of me. But when Furnival does not come to me, should I go to him?"

Juanita glanced again at Lew Melody; he was merely rolling one of his incessant cigarettes, and his face was as calm as the face of a sphinx.

"Ah, Luis," said the girl, "can you be so heartless, when those people were once your friends? Can you see them go down to a great poverty, perhaps, when a word from you would persuade my father?"

Heaven can tell how the heart of Lew Melody must have leaped when he heard this suggestion, but he knew his part, and he merely said: "They are nothing to me. Let these business-men take care of their business. Why should your father lose money to help this rancher?"

"Ah, well," said Cordoba, cocking his head upon one side as another phase of the thing entered his mind. "It would be a good loan. It would be . . . let me see . . . twelve . . . perhaps fifteen thousand dollars. One cannot place such loans . . . at a right interest . . . every day. But . . . should I go to him? No. I would lose two percent simply by asking him for his business. That would be a fool's trick. I am growing old . . . but I have not grown foolish. No, no!"

I have always seen a fate in this thing—that Juanita should have urged on a matter that ended in her own destruction. But at that moment there was nothing in her saving a great gentle-ness. And when she looked at Lew Melody and considered her great happiness, she had a consuming pity for all who might be sad in this world.

She said: "Let Luis go to them and talk for you. It would be business from you . . . it would seem mere friendship from him."

The money-lender, not displeased, grinned broadly upon his wife. "Is she not my daughter?" he said. "Yes, and she has a head. She has understanding, I tell you. Well, Luis, will you go to him from me? Will you go to him as a friend?"

I suppose that Lew Melody felt this thing was a gift from heaven, but he pretended to be disinclined. "It is a long ride, and a hot day," he said. "I should think that a letter would do well enough."

"Luis!" cried Juanita. "Do you mean it?"

"Well," he said, "will it please you if I go?"

"Ah, yes!"

"These good people," said the artful Melody with a sigh, "make us bad ones work hard to please them. I'll ride to the Furnival ranch if you wish, Juanita."

"Dear Luis!"

"Tush!" said the money-lender. "This may be a good business stroke for me. But look . . . because it is the wish of Juanita, I shall be generous. There happens to be much money lying idle in my safe. Why should it not work? So I will give them a banker's rate . . . at six percent. Now there is generosity, Luis!"

"Foolish generosity," said Melody.

"Well, I shall be soft-hearted for once. But go quickly, Luis. I am eager to learn what he says. Unless he is a madman . . . go quickly. There is much money idle in my safe. Tell him . . . it can he arranged by mail, if he cannot take this trip to see me."

It was in this manner that Melody was persuaded to do the thing that lay the nearest to his heart—by the girl and by her father. In the light of things to come, you will see if this was not the work of a controlling Providence that had a care for the sorrows of poor Sandy Furnival.

So, sauntering idly, for fear lest haste on his part might excite the suspicions of the Cordobas, after all, Lew Melody went down to the street to the Gray Pacer, and there he found a down-headed roan mustang with both ears drooping lazily forward, enjoying a sun bath. And, in the meager shadow of his neck, sitting cross-legged in the dust, his back reclining against the forelegs of the little beast, sat a bareheaded boy of fifteen with a young-old face—a philosopher above, a young satyr below. He was blowing on a harmonica, his eyes half closed in enjoyment of the weird strains that he brought forth.

"Slim!" Lew Melody exclaimed, and ran for him.

But Slim held up one restraining hand. "Listen here," Slim said, with a corner of the instrument still in his mouth. "If this ain't swell harmony, I'm a goat." And he repeated the last strain.

"You'll be a violinist," said Lew Melody. "That's fine."

At this, a gleam of satisfaction crossed the features of the ragged, dusty boy. He stood up and held out his hand. "Hello, Lew," he said. "How's things?"

"Where the devil have you been?" asked Lew Melody. "And why haven't I heard from you? And what became of the last suit of clothes I got for you?"

"I was rollin' the bones with Arkansas Joe down to El Paso," said the boy, "and he had the dog-gonedest run of luck that you ever seen. He got his point five times runnin', and, when I doubled my bets and staked my new clothes along with the rest of my pile, darned if he didn't crap and get the whole lot! That was luck. What?"

"That was luck," Lew Melody agreed, and grinned. He thrust a forefinger into the lean paunch of the boy. "When did you eat last, Slim?"

"Leave me be!" Slim said angrily. "My last meal was a fine breakfast."

"What did you have?"

"Roast chicken," said Slim. "Roast chicken done brown, and roast potaters in the ashes, and coffee that would make you roll your eyes."

"That sounds enough," Melody said. "Where did you swipe the chickens?"

"*Aw*, down the line."

"When was it? Yesterday?"

"Naw. The day before."

"Here's a ten-spot. Blow yourself to a real meal again."

"Thanks," said Slim, stowing the coin with a dexterous palm.

"Why did you fade away, Slim? I thought that you'd stay around with me for a while."

"A hand-out once in a while is all right," declared Slim, "but mooching steady all the time is beggin'. D'you think that I'd be a beggar, Lew?"

"Of course not. How have you been making any money, though? Riding herd a little?"

"Work," Slim explained, "don't agree with me none. It sort of riles up my blood and gets my head to achin'. When I start to workin', I begin to see pictures, and all the pictures is of some place where I ain't. Funny, ain't it?"

"Very queer," said Lew. "But what brought you back just now?"

"I thought I'd blow in for the wedding and the big eats. There'll be big eats, I guess?"

"Oh, yes. More than you can hold."

"I dunno," said Slim. "When I lay myself out to really eat, I can wrap myself around a whole grocery store, pretty near." He stepped closer to Melody. "A bo down the line," he said, "told me about a couple of birds that come up to scalp you. Name of Azatlán. They ought to be in Barneytown right now."

"I've seen one of them," said Lew Melody. "But thanks for letting me know. That's friendly, Slim."

"*Aw*, it ain't nothin'," said Slim. "Speakin' personal, I been sort of achin' for a scrap. I been practicin' with this right along. Watch." With a lightning gesture he conjured a revolver from his clothes and made it disappear on the opposite side of his body. There had been hardly more than a flash of steel in the sun.

"Fine," said Melody. "That's the real stuff. How much time every day?"

"Two or three hours," said Slim. "And then another hour, pullin' and shootin' quick." He added with a sigh: "But I ain't so very sure of my stuff yet, Lew. Well, it's comin', though. I remember what you taught me, pretty well. But I get to pulling with the forefinger instead of squeezing with the whole hand, the way you said."

So, when Lew Melody slipped into the saddle on the great, gray stallion, the boy jumped onto the back of the roan mustang and they started off together, the pacer sliding along like flowing water, and the mustang pounding hard to keep up. They twisted out through the narrow streets of the Mexican quarter of Barneytown, and across the staggering old bridge across the river, and so on through the broader streets of the eastern town. Then up the hills beyond toward the Furnival ranch they went, until the sharply flashing eyes of the boy detected something moving in a course parallel with theirs, on the farther side of the hill up which they rode that moment.

"Lew," he said, "there's a slick bird trailin' us on the far side of the hill."

VII

"Did you have a glimpse of him?"

"Only the peak of a hat."

"Broad or sharp?"

"A Mexican peak, Lew. Might it be . . . ?"

"I'll see," Lew Melody said, and, twitching the stallion to the right, he turned the fine creature into a silver flash of light that drove up the hillside, leaped a fence on the crest, and shot on like a winged thing floating near the ground, to the farther side of the hill, with poor Slim flogging the best speed out of the mustang but falling more and more hopelessly to the rear with every stride.

So sudden was that charge that the rider on the farther hillside was taken quite from the rear and most wholly by surprise. When he jerked his head around, it was only to see Lew Melody already almost upon him and within pointblank range for pistol shooting.

At that range, men took no liberties with Lew Melody, from the Río Grande to the Cascade Mountains. His work was too swift and far too sure for any comfort. So the man, a lean-faced individual with very long, Indian-straight black hair that jutted out beneath the band of his hat, stopped his horse and waited for Melody to come up. The Gray Pacer was brought to a swerving halt that made him face the other directly.

Melody hooked a thumb over his shoulders. "The road is yonder," he said. "There is no trail here, my friend." He spoke in Spanish, and the other answered sullenly.

"I ride where I choose to ride, *señor.*"

"We do not find men by riding cross-country for them," said Melody. "When we wish to meet them, we ride down the roads. Or, better still, we go to their houses and call them to the door and say . . . 'Defend yourself!' "

"*¡Señor!*" exclaimed the Mexican, with a glitter of danger in his eyes.

"Yes, *señor,*" Melody said. "Yes, Miguel Azatlán!"

The guess struck home so sharply, that the other turned a pale yellow with the shock of it. "You have my name, then?" he muttered.

"I have your name," said Melody. "But you are not a full-blood brother to those bull-faced fools . . . Pedro and Cristobal. You are not?"

"Their father was my father," the other replied, more sullen than ever, but more afraid than sullen.

"You have come up here to talk with me concerning the death of Pedro a year ago?" asked Melody.

"I did not say so."

"But I know your thoughts. It must be that we have mutual friends. Now look around you, Miguel. Here are open fields. There is no one near us except the boy, yonder, and he will

221

report the matter fairly and say that it was a fair fight, no matter which of us drops. Why should you not say what you have to say now?"

"I do not know what you mean," said Miguel, a little more yellow than ever. "I have nothing to say."

"Not even six words?" Melody asked contemptuously. He pointed to the holster at the hip of the Mexican. But Azatlán regarded him in a glowering silence. "Very well," said Melody. "It is to be in the dark, then, after all." And, turning his horse fairly around, he presented his back to the Mexican and rode away.

At this tempting target, Azatlán gripped his revolver butt. But still his hand brought it only half out. There was something so light in the carriage of Melody, so suggestive of an animal readiness to whirl and shoot and not miss, that he changed his mind and jammed the gun back into the leather cover.

At the hilltop, Slim rejoined his friend, grinning broadly. "I didn't hear nothin'," said Slim, "but I seen plenty. That sap is gonna dream about you, Lew."

"The rat is a night worker, it seems," Lew Melody said. "He'll try his hand with me when the lights are out. Over yonder is the Furnival ranch, kid. I have to go there by myself. I suppose that you won't be lonely?"

"Me? I keep my company with me," said Slim, and, turning the mustang under the shade of a tree, he slid off and lay flat in the pale brown grass; the outlandish strains of the harmonica followed Lew Melody down the road a step or two.

He went straight up to the ranch house, but, when he rapped and waited, his heart in his mouth, it was not the familiar light step of Sandy Furnival that came up to the door, but a trailing noise of slippers. The Chinese cook opened to Lew.

From the pidgin English of the cook, Melody learned that Furnival was superintending the building of a stack of straw behind the winter sheds for the cattle. So, to the sheds went Lew and found Furnival himself on top of the stack, taking two corners of the great square stack while a hired man labored on the other side of the rising pyramid, and a Jackson fork dumped a quarter of a wagon load at a time on top of the pile. It was well sun faded, this straw, and it rose, now, like a rough mound of ivory against a pale sky. On top, half obscured through the smoke of chaff and dust, Lew saw the grim face of Furnival, set with labor and enjoying his task. He thought it characteristic of the man that, with ruin just around the corner of his life, Furnival should be carrying on the routine work of the ranch with such methodical pains.

A little shudder passed through the body of Lew Melody and set all his lean muscles twitching. For the only thing in the world that he feared, I am sorry to say, was hard work.

The business ended as he approached. The derrick boy turned to stare at him; the teamster on top of his load paused with the ponderous Jackson fork raised in his hands. Furnival himself advanced to the edge of the stack and shouted down: "What you want, Melody?"

"I want to talk to you."

"About what?" asked Furnival coldly.

It was very irritating to Lew Melody. He came there intent upon being his mildest self, but when one wishes to have a quiet bull terrier, it is not well to bring it near to a growling dog. "About your own business," Lew snapped out, "if that interests you."

Now, Furnival was a somber fellow, and I suppose that of all the people in the world, the one he was least fond of was this tall, graceful, handsome young man who sat on the back of the famous Gray Pacer and looked up to him from beneath a gaudy Mexican sombrero. However, after he had paused for a moment, he seemed to decide that it would be better to talk than to explode. So he waded over the loose top of the stack, gripped a derrick rope, and slid down.

He came to Melody, wiping the perspiration and the dust out of his eyes and shouting over his shoulder: "Keep on! This ain't no half holiday!"

The derrick-horse driver came to life with a start, the big Jackson fork was fixed, and then went groaning up into the air with its dripping load of straw.

Melody was now standing at the head of the stallion.

"What'll you have?" asked Furnival.

"You're in trouble," Melody said with an equal sharpness.

"I ain't called for a doctor," said the rancher.

"You're about to be broken up small," Lew stated as coldly as ever. "And you know it."

"What might that have to do with you?"

"I haven't come here for your sake. I suppose that you can guess that."

"We ain't gonna argue that point," Furnival said darkly. "Now lemme hear what you got to say. I'm a busy man."

"I've come to find out what money you need to float you through," said Lew Melody, "and offer you a loan. . . ."

I suppose it was a staggering blow to the rancher. In his hard life, he had never received gifts, he had never taken help. He had moiled and toiled his way to the possession of all that he owned. Help from anyone would have been an absolute novelty to him. But help from a man like Melody, who he considered an enemy, was very strange. If he felt a shock of surprise at first, it was followed at once by a total suspicion. Things that are too good cannot be real.

"You want to offer me a loan?" he asked gravely.

"From Cordoba."

"Ah," grunted Furnival. "From the greaser, eh?"

It was a rough and a pointless insult—seeing that he and the entire valley knew that Lew Melody was contracted to the daughter of the Mexican.

But if the eye of Melody turned to fire, he controlled his anger at once. Furnival, seeing that effort at self-control, marveled more than ever. For certainly Lew had no saintly repute for patience.

"From Cordoba," Melody responded coldly. "I suppose that money from him would help you as much as money from anyone?"

"I dunno," muttered Furnival, still peering intently at the younger man to make out some hidden meaning. "I dunno that I foller your drift, son."

"Open your eyes, then, and look sharp. Is there anything that you can't understand? The bank has cornered you. . . ."

"How did you find that out?"

"From Cordoba."

"And now Cordoba wants to corner me the same way? No, Melody . . . if I'm gonna go bust, I'll let white robbers pick my bones. Thank you."

A veritable saint would have begun to show some emotion by this time, I believe. As for Lew Melody, he was in a white heat.

"I'm making the offer for the last time!" he cried. "Will you take Cordoba's money at six percent interest, or will you not?"

VIII

It was the crowning shock to Furnival. Naturally it was not the first time he had taken a loan; that was the direct cause of his downfall. But when a rancher borrows, he usually pays very dearly for it. The cattle business is too uncertain to make banks lend gladly. A famine season may ruin the most prosperous rancher, and so the rates run high on cattle money. Now, of all times, Furnival having his back against the wall, money at six percent was like money donated freely. He glared at Melody, hunting for the joke behind this suggestion, but, when he found the eye of the younger man bright and steady, he looked wildly around him, then back again to this minister of grace.

"Lew," he said finally, "this is a funny thing that you're talkin' about. I'm about down and done for. I suppose that you ain't meaning it when you talk six percent?"

"Exactly that. You can have what you want at that rate."

"Young feller," said Furnival with a rising voice, "d'you know what I'm in the hole?"

"Only vaguely."

"I need eighteen thousand dollars before I can hold up my head!"

"Eighteen thousand dollars," Lew Melody stated, "is exactly what you may have." He added: "Or call it twenty thousand, which will leave you some spare money in the bank to work on."

The sun was burning hot, but Furnival took off his hat and exposed his face as though to a cooling breeze. "Say it once more . . . slow and careful," he said.

Lew Melody repeated the offer.

"But why in heaven's name will he do it?" cried the rancher.

"He knows that your ranch is worth it."

"Aye, it is!" exclaimed Furnival. "And more, too. And if I can meet the bank, I'll be so far ahead by the end of the season that I could pay off the whole eighteen thousand. I got my hands on gold . . . a regular mine . . . everything is busting my way . . . except for cash, and the lack of cash was killing me. But now . . . why, I'd be free, Melody!"

"Cordoba is not a fool," Lew said. "He wouldn't lend the money if he didn't know that you were worth it."

"It ain't him," said Furnival. "It's you, Melody, that's doin' this for me."

"I tell you, it's not, Furnival. I give you my word. . . ."

"You're lyin' to me," snapped out the rancher. "It's you that persuaded him. Whoever heard tell of a money-lender sendin' out beggin' to make a loan . . . and at six percent. Why, it's not more than charity, Melody."

Nothing else could have torn through the outer shell of his strength so effectually, for there was nothing else that Furnival so understood as he understood money and money matters. This was an eloquence of dollars and cents that went to his soul.

While Lew Melody persisted that there was no charity in it, and that it was a matter of the sheerest business, Furnival took him by the arm and said: "We're gonna walk into the house where we can talk more comfortable."

He fairly dragged Lew to the house and up the steps of the verandah through the door. The same door where, not long before, he had met Lew with a shotgun in his hands and a sharp command never to show his face again in the Furnival house. But that was forgotten now. No, as they entered the living room, he turned about and gripped the hand of Melody.

"I said once that I'd never see you inside my house again, Lew. Well, I was a fool. I didn't know you. I was blind to you. But when a man gives back good for bad, the way you're doin' now . . . why, it makes me want to stand on top of the house and talk to the world about it."

"You'll not tell a soul," said Melody.

"But I shall."

"Furnival, you'd embarrass me."

"Hey, Sandy!"

"For heaven's sake," Lew hissed when he heard the name of the girl he loved.

And then her sweet voice from the upper part of the house made answer, and he heard the quick, light step come through the upper hall.

"I can't stay. You mustn't tell her about it," Lew said, completely miserable. "I'm going now. Let me go, Furnival!"

"Let you go? I'll see you damned first!" He laid a gigantic grip upon the arm of Melody. "Hey, Sandy! Will you hurry up?"

Sandy came in a breathless whirl to the open door, and there she stopped short and threw her hand up before her face. For it was a cruel thing to bring her so suddenly into sight of the man she loved.

But Furnival was in the midst of a speech-making effort, the first in his life, and the glow of his enthusiasm did not permit him to see the pain and the white shock in the face of his daughter.

"I dragged Lew into the house," said the rancher, "because you got the lingo to talk right to him, and I ain't. I dragged him in here, first, to tell you that he's saved us, Sandy. Why he done it, I dunno, except that he's naturally white. But here's the work of my life . . . this here house . . . that chair and that table . . . and everything beyond that window, from the straw to the cows . . . the whole work of my life was gonna go up in smoke, Sandy. And now Lew comes in to save me, after I've treated him like a mangy dog. I say that it warms my heart."

"No, Sandy," Lew Melody broke in. "I have no money. I could not do it. It is the money of Cordoba, and he deserves the praise."

"You hear him?" The rancher laughed, swelling with joy. "Why, he's modest, too. Darned if I ain't seein' him for the first time. Sandy, are you struck dumb? Ain't you got a word?"

"Bless you, Lew," Sandy said, and went up to him and smiled in his face.

"I'll go see Cordoba and arrange things with him," said Furnival. "You might fix up a snack or something for Lew, Sandy. I'm not gonna be back till the middle of the afternoon at the earliest. So long!"

He was through the door with a rush like that of a happy boy. His daughter and her lover remained gravely behind, like old people, indeed.

"As soon as he has gone, I'll go," said Lew. "As soon as we hear his horse."

She shook her head. "There's no need of that," she said.

A heavy silence fell between them, until the rapid *clattering* of the hoofs of the rancher's horse began and died off down the road. Then Lew Melody picked up his hat and turned toward the door.

He had almost passed through it when a low cry from Sandy stopped him; I dare not think what the future might have been for them if that cry had not been uttered. But Melody turned and saw Sandy leaning against the wall, very pale and very drawn about the mouth.

"What is it, Sandy?" he asked.

"I don't want you to go," she said. "I'm too weak to let you go just now."

He went back to her and took her cold face between his hands. "Do you think it's right?" he said.

"I don't know," said Sandy. "Is it wrong?"

They were both trembling; they were both pinched of face and great of eye.

"Only I thought . . . ," said Sandy.

"Tell me," he coaxed.

"That it was our last chance for a little happiness together, Lew."

"It is our last chance," he said.

I don't like to repeat what was said then by Sandy, but all her heroism and that touch of saintliness that I think most good women possess—for a few great moments in their lives— vanished from Sandy and left her weak and all too human. But she cried out: "Ah, my dear, why should she have you? Is it only because she rode a horse up into the hills to find you? Is it that, which gives her the right to have you? But I won't submit to it. I'll fight . . . because it's my life and my happiness that I fight for. And I love you . . . and you love me . . . tell me if you do!"

I am glad that I never had to feel such an agony as went thrilling through the body and through the soul of Lew Melody as he listened to her and stared drearily before him at the wall.

IX

Slim had not lain under his tree long when he heard something behind him, no louder than the rushing of a bird's wing through the air, but it made him drop the harmonica and whirl over on his belly with his revolver slipped into his hand by a gesture of wonderful speed such as Lew Melody himself had seen and approved. When Slim had turned upon his stomach, he found that the barrel of the gun was pointed straight at the piratical form of Miguel Azatlán, who was just half a step from the far side of the tree, sneaking along stealthily with a sort of congealed malice in his face. He stopped with a shock at the sudden change in the posture of the boy. But, after the first start, he was inclined to regard the leveled revolver, in such young hands, as little more than a poor joke. So he grinned at Slim.

"Be careful, my son," he said in Spanish. "There might be a bullet in that."

"Might there be?" said Slim, showing his teeth as he smiled. "And there might be a pair of 'em . . . and there might be three pairs, too. And every pair might be meant for you . . . you yaller-skinned, rat-eyed, long, drawn-out, blue-mouthed alligator!"

"I shall make you yell for that," Miguel said, turning into a demon at once. "I shall teach one young *gringo*. . . ."

"Say, greaser," said the boy, "you got a tassel on the side of your hat that you don't need. So I'm gonna take it off for you."

He had his aim on the tassel, well enough, but that aim was a little too close. He clipped off the tassel, but the big-faced bullet tore into the body of the sombrero itself and ripped through the tough felt and sliced away the hatband and, in short, knocked the sombrero so neatly off the head of the Mexican, that it spun away through the air and left him suddenly bareheaded.

Miguel Azatlán clapped his hand to his bare sconce with a shout of surprise, and then he snatched out a gun only to hear the sharp voice of this evil young American ripping at his ear:

"Drop that gun, greaser! Drop that gun, or I'll salt you, sure!"

Miguel hesitated, then, being lost in fact, he dropped the gun in all obedience and glowered at Slim. "Young murderer!" he gasped.

A lie began to expand in the fertile brain of Slim, and grow into a rosy dream of fiction. He began to narrate: "Sometimes I lay down by the old río and snooze in the bushes. Pretty soon, I hear some sap comin down for water on the far side of the river. Then I up and draw a bead on him and give him a yell. And when he looked up, he got it."

"Son of a devil!" snarled Miguel. "You will be buzzard food before many days . . . you and *Señor* Melody. I spit on you and scorn you."

So he turned himself about and walked away with as much dignity as he could muster. Slim, however, picked up the revolver and gloated over it. It was of a new make, in perfect condition, and all of the six chambers were loaded. The armament of Slim was, in this fashion, doubled on the spot. However, it was no time for him to linger. Since Miguel had been affronted in this fashion, there was not much which he would not attempt, and there were too many ways of getting, unperceived, within at least rifle range of this tree. So Slim gathered up the

231

reins of Sam, the mustang, and jumped on his back to find a new resting place.

But, as he did so, he heard a *clattering* of hoofs. He knew that it was not Lew Melody coming down the road, for the sound of the pacer's rhythmic tread was unmistakable to his sharp ears, so he waited with some curiosity.

What he saw, breaking around the bend of the hill and beating up a cloud of dust from the road, was none other than Furnival himself. The rancher was riding hard, and, although he was on a willing horse, yet its pace did not suit him, and he mended it from time to time with a stinging cut from a quirt, so that the wind of that gallop made the brim of his hat furl up stiffly in front.

That was enough for Slim. He considered that flying figure for one instant, and, comparing its gait with the best pace that he could get out of old Sam, he knew that he could never overtake the flying horseman to ask any questions. Yet he was greatly alarmed. He was too well acquainted with the habits of Lew Melody to be surprised by a disaster of any kind worked by his hands.

What first leaped through the brain of Slim was that Melody might have had trouble with one of the men at the Furnival ranch and that he had shot the man down. Now Furnival himself was rushing for the nearest doctor; that was the meaning, he thought, of such ardent riding on the part of such an elderly and sedate man.

With Slim, as the saying goes, to think was to act. If his idol, Lew Melody, had recently shot down a man, then Lew himself was now in very real trouble. And a man in trouble needs his friends. This was thinking enough for Slim. He turned the roan mustang toward the ranch of Furnival and rode thither at full speed.

But the very first thing that he saw disarmed the greater part of his suspicions. For he discovered that the derrick behind the cattle sheds was still working busily, lifting forkful after forkful of straw to the top of the growing stack, from which a faint smoke of dust and chaff was rising. If there had been a shooting scrape on the place, it seemed most unlikely indeed that the men would be working on in this fashion. If they remained at the stack, it would be to sit in a cluster and talk over similar affairs that had occurred in the valley—particularly if such a person as famous Lew Melody were concerned in the matter.

So Slim paused and took patient thought before he decided upon his next step. It even occurred to him that he might return to the vicinity of the tree where Lew had left him, but when a boy of Slim's age has decided that something may be wrong, and that it concerns the welfare of a friend, he cannot sit down and fold his hands. In another moment Slim had started for the house of Furnival.

He went to the front verandah, dismounted, and stood a moment at the front door. There was not a sound from the house. Yet Lew Melody was not with the working men, and had not returned to the oak, and was certainly not with Furnival himself, who had ridden so hard in the direction of Barneytown. It began to seem like an exciting mystery to Slim when, far and faint in the house, he heard the sound of a girl's voice, and, a moment later, the familiar murmur of Lew Melody.

It was such an immense relief to Slim, that he was about to turn away with a sigh, but then he grew interested, not to eavesdrop upon the pair, but in the nice experiment of seeing how sharply he could attune his ears to those light sounds.

There are ways and ways of listening, but few have the power to throw their attention in a definitely concentrated direction. Yet, from the wide and circling horizon of noises around him, Slim shut out from his consciousness the yelping of a far-off coyote—a mere pulse in the air—the sharper conversations from

the hen yard behind the house, the dreary *squeaking* of the derrick pulley, the lowing of a cow like a doleful horn in the
distance—all of these noises were closed out of the ear of Slim,
and he heard only the delicate stir of voices within the house
itself. Then, having shut out all else, as a burning glass focuses
the sun to a point of fire, so Slim centered his attention and
received reward. For, at once, he could distinguish the thread of
the conversation. The merest puff of wind would have shattered
that dainty web of sound, but no wind came, and presently Slim
was fascinated by the picture that those voices were painting for
him—a picture so startling and so grim that he could not believe
the ears with which he heard it. For he had looked upon Lew
Melody as the happiest man in the world, and now he could
peek behind the curtain and see the truth. Only a brief glimpse
of the truth, but that was enough.

"I shall manage in some way," was the first thing Slim heard
Sandy Furnival saying.

"Ah, Sandy," said Lew Melody, "I wondered why I should be
punished like this, but now I can understand. It's because I've
lived for myself and hunted for nothing but my own fun . . .
and my fun was making trouble for other people. I've lived by
the gun, and now I'm punished for it."

"You'll be happy, Lew."

"I shall be?"

"She is very pretty, and she loves you. And so do all the
Cordobas. But how could they help it? And you'll have money.
That helps to smooth out life, I know."

"When she came to me like that in the mountains . . . I had
to do something to save her name. Was there anything else?"

"You have to marry her, Lew. It is the only right thing. Do
you think that I shall ever reproach you for it?"

"I know that. And it only makes the pain harder to bear."

"Besides, perhaps I shall be happy, too, after a while. There are things for one to do. And Father needs me. I shall find some sort of happiness. But, oh, how I wish that I had never broken out at you today. It was only because Father brought you in so suddenly . . . and said so many kind things about you . . . just for a moment I thought that my heart would break. Because I love you so. Do you forgive me?"

Slim tiptoed from the verandah with a white face.

It was much more to him than if he had looked in upon a frightful murder. He was fifteen, and at fifteen the ideals are as rigidly established as lofty walls of steel. So it was with Slim. Here was his pleasant picture of the future life of Lew Melody pulled down around his ears. He had seen him as the husband of a lovely girl, the son-in-law of a rich man; trouble seemed annihilated for Melody. But here was the truth! And that a man should marry a woman he did not love, even from a sense of duty, seemed to Slim—thief, vagabond, and incipient gunfighter as he was—the most deadly and blasting of sins.

"Something has got to be done," Slim whispered.

X

Such a decision as Slim had come to was proper enough, but what under heaven could be accomplished, he did not see so clearly. What he was determined upon, however, was that this false marriage should not take place. It was true that he knew Juanita and liked her very well, but he had seen Sandy, also, and to see her, as the poet says, was to love her. Moreover, he felt that this project of Melody, to marry one woman while he truly cared for another, was a crime so dreadful that anything was permissible to prevent it. Therefore means, no matter how brutal, did not appear to Slim as things to be rejected. His only difficulty was to find the way in which the thing could be done.

In the first place, he decided that he could not endure to meet Melody face to face at once. There would be too great a danger of his tongue running away with his discretion, and Melody must not now suspect what was in his mind—for nothing he could say, he very well knew, could alter the mind of Lew.

So he rode the roan mustang straight back toward Barneytown but at a slow gait, and slowly he was passing through the streets when he came past my house just as I was busy in the garden watering Lydia's hedge of sweet peas, which is the joy of her life, I think, beyond anything else in the world. Well, it is a pretty thing, that hedge, and I think that, when it calls the eyes of the townsmen toward our house, it sends them by with a happy thought of their clergyman.

However, the sun was very hot, and, when I saw Slim, I was glad to retreat to a corner of the garden under the shade of a tree and turn the hose into the trench to run as it pleased—a thing that Lydia greatly objects to. I waved to Slim, and he rode his horse up close to the fence. He was proud of his ability to talk with men like a man would, and now he drew himself up in the saddle and looked in a patronizing fashion over the brilliant wall of the fragrant color that the sweet-pea hedge raised into the sun. The aroma of it went like a secret blessing half a block away, when the wind was blowing softly.

"That ain't a half-bad garden," said Slim. "But, Jiminy Christmas, Mister Travis, what a pile of work you and Missus Travis must put in on it!"

"Quite a bit," I agreed. "Quite a bit, but it's worth it. Don't you think so?"

"Well," said this imp, "we all got our own tastes, you know. Speakin' personal, I'd say that these here sweet peas smell pretty sweet, but they smell like work, too, and I dunno that I care for the smell of work."

"Work," I said a little sententiously, I fear, "is the only great happiness in life."

The eyes of Slim opened at me. "Might that be a joke?" he asked with a frown of wonder on his young-old face.

"Not at all a joke," I assured him. "Because, you see, man is intended to labor."

Slim blinked. "I dunno that I see that very clear," he admitted.

I am always glad of an argument, even with a youngster, because an argument will open the mind. I have noticed that I am always more violent about a matter of which I am only half convinced. And one never half persuades the other fellow without becoming half unpersuaded oneself. However, there are certain things about which one feels a calm conviction. When they are challenged, one merely smiles down at the challenger, very much as I now smiled down at Slim.

"I'll explain," I said. "Do you know really anything in the world that is happy without work? Consider the squirrels and how hard they labor almost all the year."

"*Hmm*," Slim said, and looked restlessly about him. Presently he pointed. "How much work does that do?" he asked.

It was a rascally blue jay perched on the top of a sapling, which flaunted back and forth in the sun, making it look like a rare jewel.

"Ah, that is a pirate, a marauder," I said.

"What I ask is . . . is it happy?" Slim said calmly.

"Why, one can never judge entirely from appearances," I answered rather feebly. "I admit that it looks rather pleased with itself, but that's probably because it's thinking of the last bird's nest it robbed . . . the scoundrel."

"All right," Slim said patiently. He made his point. "It's happy. And does it work?"

"I don't suppose it does, a great deal," I said. I was immensely embarrassed, but for a moment I could not think of a favorable direction in which to turn the conversation. "But, after all," I continued, "birds and beasts cannot be judged by the same standards that we use for men."

"I dunno," said Slim. "They ain't so different. They're born, the same as us . . . they live and eat and sleep and drink and die, the same as us. They get mad and they get glad, the same as us. They got their friends and they got their enemies. Ain't they a good deal like us, maybe, after all?"

"My dear child," I said, taking on a more pulpit-like manner, "do you not see the great difference? No, perhaps you do not, because it is not apparent to the naked eye . . . only to the inward glance which rests upon the spirit."

"I dunno that I foller you," Slim said, and he politely stifled a yawn.

I grew a little angry, I admit. "Slim," I said, "have animals souls?"

"I dunno," Slim answered. "Why not?"

It was staggering. I stared at that young pagan for a mute moment, and then I said: "Why . . . er . . . isn't it apparent?"

"I dunno that it is," said Slim. "How d'you make it out?"

"Do you dream," I asked, "that there is a heaven for dumb beasts?"

"I dunno," said Slim. "Why not?"

"Because they have no souls to go there!"

"That's what you said before," Slim remarked dryly.

"Can they speak? Can they reason?"

"I dunno that a lot of talk is much good," said Slim. "I never heard no talkin', and I never done none that said half of the things that was inside of me. Did you?"

I could not help biting my lip. "Slim," I said, "could your horse, yonder, reason and talk as we are talking now?"

"Can you smell what's in the wind the way he can?" Slim asked. "Can you see as far? Can you hear as well?"

"Physical properties only," I declared. "What is the soul and the heart of a beast compared with that of a man, Slim?"

"I dunno what you mean," said this irritatingly blunt child.

"Consider, for instance, the affections," I said. "What is so beautiful in the world as love? And can a beast really love, Slim?"

"Well," he said, "how many folks is there in the world that you'd die for?"

"Is that to the point?" I said. "However, perhaps there are some. Death is a good deal, however."

"Could you name one gent that you would die for . . . I mean, step right out and die for the sake of doin' what he wanted you to do?"

I countered rather adroitly by saying: "Of course a man who asked me to die for him would not be. . . ."

But Slim struck brutally across the fine current of my ideas. "Well," he said. "Sammy, here, would die for me. He's pretty near done it a couple of times. He'd run till he dropped."

"A mere instinct!" I cried. "Being trained to that work, the poor creature does not understand anything except to run as long as the spurs tickle his ribs."

"You get into this here saddle and ask him to run for you," said Slim. "Only, you better ride him where the ground is soft."

I flushed a little at this insinuation cast upon my horsemanship, but I was not tempted to mount the little brute. "Ah, Slim," I said, "who is guilty of giving you an education without any religion?"

"I dunno," said Slim, "whoever done any educating of me, except Lew Melody, with a gun. Maybe he ain't good enough for you?"

He said this with the cold smile of one who names a perfect man and dares criticism to show its face. But I was not in a humor to assail Lew Melody.

"Ah, well," I said, "I would need a great deal of time to convince you. Life will teach you, however. The trouble is that life is a painful schoolmaster. And religion comes easily into the mind of man at two times only . . . his childhood and his deathbed."

"I'd like to know one thing," said Slim, "and that's this talk about hell. How much real stuff is there in it?"

I could only say: "I don't know. But some of us feel that there must be some punishment hereafter for sins which are not punished on earth. Just as we hope that there is a reward for the good that is done."

"What would you say," said Slim, "is the worst thing a man could do?"

"Murder, I suppose."

"*Aw*, I dunno," Slim said. "I've seen murder. It ain't so bad. It's over quick, anyways. But what about a gent that loves a girl and marries the wrong woman. Ain't that about as bad as you can think?"

I did not know, at that time, what Slim had overheard. I was inclined to smile, but this touch of idealism in the boy sobered me.

"It is a very great crime," I said, and the thought of Lew Melody and Sandy Furnival did not enter my stupid head. That I had confirmed Slim in his secret thoughts never occurred to me, but his determination was simply that he must save his friend from the dark of hell itself by preventing this marriage with the daughter of Cordoba.

XI

From a secret coign of vantage, Slim watched the return of Lew Melody to the house of Cordoba. He saw enough in the manner of Lew to convince him that what he had heard at the door of the house of Furnival was not an illusion, but a gloomy fact. For Melody did not sweep down the street at the full and reckless speed of the Gray Pacer, whirling a cloud of dust behind him, but at a dreary and a trudging gait, as though the horse beneath him were exhausted with much work. Yet the Pacer was fairly dancing to be off and away at the full of his stride.

Something had happened in the mind of Melody like the drawing of a curtain that darkens a room. From the window of the Cordoba house, a silvery voice called, and Lew Melody looked up with a smile to Juanita. But it was a forced smile, and an observer as keen as the hidden boy could not fail to note the difference.

All that he saw convinced him more and more. He decided that there was new and perhaps greater trouble coming, which inspired him to do two things. The first was to run to a Mexican restaurant and there eat the quickest and most filling meal he could get—which was a few tortillas wrapped around cold *frijoles*. That meal would have been lead in the stomach of any other than Slim, but he returned untroubled to his post from which he could survey comfortably the whole front of the Cordoba house, without being seen in return. There he curled up and fell into a semi-sleep, for this young animal, like any fox, could sleep with his eyes partly open—as one might say. At least, he was perfectly capable of doing all but lose consciousness while he kept his observance upon one point. That point was the house of Cordoba.

He had an animal patience, too. No cat ever starved and waited by the hole of a mouse with more equanimity, apparently, than did young Slim. For one thing, he was very tired, and therefore he remained in that semi-sleep the more easily. His place was the flat top of a roof, sheltered from view from the street by other projecting and over-lapping eaves above him. Here he remained for long hours. Sometimes he roused enough to change sides and curl into a new position of comfort. Otherwise, there was no change. But his skinny body was drinking up rest as the desert drinks up rain.

At length he saw the form of the person, for whom he was waiting, slip out from the patio gate of the Cordoba house. Slim was instantly wide awake. What he had seen was no more than a dull silhouette, for it was now late at night, and there was nothing but the shining of the bright mountain stars and an occasional yellow bar of lamplight that struck softly across the street. He was very cold as he sat up on the house top and yawned and stretched the sleep from his body.

But, in the meantime, he was using his eyes industriously. There was no room for doubt. Even if the outline of the man had not been familiar to him, he would have known the furtive lightness of step with which the other now turned down the street—he would have known the very speed of that walk.

Instantly Slim was out of his spy's nest. He dropped down the face of that house like a wild mountain goat jumping from ledge to ledge. So Slim lowered himself to the ground in an unbroken streak. And he set off in pursuit of his friend, Lew Melody, for it was he.

Never was there such anxious caution as that of Slim at this moment, for he knew by the very manner of Melody that, no matter what his goal, it was one to which he wished to go unaccompanied. When one is shadowing a fox, there is need of more than fox-like cunning. If Lew Melody was a drifting shadow that went rapidly down the street, Slim was a shadow, also. His bare feet gave him a great advantage. There was no possibility of striking out a noise as his heel dislodged a small stone. It was as though he were equipped with another pair of eyes in his toes that told him beforehand the nature of the ground over which he was passing.

They were out of the skirts of the town before Slim had the least idea to what the trail might lead him. For when they were clear of the house, Lew Melody went straight for the heavily-wooded river bottom.

Slim, crouched behind the corner of a fence, took counsel with himself, and he was quaking in every fiber of his being. He understood now. For he was not ignorant of the stories that had been alive in Barney Valley during the last eight years, of how Lew Melody rescued himself from *ennui* by hunting trouble in the jungles of the Barney River bottom lands. In those tangles of willow, the floating life of crime that moved up and down the valley on the trail to Mexico and out again paused to recruit itself. From those darkly forested places, there issued the covert figures that stole into the town to pilfer what they could lay their hands on.

It was on that account that every yard in Barneytown contained a dog as fierce and as formidable as the pocketbook of the house owner could afford to buy. It was on that account that the streets of the town were deserted at night. Nothing but petty crimes were to be feared, to be sure, for the criminals with greater thoughts in their hearts postponed the execution of them until they came to more favorable sections of the country. It was the fear of this same night prowler, who advanced in front of Slim, that restrained them. Time was when they had come up out of the tramp jungles of the bottom lands and committed wild and nameless crimes in the little village. But that time was gone. The fear of the law had been impressed upon them by a man more wild and more tigerish than they themselves—Lew Melody.

I, of course, have never seen him in his element—in his glory, I had almost said. Yet even a minister could be forgiven if he pointed out the majesty of this man's courage, no matter how it was linked with savagery. Here he was stalking through the night toward a place where there might be a dozen bold, strong, cunning men, all bound to be turned into mortal enemies of his the instant he was seen. For when he was seen, he would be recognized. Certainly no hurrying exile ever passed down Barney Valley without receiving, beforehand, some warning from his peers of the man-slayer who would lie in his path at Barneytown.

How much would I not have given to have seen him that night, as Slim saw him, gliding on without sound, scanning all things around him with piercing glances, and never knowing what dark alley mouth, or what fence corner, or what copse of trees, or what thicket of brush contained enemies on the lookout for him and as ready to shoot—if they could do so in safety—as you or I would be ready to set heels upon a loathsome, poisonous spider.

It was very long after this that Slim told me all the thoughts that had passed through his mind as he lay there at the corner of the fence, watching his hero pass on down toward the darkness of the bottom lands, and I, hearing them, could understand and sympathize. It was like stepping of one's own free will into the region of nightmare. For a time Slim hesitated, while the form in front of him first faded and then was lost in the dark of the first trees.

But the instant his eyes lost sight of the man, Slim knew that he could not let him go on alone. He started out at once and ran fast through the dark—fast but softly, as only Slim knew how to run. He wound through the blackness of the copse into which Lew Melody had run—until something sprang on him from behind like a beast of prey, and struck him to the earth.

There had never been a time when Slim had been handled like this. Not even the brutal force of Stan Geary, when that monster used him like a slave, had so paralyzed Slim. He was caught in hands that bit through flesh to the bone with the strength of their hold. In an instant, Slim was helpless, pinned down upon his face.

He had only one thought—of Miguel Azatlán.

Then he heard the voice of Lew Melody, turned to iron: "Slim!"

He was too shocked to make any reply, and so he found himself picked up by the back of the neck and dragged into the dim starlight of a clearing. He was set upon his feet and stood, wavering, before this changed man.

Be sure that this was not that Lew Melody who had been saved from great peril on a day by the testimony of Slim in a courtroom. It was not that man, but quite another—an animal of glistening eyes and stern face, a panther-like creature with no human tenderness in his soul.

"You've followed me, Slim," Melody said.

"I follered you," admitted Slim, shaking.

"D'you know what I came within an ace of doing?" asked Melody, towering above the youngster. "I came within an ace of putting a bullet in you and letting you lie."

"Lew," said the boy, "I didn't mean no harm."

"But I did," answered Melody. "I had the knife ready when I jumped at you, Slim. And only by the grace of God I knew when my hand gripped you that you were a boy and not a man. Otherwise, you'd be lying back yonder with your throat cut and a few heaps of dead leaves kicked over you. What do you mean by trailing me?"

"I meant nothing wrong," poor Slim muttered.

"You meant nothing wrong!" snarled out Lew Melody. "You meant nothing wrong! Why, you young fool, I knew that I was being shadowed the moment that I left the town, and before that. I knew that I was being followed from the gate of Cordoba's house, and I waited until I could hunt the hunter."

A chill struck through the body of Slim. "How could you tell, Lew?" he faltered. For he was certain that he had not been seen.

"How can you tell when there's a cold wind blowing on your

back?" asked Lew Melody.

"I didn't know," said Slim. "But I thought that you was head-ing for trouble. That's why I. . . ."

"Why did you think that? Why did you watch the Cordoba house?"

"Who said that I watched it?"

"For hours . . . or you wouldn't have seen me leave it."

"I only happened along. . . ."

"You lie. And what made you think that I was started for trouble? Slim, I think that you've done a worse thing than lie to me today. And if you have. . . ." He paused, breathing hard. "Go back from the river bottom," said Lew Melody. "Don't try to trail me again. Because, if you do, I'll make you wish that you were never born. Now run for it!"

And Slim turned and ran—ran as if a ghost were pursuing him.

XII

Look in with me upon a little domestic scene in the river bot-tom near our town, on this night when Lew Melody went on his last manhunt.

It was a clearing on the bank of the river, which runs broad and smooth around a bend, at this point, with its quiet shallows at the edges, dotted with stars. There had been a big and cheer-ful fire earlier in the night—a fire that tossed armfuls of leaping flames far higher than the tops of the big trees around the clear-ing. That flaring light made every tree stand out as cold and bright as the sun on a stormy day when the clouds are herded fitfully across its face. But now the great fire had fallen away to an extensive bed of coals that cast a soft light through the clear-ing, and the trees were solid with shadow. Still, in the center of the open space, near the fire, there was warmth enough, and there was light enough for men to sit in comfort and talk, smoke, and play cards. And that is what they were doing, the six men of this party.

First there was a long, lean man with a grave and thoughtful face, smoking a cigarette with half-shut eyes, as though he were seeing, in his dreams, another scene than this. Beside him a bull-necked fellow had spread out a little sewing kit and was busily mending a rent in his coat, which he had taken off and held in his lap. From time to time, he lifted the coat and examined his work with a careful scrutiny, to see whether he was mending smoothly enough. Just beyond them was a jovial face—a very youthful face with gray hair in odd contrast above it. He had his arms locked around his knees, and he was talking softly—telling his yarn in such a quiet voice that he would not disturb the game of blackjack that continued nearby.

At this game—which was played upon a spread-out slicker—sat two people who you have seen before—Miguel and Cristobal Azatlán. But with them was an American who wore a derby hat, oddly out of keeping in such surroundings as these. He was a pale, sickly-looking youth with the long fingers of an artist.

It was a very quiet scene, and there was no noise except the voice of the narrator, just raised above the silky flow of Barney River.

Let me introduce you to these men again, by name and nature. The grave gentleman with the lean face was Doc Ransom, a confidence man of the old school, and what he dreamed of was the palmy height of his career, when he sat in far other company than this, and spent the money that he had cheated out of the pockets of better men than himself. The bull-necked individual was Tony Mack, who not only understood how to use a needle as well as any housewife, but who was also expert in certain devices that would lift the door from a safe. He had performed these operations in many of the largest cities in the country, and he was now destined, after a streak of bad luck, for the flourishing city of El Paso, where luck and dollars would flow back upon him again. The third of this trio in the foreground was also a known man, for he of the rubicund face and the gray hair was none other than Smiling Dan Harper, whose greatest accomplishment was his ability to get his gun out of the holster before the other man, and then shoot quicker and straighter. He had demonstrated his ability in so many lands that sundry sheriffs all over the West were very tired of his exploits in self-defense. He dared not kill again without risking his neck at the end of a hangman's rope. But still, behind those pleasant, smiling eyes, there was the consuming passion—the same passion, in a way, that was now leading Lew Melody toward this very spot.

The Azatlán brothers are already known to you, and he who was playing with them, the sickly youth with the hands of an artist, was a boy from great New York, 2,000 miles away. He was a talented youngster who began in a small way as a sneak thief, but, while he was still in his teens, he formed the more exciting habit of walking into small stores in outlying districts of the great town and presenting his gun under the nose of the fear-stricken clerk while he demanded the proceeds of the cash drawer. But, having served a sentence—abbreviated for good behavior—he reverted to his earlier talents in a modified form and became a second-story man, able to open a window without sound, and able to smell out the hidden treasures of a home in their most secret places. He, also, had had a streak of bad luck, but he was turning his face toward more southern and more profitable scenes.

This was the sextet who waited in the hollow clearing for the coming of Lew Melody—although, if they knew that he was at hand, if they knew that he was at this moment lurking at the edge of the forest, watching and weighing them one by one with an unerring instinct—you may be sure that they would not sit so quietly, but would scatter to the trees like so many frightened rabbits.

But let us pick up the tale that our friend, Smiling Dan Harper, was telling. It may lead us into some amusement.

"When I hit the inside of that boxcar, I sat down and eased up a mite, and pretty soon I heard someone come along and drop the lock on the outside of the door. But I was too fagged to worry about that. The train started up in another minute and I went to sleep, with the car swaggerin' and swayin' along that jerkwater line. We kept on moseyin' along . . . I dunno how long. I was dead to the world. Finally there was a lot of jammin' around, and then I felt that boxcar go rambling smooth as silk onto a sidin'. The brakes come on and we squeezed to a stop.

" 'In the mornin',' says I to myself, 'they'll open up this here car to shove a load aboard, and they'll laugh when they find that there's a carload already aboard her.'

"So I went back to sleep and slept for a long time. When I woke up, the sun was shining through the cracks of that old car. I peeled my eye through one of the cracks, and all I could see was trees that was walkin' down to the side of the track. Then I peeled my eye on the other side, and all I seen was trees walkin' down to that side of the track, just the same way.

"Well, I wait for a couple of hours . . . till my empty belly begins to bother me. Then I up and make a racket. I just hollered, at first, and then I started kickin' the sides of that car and yappin' real loud. I kept that up for pretty near an hour. Seemed like I was makin' enough noise to be heard right over the top of the mountains, but, when I got through, I listened and didn't hear nothin' but a sort of an echo of the noise I'd made, rollin' and roarin' through my ears.

"I sits down and has a think. By the sun and the warmth in that car, I know that it's pretty well along toward noon, and so the station agent is reasonable sure to have been around. I take a long rest and try to figger it all out, but it sort of puzzles me.

"Well, as I was sayin' before, I hadn't done much sleepin' since the posse started after me, so, instead of worryin' none, I took the kinks out of my belly by tightenin' my belt, and then I curled up and went to sleep again. When I woke up, there was a sound of a shufflin' step outside the car.

" 'Some lazy bum of a shack,' says I to myself, and then I hollers out . . . 'Hello, pal! Gimme a lift out of this, will you?'

"That shufflin' noise stopped, and then it went scamperin' away toward the trees . . . I never heard the sound of no man runnin' that was just like it. The next minute, while I was tryin' to peel my eye through a crack in the side of the car, I smelled bear as plain as you ever smelled bacon in the mornin'.

"Bear was what it was! There ain't no mistakin' that smell. And that showed me where I was. No bear would come wanderin' around the sidin' of a real town or even of a real station. No bear would come inside of ten mile of a place full of switchmen and what not.

"What had happened was that the train had sided that car in the middle of the mountains. I could remember seein' cars that had stood out on little sidin's like that one for half a year, till their wheels was froze to the rails with rust. And how long would it be before they come to get that car again?

"I sat thinkin' it over, and feelin' my face get cold with sweat. But there was no use just settin' and waitin'. I got out my knife and started to work on the side boards of that car. Dog-gone me if that wood wasn't like iron. It pretty near turned the point of the knife. It was an old car, but it looked like it had been boarded up new all around pretty recent. So I got sort of peered and gave the knife an extra hard jab. And the blade busted right off!

"Well, there I was, pretty well strapped, you might say, and feelin' pretty sick, inside and outside. All that I had in my hand for a tool was a dog-gone' bit of a busted-off blade of a knife, and it looked like there wasn't much more use in tryin' to work with a tool like that than there was to start in scratchin' that hard wood with my nails.

"But there wasn't any use in settin' still. I had to do something, or else go mad. I got to work and I walked around that car, and every plank I tested out by punchin' at it with the blade of that knife. And, finally, I got hold of a plank that seemed a lot softer than the rest of 'em. So I got to work on it right away.

"Well, sir, it was just scratchin' and nothing better. After about an hour, with my hands sore and my arms tired, I'd only made a couple of rough white streaks across that plank. I sat down to take a breath and think it over again. I could do a long turn without food, I knew, but without water, nobody can last very long. And there was a hot sun over the top of that car, and the inside of it was like an oven. I needed water awful bad. Seemed like I'd been dry for a week already. And I knew by what I'd heard that a gent can go only about three days without a drink. I asked myself how many days would it take me to cut through the wall of that car? Just thinkin' about it throwed such a scare into me that I knew that I'd have to keep to work if I didn't want to bust down with the shakes. I grabbed up that knife again and set my teeth and sailed into the plank."

"*Psst!*" came the warning hiss of one of the gamblers.

At the same moment, a light-stepping shadowy form of a man came out from the trees and approached the glow of the fire.

XIII

Miguel Azatlán, having seen him most recently, knew him first and gave his brother the tidings in a murmur that was, never-the-less, heard plainly by all the rest: "Be ready, Cristobal. That is *Señor* Melody."

Tod Gresham, the boyish second-story man and nimble-fingered thief, was so filled with alarm that he jumped half to his feet and prepared to bolt for the woods. It was the long arm of Doc Ransom, the confidence man, that darted out and caught him and dragged him back to the ground.

"It's Melody!" gasped out the robber.

"Maybe it is. But here are six of us," said Doc Ransom. "Sit tight, my boy. We may need one another, but we don't need to run. Sit still and watch, and shake your gun loose, so you can get it quick."

This admirable advice was received by the youthful thief with a shudder of distaste. It was true that he went armed and that he had worked with the trigger of a gun as much as most men of his profession. Yet he had no liking for this work that seemed about to lie ahead of them.

"Guys like you," he snarled softly to Doc, "are just the sort that he uses for his meat . . . leave your hands off that kale."

The last was directed to Cristobal Azatlán who, seeing that there was a momentary disturbance, decided to profit by raking in all the stakes that were on the slicker and pocketing them. At the bark of Tod Gresham, he refrained, with a rolling up of his eyes like the glare of a bull before it charges.

In the meantime, Lew Melody had advanced into the rich circle of the fire light and hailed them with a sort of quiet cordiality: "Hello, boys!"

"How's things?" said the white men.

"*Señor,*" murmured the two Mexicans.

They were sitting close together, these two dark-eyed sons of trouble, and lean Miguel whispered at the ear of his half brother: "Why not now, Brother?"

"Is your gun ready?"

"I shall use a knife. I trust it more."

"No. While you draw back your arm to throw the knife . . . even if you are quicker than a striking snake, he will have his revolver out and he will kill us both. We must work with guns only."

"As you please. But quickly. I am nervous, Brother."

"Not yet. See how cool the devil is. Perhaps he has friends, yonder, in the brush. If he did not have them there, how would he dare to come in this way to six of us?"

"True."

"One of us must try to come behind him . . . or else, one on either side of him. Then watch me . . . when I start my hand, start yours. One of us he is sure to kill. I hope it is I, not you, my brother."

"As God wills, so must it be. Farewell."

"Farewell, Brother. We shall never speak to one another again in this world."

So, in whispers inaudible a foot away, quickly, with the resignation of stoics, they determined to kill or be killed.

Lew Melody, meanwhile, had entered into a cheerful conversation with the others.

Smiling Dan Harper led the talk with: "We hear that you aim to settle down, Melody?"

"Is that what marriage means?" Melody said.

"I suppose so."

"Well, you ought to know, Harper."

"You know me?" cried Dan Harper in surprise, and in alarm, also.

"Oh, yes."

"How does that happen?"

"I knew Sam Arnold."

"Was he a friend of yours?" Harper asked, his voice becoming a little strained.

"We used to have fist fights when I was a kid. Well, I don't think that I could call him a friend. Did he put up a real fight with you?"

Dan Harper hesitated an instant. It was two years ago that he had killed Sam Arnold. The face and the voice of that unlucky boy floated back upon his memory too vividly.

"It was a bad evening's work for me," said Harper, watching the face of his inquisitor with a sort of critical anxiety. "We'd been drinking, and then we started playing cards. I thought that Sam had too much luck. He said that it was just the swing of the cards. But when a feller wins seven hands running . . . well, you know, Melody."

"Sure," Melody responded with the utmost good nature. "Someone said that you shot him under the table."

The face of Dan Harper contracted. "As I was jumpin' the gun out of the leather, the damn' thing went off. . . ."

"I understand," Lew Melody said, and smiled. "They tell me that you got two more slugs into Arnold as he was droppin' to the floor."

"That's a lie, and a loud lie! I'd like to get the dirty dog that told it."

"Maybe it is. It's a queer thing how facts are lost when a story has been told a few times, isn't it, Dan?"

"You're right," declared Dan, welcoming this friendly tone.

He felt that there might well be a reason behind this friendliness. If Lew Melody had come into the jungle bent on action, he certainly could not wish to attack all six of them at the same time. He must establish a friendship with a few of them—or a state of neutrality, at least.

"To say that I'd shoot a man that was down!" cried Harper. "That's a rotten thing to spread around. I'd like to get the rat who said it."

"I've forgotten," Lew said. "It was some fellow from

Montana. He told us quite a lot about you."

"What else?"

"Why, I remember that he said that Shep McArthur was a friend of yours."

Here Tony Mack, whose glittering eyes had never left the face of the young gunfighter, broke in: "Well, that was the truth. You and Shep was bunkies, Dan. Ain't that right?"

"We was," admitted Harper. "He was my best friend in the world. He left me one summer. Heaven knows whatever became of him."

"I can tell you," Lew Melody said, "one part of the story. I met him right here. There was a fire that night . . . a good deal like this one tonight. I remember that Shep McArthur was boss of the fire and was telling the boys what to do. He told me to get some wood for the fire, and he spoke very sharply. I'm a very sensitive, nervous sort of a chap, Harper. When he spoke to me that way, I couldn't help objecting. And in another moment . . . you know how it is . . . we had our guns out. I was unlucky enough to hit him with the first shot." He was speaking with an oiled gentleness, but the eyes that he fastened upon Dan Harper were the eyes of a tiger. He held the entire group fascinated. "That bullet went through his leg, Dan. He shouted that he had enough as he dropped, and I stopped shooting, of course. But the minute he saw me lower my gat, he raised his and started pumping lead at me as he lay on the ground. His bullet nicked my ear. I'll always remember McArthur because of the chip on the rim of this ear." He touched the place gently with his fingers. "So you understand, Dan, why I had to kill him?"

"I understand," Dan Harper said huskily. All the muscles in his throat were distended by the grip of his teeth as he ground them together.

"I'll sit down by you, Mack," said Melody, "if you don't

mind." He made himself comfortable by the fire, sitting at the extreme point of the arc of which Cristobal Azatlán made the other tip.

"You know me, too?" said the yegg.

"I know that Dan Harper and Tony Mack often travel together," said Lew. "That's why I suppose that you're Tony Mack."

"Our friend seems to be a mind-reader!" exclaimed Doc Ransom, who had been using the last conversational interval to shift his gun to a more convenient pocket. "He seems to be able to select names for all of us. What about our two friends on the left? Could you name them?" Ransom asked.

"Miguel and Cristobal Azatlán," responded Lew Melody, "We have met before. I might almost say that we are old friends. I knew their brother a year ago."

The deadly irony of this remark caused even the calm of Doc Ransom to break a little, and he flashed a side glance at the two Mexicans. But they sat with faces of stone, smoking and hearing nothing.

"Here is another," said Ransom, pointing to Tod, the sneak thief and burglar. "You have given four names out of six, and I suppose that you could name this gentleman, also?"

Perhaps I have pointed out that Lew Melody had, one by one, created enemies out of four of the six men in the circle around the fire. It was impossible, surely, that he could intend to throw down the glove to the entire six. But now he lighted a cigarette and waved an open path through the mist of his first expelled breath so that he might study Tod Gresham more intently.

"I don't know your name, partner," said the gentle voice of Lew Melody, "but I can tell how you make your living."

Tod started nervously. "Tell me, then," he said, filled with defiance.

"Why, that's easy enough. You make your living with your hands . . . and yet you don't work."

The sneak thief clenched his fists and glared at the other, but, after a moment's reflection, he decided that, if such a formidable warrior as Dan Harper had decided to pocket up a cause for battle, certainly he, Tod Gresham, could afford to follow that example.

"You have named four and the occupation of a fifth," Doc Ransom declared, turning his cool glance straight upon Melody. "And what about me?"

"You're another who hates work," said Lew Melody. "Talk is enough for you, is it not? You can talk money out of the purses of other men, I suppose."

It was the final blow. One by one, he had slapped each of the six in the face.

XIV

When Slim bolted away from Lew Melody, he had no thoughts of turning back, after a little time, and attempting to resume the trail. For he felt very much as though he had walked after a tamed house cat and found it transformed suddenly into a panther. The thought of that stalking panther drove him on until his breath failed, and then he slowed to a walk. His feet were now in the velvet dust of the old town, and that softness was grateful to them, for as the ecstasy of fear subsided in him, he was aware that they were cut and bleeding and tingling with pain—with such abandon had he raced through the dark of the night.

He paused, finally, to take stock of possibilities. What he was convinced of was that Lew Melody had gone out to throw away his life because life had become a burden to him, and, in some way, this thing must be avoided. All that he could think of on the spur of the moment was to go to the house of Cordoba—

not that Cordoba himself was a fighting man who could rescue Slim's hero, but Cordoba was rich, and Slim knew that money works with a thousand strong hands.

So he went to the black-faced house of the money-lender, where the stars struck out a few highlights from the blank windows. He knocked at the front door, first, but he got no response. Then he clambered to the balcony and tapped again, loudly, at the upper door that opened upon that balcony.

Finally he heard muffled voices. Then a light gleamed inside the room and the voice of Cordoba, shaken with excitement, called: "Who's there?"

"Slim," said the boy.

A lamp was suddenly interposed between the curtain and the window of the door, so that a strong shaft of light struck out upon Slim, leaving the holder of the lamp in darkness. Then the door was unfastened and opened.

"What do you wish, young man?" Cordoba asked, repressing stronger language because he knew that Slim was a close friend to Lew Melody.

"I want help for Lew," said the boy. "He. . . ."

"What sort of help for a man soundly asleep . . . too soundly asleep to hear your rapping?" growled out Cordoba, yawning.

"Go look in his room, if you don't believe me," Slim said, furious at every delay.

Cordoba scanned him once again—cast an anxious glance around the room to make sure that there was nothing this young vagabond could steal when his back was turned, and then hurried to the room of Melody. He opened the door, and then came hurrying back, this time with a pale face.

"He is not here," muttered Cordoba. "He is not here. But I saw him go to his room . . . how . . . ?"

"He's in the river bottom."

"No, no!" groaned Cordoba. "He vowed that he would give

up such . . . how can you know that he is there?"

"I follered him till he found me out and sent me back. He's bound for the river bottom, and to raise the devil there."

"Ah," groaned the unhappy man, "why should he do such a thing as that . . . now?"

"Because he ain't happy," Slim said, trembling with emotion.

"We saw that he was moody tonight . . . all young men will be that way. They are like calves or colts. They have whims. But . . . boy, do you know that his marriage is less than a week away?"

"And ain't that the thing that's eatin' him now?" cried Slim.

"*¡Diablo!*" gasped out Cordoba, and could say no more while he stared at Slim as at a ghost.

"Where was he today?" Slim went on bitterly. "Where did he go today?"

"To *Señor* Furnival, yes. But what of that?"

"To Furnival? The devil, no! Maybe he seen Furnival . . . but the one he stayed to talk to was Sandy."

Cordoba put down the lamp because his hand had begun to shake so that he dared not continue holding it.

"You are talking of something that means more than your words," said the money-lender. "Ah, may we keep sorrow from Juanita's life. A blow is about to fall . . . I have felt it, and I have dreaded its coming. Boy, tell me whatever you know."

"I know that Lew Melody is eatin' his heart out because he's got to marry Juanita," Slim stated.

There is little tact in boys. Besides, Slim was desperate. It was the picture of Lew Melody's peril that crushed him, not the troubles of the old money-lender. And when Cordoba stretched out his hands in appeal and cried—"How can that be?"—the answer of Slim was brutally to the point:

"Because it's Sandy that he loves . . . don't everybody love her? And ain't Lew the only gent that she ever looked at?"

In this great crisis, Cordoba gathered all his strength and became calm. "Speak softly," he said. "If there is any truth in what you say . . . but there cannot be. But not a whisper of it must be heard in this house . . . or it would turn my home into a hell. Now tell me how you could know this? But you could not know. It is a guess . . . a dream."

"Cordoba," Slim said fiercely, "I heard 'em talkin'. I stood at the door when they thought that I was a mile away, and I heard 'em talkin'."

Cordoba sank into a chair and supported his face in both uncertain hands. "It is the end," he groaned. "It is the black day of our three lives. What is my sin that this should be done to me now? But he . . . treacherous devil. He has crept like a snake into the heart of my girl."

"He done the right thing as he seen it," Slim tried to explain. "When Juanita rode up to him in the mountains . . . he had to try to keep her from bein' talked about. He wants to go through with it, but I tell you that, after he seen Sandy today, he'd rather die than marry anybody else. I tell you that I stood there and heard 'em talk like they was both gonna die the next minute. And now Lew is down in the river bottom huntin' for trouble . . . and God knows that he'll find it. Them Azatláns are there, and I know that Tony Mack and Smilin' Dan blew into Barneytown today. He'll run amuck with the whole gang of 'em . . . unless you do something to stop him."

"He must be stopped," gasped out Cordoba, staring wildly about him. "Think for me, my boy. Find a way! How shall I do it?"

"Ain't you got a house full of servants? Ain't you got friends? Get half a dozen gents with guns and send 'em for the bottom lands. They'll find him there, and I'll be one of the gang. I'll do as big a share as any other man . . . only, by myself, I couldn't handle Lew tonight. He's gone sort of crazy. I thought he was gonna kill me for follerin' him."

The door into the room of Juanita had opened some moments before, and now she ran out at them, a slender white form. "It is too late already!" she cried. "Do you hear?"

Up from the river bottom, in the breath of silence that followed, they heard the sudden chattering of guns—many guns in rapid action like a mutter of musketry in the distance. But Cordoba forgot everything else. He ran to his daughter and caught her by the shoulders and turned her so that the light struck across her face.

"What have you heard, Juanita?" he snapped.

"I have heard everything," she said.

"It is all a lie," moaned Cordoba. "There is no truth in it. You shall not believe, my sweet girl!"

She tore herself away from him. "Why do you speak of me, always," she cried. "*Don* Luis is being murdered in the river bottom! Raise the town. Do not wait to saddle the horses. Ride bareback. Ride, ride! I shall come as I can . . . will you go? Will you all stand still and drive me mad?" And she rushed back into her room.

Her mother came hurrying in as Juanita tore off her nightclothes and began to dress haphazard. In the distance there was the voice of Cordoba thundering to his neighbors— the sound of other windows opening, with a slam—other voices shouted in reply.

"What are you doing?" sobbed the *señora*. "Where are you going, Juanita?"

"I am going where I may help him for the last time," said the girl.

"God pity us!"

"Have you heard, too?"

"Everything. But it must be a lie!"

"A lie? I heard the guns in the hollow. And I know that he is dying now."

"You must not go. Juanita. . . ."

The girl knocked away the hands of her mother with a furious strength. "Do not touch me. I must go. If I may hear his last words . . . perhaps he will see my face . . . the last face in his life. . . ."

"Juanita, it will kill you . . . it will break your heart. You will die of it!"

"What is *my* life?"

"He has lied and pretended to you. . . ."

"Ah," the girl cried savagely, "if you say such things of him, I could kill you!" She had dressed while she talked, flinging her clothes upon her body and now, stamping her slender feet into her boots, her short black hair whirling about her head, she rushed past the *señora* and across the big room, and past the piano where her mother had played while she taught Lew Melody to dance—and to dance his way, so, into the heart of Sandy Furnival.

She thought of these things as she fled down the back stairs of the house. When she reached the courtyard, she found a swirl of men and horses there—saddling, arming, shouting.

"Don't wait for saddles!" cried Juanita. "There is no time! There are men dying in the river bottom. God reward you if you hurry!"

But, fast as they fled down the road, she was up with the leaders, before they reached the woods. She was up with them, flashing along on the bare back of the pinto mare, which had been given to her by Melody himself.

A reward because she had taught him to dance!

XV

When Lew Melody had, in his own fashion, insulted the half dozen grim fighters who sat around him, a little pause followed, and during that pause his hand went slowly to his lips and down again, as he puffed at the cigarette.

All were fascinated by that hand. It was as slender, almost, as the hand of a woman, but the square-tipped fingers and the round wrist, in which the cords thrust out at every movement, told of the gripping strength that was there. It was neither grace nor beauty in that hand, however, which so charmed the watchers, but the peculiar steadiness with which it moved and, every moment or so, flicked the ashes from the fuming end of the cigarette. For, very obviously, he now stood in danger of his life from six men, and each one of them was capable of struggling like a tiger. Yet he continued his smoking with the same deliberation—even when Miguel Azatlán, rising to put a fresh clump of brush upon the fire, moved to another part of the circle, a point at which he was just opposite to his brother.

But Lew Melody did not appear to see. Neither did he seem to care when the heat of the glowing embers of the fire ignited the dry brush and sent a *hissing* column of flame aloft in the air, where it stood like an orange pillar, wagging its head and snapping off wild arms of brightness that vanished instantly in the black of the night.

Yet he was now at a greater disadvantage than ever. Only a gunman of such uncanny expertness as himself could have shot with any certainty in the dull light of a moment before, but in the full flare of the fire, each of the six would have immensely improved chances.

No one spoke. And yet the loudest speeches, the most blasphemous insults could not have filled the air with such a tensity of excitement.

Then, from the town, an excited dog began to bark, the noise coming in sharp little pulses through the air and dropping into the clearing.

"Damn that dog," said Tony Mack.

"I'd like to kill all dogs in the world!" snarled Smiling Dan Harper. "I've had their teeth in my legs too often."

"Then start right in close to home," muttered Tod Gresham, who was trembling and gasping in a nervous frenzy of excitement.

"Start where?" said Tony Mack, who was slow of wit.

"Here!" screamed the boy, and snatched at his gun.

When he leveled it, he found that he was covering not Lew Melody, but the squat form of Tony Mack, for, at the voice of the boy, Melody had dropped his cigarette and flung himself at the yegg. Even that stoutly muscled body was helpless under his handling. They whirled—and Tony Mack staggered helplessly back toward the fire as Melody leaped for the trees.

The first bullet to follow him was that of Tod Gresham. It clipped his coat at the point of the shoulder. The second was from the gun of Miguel Azatlán, and his brother's bullet *whirred* past the ear of the retreating fighter. But before there was a chance for more action, Tony Mack pitched back into the midst of the fire, beat down the flames, scattered the flaring brush far and wide, and threw the whole group into confusion. Tony Mack himself rolled with a scream from that terrible bed and started, still yelling with agony, toward the broad, black coldness of the water.

Lew Melody had turned from his flight toward the trees and dropped flat on the ground with two guns stretched out before him. His first shot caught the tall body of Miguel Azatlán squarely in the stomach and, plowing through his flesh, broke the backbone. He died without a groan. His second shot landed below the hips of Tod Gresham and passed through both thighs. He fell with a shriek of pain, for his flesh was frightfully torn.

Then Melody was up and flying toward the trees again, for there was no other easy target before him. The remaining three—Smiling Dan Harper, Doc Ransom, and burly Cristobal Azatlán—had sought better cover by throwing themselves upon the ground in imitation of his own maneuver.

As he ran, he swerved like a football player running through a broken field, and, although the bullets sang wickedly around him, he reached the very border of the trees before he was struck. He did not know where the shot landed. But from head to feet he went numb, while the heavy blow knocked him forward upon his face.

The wild, three-throated yell of the enemy called back his senses from a fog of pain and shock. He turned on the ground and fired at a leaping form that ran toward him, gigantically big and black against the firelight.

That grotesque figure seemed to be snuffed into nothingness. In reality, Smiling Dan Harper had gone to the ground with a bullet through his head.

But there were two other points of rapidly jetting fire—the weapons of Azatlán and Doc Ransom. Twice, long ripping thrills of flame passed through the flesh of Lew Melody before the sheer ecstasy of pain enabled him to roll into the covering shadows of the trees. He managed to gain hands and knees, and so to drag himself behind a trunk.

There he lay with his back to the firelight in the clearing and his face turned toward the heart of the woods, for he had a feeling that if they came at him, it would be from the trees.

Presently he heard a *crackling* farther into the woods. They were searching for him there, not dreaming that the extent of his wounds had chained him to the place to which he had first forced himself.

Somewhere in his body there was a painful pulse, every throb of which was driving life from his body, and he knew that he was fast bleeding to death. He was not sorry for it. It seemed to Lew Melody, as he lay there in the dark, that it was the only way to extricate himself from the frightful tangle of his life—the knot could only be cut. If he had one desire, it was to see the forms of his two last enemies in the sextet come into view and range of his gun.

But that was too much to pray for. Here, in his last and greatest battle, he felt himself dying, and he could not help a certain boyish thrill in the knowledge that the world would talk of this deed long after it had forgotten the better work of better men than himself. He had snuffed out two lives and laid another low and held off three more. It was a comfortable night's work even for Lew Melody.

Another *crackling* in the brush told him that the pair of hunters had turned back toward the edge of the fire. Hunting as they were hunting, stealthily, with a deadly caution, there was little chance that they would fail to see him before he saw them. He made himself ready to accept a bullet, and, in return, he steadied himself and quickened his nerve to drive an answering bullet back at the jet of fire. A little below the tongue of flame he would direct his own aim, for they would doubtless be stretched along the ground. So he waited, with the life ebbing from him at every moment. And a lifetime, I suppose, whirled through his brain with the passage of each second.

Then he heard the noise of Tony Mack—frightfully burned, to judge by his groans—as he dragged himself from the water back toward the dry land—a groan for every breath he drew. Perhaps that rascal had been injured enough to end him with the others. There was a grim satisfaction to Lew Melody in that thought.

There was a new sound, now, a distant muttering like soft thunder that rattles beyond the edge of the horizon. But this grew faster than the noise of any thunderstorm sweeping across the face of the sky. It swelled and whirled closer—the pounding of the hoofs of many horses.

Then, with a great crashing, the cavalcade struck the outskirts of the woods.

Slim, Melody thought to himself. *But it's too late.*

The meaning of that noise was not lost upon the two hunters in the dark. There began a brisk *crackling* as they rushed from the brush covert in an opposite direction, and, at the same time, the first riders lunged into the dull glow of the firelight that filled the clearing. Lew Melody, turning himself with an infinite labor, saw Juanita—the first rider, on the pinto mare that he had given to her.

"Luis!" she cried.

It was not she for whom he wished, but since she had come, he answered faintly: "Here."

She was at his side in a flash, and men thronging after her—a great dismounting, snorting of horses, *creaking* of leather, *jingling* of spurs. He was pleased with these sounds. They came to him as out of a sleepy distance, for a black burden of rest was falling upon his eyes.

The face of Juanita, as she leaned above him, was a dull blur. Only her voice had life and light as she spoke to him. And then her sharp cry of agony. "Help! He is dying!"

Professional hands took charge of him. Vaguely he recognized the voice of the Mexican doctor. Lights flared up around him. No, he was being carried into the clearing and now he was put down by the fire, which was freshened until it filled the eyes of Lew Melody with yellow lightnings.

Then, from Juanita: "He will live, Doctor?"

"I cannot tell," said the doctor. "If he wants to live . . . perhaps."

Lew Melody heard no more. He had fallen into a blissful sleep, so it seemed to him—or was it death toward which he sank? No, for he was called back by burning pains. The doctor, with two assistants, was hastily drawing wide, gripping bandages, about his wounds. That pain gathered like a great crescendo of music, and crashed upon his brain.

And he fell into darkness again.

XVI

Juanita was not in the clearing. She had remounted the pinto mare and now she was flying up from the river bottom, and twisting through the thick shadows of the Mexican town, and then the hoofs of her horse struck out an echoing roar from the old bridge that staggered across Barney River.

Before her glowed the lights of the American section, with its broader streets, and now she was passing through it with the scent of freshly watered lawns coming, cool and fragrant, upon either side. Then she was beyond those lights of the town and stretching up the weary rise of hills to the east.

The pinto mare, laboring with all her might, seemed to be standing still, and the girl flogged her onward remorselessly. So, reeling with weakness, completely run out, the pinto reached the house of Furnival, and the shrilling voice of the girl reached the ears of the sleepers in the house; yes, it passed behind the house and, needle-like, pierced the heavy sleep of the men in the bunkhouse beyond the main building.

A moment later and Furnival was at the front door. He opened it upon a wild-eyed creature, trembling, and crying to him: "I must see the *Señorita* Furnival . . . quickly, oh quickly! It is the life of *Don* Luis!"

And here was Sandy herself flying down the stairs, already half dressed, and drawing on the last of her clothes and doing buttons with flying fingers.

"They have killed *Don* Luis . . . in the river bottom. Six men . . . and they have killed him, but he will want to see you before he closes his eyes. He is dying, *señorita!*"

Here were two races and two differing souls face to face, and Sandy was as white and as cool as the Mexican girl was shaken and wailing.

"Will you help me saddle a horse, Father?" she said, and was through the door at once.

Furnival, in his nightclothes, followed. It was he who flung the rope that captured the horse; it was she who dragged out saddle and bridle. Between them the animal was instantly ready. Then she was off—no, with the spurs ready to thrust into the flanks of her mount, she stooped to Juanita, standing at her side.

"I understand," she said. "It is more than I could have done for you. God bless you for it."

Then she was gone.

How she rode that night. I was an eyewitness, for the news from the river bottom had come back on wings to the town, and half of Barneytown was in the saddle, I think—myself among the rest—when a foaming horse flew down the street and someone cried: "Sandy Furnival!"

Like a bolt from the sky, she was past us. I rode as hard as I could, but the thundering hoofs of her horse were on the bridge long before I was there.

I cannot tell how she found her way so straight to the clearing. Perhaps there were other hurrying horsemen already streaming in the same direction, for the whole valley would burn tomorrow with the tale of how Lew Melody had fought six men hand to hand.

But when she stormed into the hollow, she was met by a deadly silence.

It is death. I am too late, Sandy thought in her own sick heart. So she slipped from the saddle and ran to the quiet form beside the towering fire, all of whose ruddiness could not relieve the pallor of his face.

His eyes were closed.

"It is death?" whispered Sandy.

"I cannot tell," said the Mexican doctor. "I cannot get the pulse . . . but there still seems to be a little trace of breath. . . ." He held the mirror again at the nostrils of Melody.

"Lewis," the girl whispered.

All those who leaned to watch swore to me afterward that he came far enough back from death in answer to her voice to open his eyes and smile at her.

Of course Lew Melody lived. If he had not, I should never have been able to draw from him more than half of the odd little details with which I have been able to adorn his history. Of course Lew Melody lived, and Sandy married him.

She is coming in this afternoon, for since the death of Mrs. Cheswick she has led the singing.

But now, as I come toward the end, I wonder what is balanced in this narrative—sorrow or happiness? And has the happiness of the Melodys been great enough to counterbalance the anguish that uprooted the Cordobas from their home and sent their three lives south to Mexico?

Sandy still writes to Juanita and hears from her from time to time. Mrs. Cordoba did not live long in Mexico City. Cordoba himself has failed rapidly. As for the girl herself, twice it seems that she has been prepared for a marriage, and twice something has happened to break off the match. Although Juanita does not confess what it is, I suppose that by this time we all know.

We look at Lew Melody, grown more brown and prosperous than any of us dreamed possible, and we understand.

ABOUT THE AUTHOR

Max Brand® is the best-known pen name of Frederick Faust, creator of Dr. Kildare, Destry, and many other fictional characters popular with readers and viewers worldwide. Faust wrote for a variety of audiences in many genres. His enormous output, totaling approximately 30,000,000 words or the equivalent of 530 ordinary books, covered nearly every field: crime, fantasy, historical romance, espionage, Westerns, science fiction, adventure, animal stories, love, war, and fashionable society, big business and big medicine. Eighty motion pictures have been based on his work along with many radio and television programs. For good measure he also published four volumes of poetry. Perhaps no other author has reached more people in more different ways.

Born in Seattle in 1892, orphaned early, Faust grew up in the rural San Joaquin Valley of California. At Berkeley he became a student rebel and one-man literary movement, contributing prodigiously to all campus publications. Denied a degree because of unconventional conduct, he embarked on a series of adventures culminating in New York City where, after a period of near starvation, he received simultaneous recognition as a serious poet and successful author of fiction. Later, he traveled widely, making his home in New York, then in Florence, and finally in Los Angeles.

Once the United States entered the Second World War, Faust abandoned his lucrative writing career and his work as a screenwriter to serve as a war correspondent with the infantry in Italy, despite his fifty-one years and a bad heart. He was killed during a night attack on a hilltop village held by the German army. New books based on magazine serials or unpublished manuscripts or restored versions continue to appear so that, alive or dead, he has averaged a new book every four months for seventy-five years. Beyond this, some work by him is newly reprinted every week of every year in one or another format somewhere in the world. A great deal more about this author and his work can be found in *The Max Brand Companion* (Greenwood Press, 1997) edited by Jon Tuska and Vicki Piekarski. His next Five Star Western will be *Outlaws from Afar.*